THE BLESSED BRIDGE

THE BLESSED BRIDGE

By

RUDOLPH SABOR

International Press

Published by:
International Press, Kent

First published in 2004

ISBN: 0-9546858-0-6

Printed by:
ProPrint
Riverside Cottages
Old Great North Road
Stibbington
Cambs. PE8 6LR

ACKNOWLEDGEMENTS

My gratitude is due to Dr. Maurice Pearton and to Keith and Lilian Banner, who undertook the task of ridding the text of many Germanisms, and turning them into more acceptable English. Any remaining infelicities are merely due to my own stubbornness. I also wish to put on record the tireless work undertaken by Emmi Sabor, who took great pains to read and re-read the text and rid it of a mass of typing errors.

CONTENTS

CHAPTER 1

Among Joseph Messing's post, which was sizeable on account of his 36th birthday, was a letter that produced unforeseen consequences. He laid the congratulations from relatives and colleagues aside, and regarded the grey envelope with suspense. The motto on the cover read: *In the Führer's name.* Could this be his promotion? Or - here Joseph shielded his eyes - was his son responsible for . . .? Rolf is a dreamer. He had no bad intentions, last year, but he did make life uncomfortable. No, he would not. He could not. He is practically an adult. Joseph Messing disconnected the phone, pulled the curtains together and took his reading glasses from their case.

CHAPTER 2

1840. Spring had arrived in Northern Germany, and the church was filled with Sunday worshippers. This was where Buxtehude used to sit at the organ bench, and where young Bach recovered from his exhausting walk, to hear and learn from the master.

Modern times with tall hats and coloured trousers would have made the organist and other clergy look absurd with their powdered wigs, but the prevailing sentiments had not changed. Devotion, mingled with tender, unspoken love. For Jesus? For his priestly deputy? For the young girl in the front pew? The congregation had risen for the hymn, and she listened to the boy's silvery voice, that refused to mingle with the others. It was a haunting experience for the susceptible girl, especially since amongst the perfect notes of the fifteen year old there were a few that did not respond to the singer's intention, signalling the feared break of voice.

They had never exchanged a word, but they knew they belonged to one another. And no greater contrast between two young people could be imagined. Bettina Sommer was small for a fourteen year old. She wore her two ash blond pigtails carefully braided around her head, under a white lace bonnet. The handsome, lanky boy in the scarlet cassock seemed an intriguing guest in the largely native congregation. Did he come from the south, or further still, from the Levant or the Holy Land? Yossl Messing's full, black curls enwrapped his eyes, as they kindled the girl's, as he sang. And, ah, those eyes. Big, round and raven black. This is the witchcraft that bound her to him.

'Today I shall speak to her,' Yossl vowed to himself. And Bettina considered how to be rid of her parents for five crucial minutes. Such was their daring.

For the sake of those precious minutes they invented a prayer book left behind in the pew, a promise to catch up with the parents' homeward stroll, and the boy's excuse for withdrawing hurriedly after the service, on account of his starving golden retriever - all habitual devices of Cupid.

'O, I'm looking . . . I'm looking . . . for my prayer book,' Bettina panted, as the two almost collided.

Yossl replied, ' Allow me!'

He bent down, and held the errant little volume in his trembling hands, overcome by the proximity of the girl's white skirt and an experience of exquisite upheaval.

The two sat, with plenty of room between them, on the wooden bench. The church was now darker than before, with just a few of the cleaners at work. Nobody dared to speak. At last she whispered:

'I know your name. It's Yossl. Yossl Lessing. I know where you live. Kirchgasse, number ten. I know which school you go to. And what instruments you play. The Fortepiano, the Violin, and my favourite, the Guitar.'

Yossl suddenly felt hot. Then he opened his mouth, shut it again, and opened it once more to speak.

'How?'

Then: 'I mean, how did you manage to . . .?'

There came a pause for Bettina to smile triumphantly.

Yossl rallied:

'I don't know your name. I don't know anything. But I often go through the little roads and the broad thoroughfares of our town, trying to catch a glimpse of you. In vain. By the way, Messing, not Lessing.'

'O no,' she cried out, raising her voice to almost a shriek. Two pairs of cleaners' eyes pierced the gloom and disapproved. Then Bettina began her interrogation.

'Not Lessing, but Messing? Then you are not a descendant of the great Ephraim Lessing?'

To Yossl's incomprehension she replied:

'He of *Nathan the Wise*.'

Yossl assured her that indeed he was not. That he had not even heard of the gentleman before.

'But occasionally, when the southwind talks to the willows by the river, I scribble verses in my diary.'

He patted his capacious coat pocket, brought out a volume of more than ordinary size, and prepared the greatest wager of his life. *Va Banque* (the ultimate card game in which you stake all you possess). He would read to her:

> *Black eyes,*
> *eternal enigma*
> *behind witching lids,*
> *whom do you seek in the night?*
> *Black eyes,*
> *do you mean me?*
> *Was it the wind,*
> *Spring's postillion,*
> *that has cradled your dreams*
> *in such rueful ease?*
> *Spring, what hopes can we muster?*
> *Yours is the whole might.*
> *In this sombre springtime night*
> *two black eyes*
> *shed their lustre.*

He slowly replaced the diary, all the time waiting for her reaction. At last she said, word by measured word,

'Was it the wind . . . Spring's postillion . . . that has cradled your dreams . . .?'

Then both were silent, amid the greater silence of the now empty church. When he dared to look into her eyes, he saw them half hidden behind a moist veil.

'Teach me,' Yossl pleaded with her.

'I know nothing. About Goethe. Schiller. And the man who almost shares my name.'

When Bettina spoke at last, her voice was clear.

'O, they are wonderful. Goethe's poems. Exquisite. So I think, are yours. But I only know this one. And Schiller's dramas. *Kabale and Liebe* will give you sleepless nights. And Lessing? We saw *Nathan* last Friday. It stopped my heart.'

The boy repeated: 'Will you teach me?'

She nodded her head. Then she jumped out of the pew.

'Heavens, I must hurry home!'

'What's your name?' he called after her.

4

'Bettina. Bettina Sommer. See you next Sunday. In church.'

He quickly took out his diary, tore out the page with his poem, rushed after her, and reached her by the big, heavy door.

'Allow me, Bettina. And here is a keepsake.'

He wanted to add, 'Of the happiest day of my life.' but she was gone.

CHAPTER 3

'Heil Hitler!' 'Heil Hitler!'
'Heil Hitler!' 'Heil Hitler!'
'Heil Hitler!' 'Good Morning!'
'Be careful, my friend. This is Berlin in 1934. Nobody wishes anybody a good morning anymore.'

Joseph and Rolf Messing, father and son, had breakfast together. As it was Saturday, Rolf was at leisure. When the wordless meal was over, the two sat together on the couch. Father handed over the letter that had been the reason for yesterday's shock.

'Read this and tell me what you make of it.'

The boy examined the envelope. Then he studied the text.

'Dear Herr Messing. This is to inform you that your application has been received. Before we can proceed, I must ask you to let us have an *Ariernachweis* (proof of Arian birth) of your paternal and maternal grandparents. Heil Hitler!'

Joseph Messing looked alternately at the reader and, not without pleasure, at his reflection in the large wall mirror. He brushed his sandy hair. He waited for Rolf's opinion. He straightened his black SS shirt. He got impatient.

'What is taking you so long?'

'Be on your guard, father. I advise vigilance.'

Yesterday, Joseph Messing would have shared his son's apprehension. But today he was more sanguine. He found it difficult, however, to raise objections. Had the fifteen-year old not proved his ability to divine a correspondent's mind, as opposed to the written evidence? Thus, Rolf's glossing of the text had ensured, during the past year, his father's relative immunity from danger. Except for that one unfortunate incident, when Joseph Messing entertained two high-ranking, uniformed nonentities, and the son told the company a story which featured lapsed Socialists and a bandwagon.

Rolf installed himself in the passenger seat of the Mercedes, driven by his father to Lübeck. They passed Wittenberge, Rheinsberg, Malchow, all places of memorable import to Rolf.

Joseph Messing persuaded himself, by frequently consulting his rear mirror, that his uniform was fetching and, by personal inspection, that his footwear reflected the enquirer's charm. He had to look his best on this day.

Where Lake Malchow is at its narrowest, they stopped for their picnic. This is where Joseph began to unburden his mind.

'Rolf, I think after today we shall either be crawling to Canossa or triumph in Berlin.' Joseph brushed a crumb from his lapel.

'You will find this hard to understand, Rolf. You have always been an anti-Nazi. With your romantic ideas. With your campfires. Your songs. Your - idealism. I started the same way. I was a convinced Socialist. So was your mother, when she left me - us.'

He stopped to blow his nose, extracted a flyswatter from the basket and deftly exterminated the offender.

'Then came the day when I was reborn. When I saw - no, when I experienced Adolf Hitler. His eyes, Rolf. There was Germany, hungry and poor after Versailles, and he promised us wealth and power. I knew then that I had found the saviour of our fatherland. My Führer. I joined the SS. I had to produce an *Ariernachweis,* to show that your parents were of - impeccable birth.'

His son regarded him for a while.

'There can be little doubt,' he said with a smile. 'Tall, blond, blue eyes. All of us. Typical Germans. And the aquiline nose.'

'The what?'

'The aristocratic nose of an eagle.'

'Quite. We have been ordered to Lübeck. That is where my grandparents lived. And that is where I shall obtain the additional *Arienachweis* about both grandparents. A trifle.'

'Or a noose,' added Rolf.

Thus it befell, a hundred years after his grandfather first dared to address his future wife, that Joseph Messing entered the same church, accompanied by his son. A few things had changed. Cobblestones have yielded to asphalt. Horse and coach have acknowledged the conquest of the motor car. But as the two stepped slowly, bare-headed, along the centre aisle, they experienced the same sense of awe as their ancestors. In Joseph's case, however, this was mixed with apprehension, mainly due to his son's apocalpytic augury of a *noose*.

Joseph's appointment with Church Councillor Kietz was at 7pm. His son climbed to the organ loft, while SS Captain Messing knocked at the heavy oaken door.

'Heil Hitler!'

'Yes. Sit down, Herr Messing.'

Amazing. With just five words the white-haired man had managed to set Joseph free of his uniform, and treat him as a fellow human.

'Regarding your enquiry, here are the wanted papers about your maternal grandparents. There is some doubt about the paternal side, however.'

Herr Kietz looked at his interlocutor with an amused twinkle.

'What sort of doubt?' asked Joseph, dismayed.

The Church Councillor took a large, leather-bound volume from one of the shelves and murmured:

'Page 217. 198-206-218 - here we are, page 217.'

Without a care in the world he invited Joseph to inspect the entry.

'Yossl Messing, born 12th March, 1825. Religion:
Protestant.
Bettina Sommer, born 4th August, 1826. Religion:
Protestant.'

'Well?' Joseph asked indignantly. 'Where is your doubt?'

Herr Kietz, always a friendly smile gleaming between short beard and thick lips, pointed to the top of the page.

'Moses Messingsky (the father) changed his name to Messing on 3rd June, 1818, and converted on the same day to Protestantism.'

The Church Councillor closed the book, the twinkle now extending from his narrow eyes to his beard. He leaned back in his armchair, having evidently enjoyed a filling high tea. He observed the SS Captain, his handkerchief, his sweaty forehead, his bewilderment, with equanimity.

'Converted to Protestantism, Herr Kietz. Converted from what? From Catholicism? It does not say. Many of our best members were formerly Nationalists, Democrats, Socialists, even Communists. But they were good Germans, nevertheless.'

'Moses? Messingsky?' Herr Kietz asked, delicately.

Joseph thought for a while.

'We have no conclusive evidence, do we, that Moses Messingsky was in fact . . .'

'Of mosaic descent?' the Church Councillor assisted.

'Quite so. And therefore I would suggest . . .'

Here the Church Councillor allowed himself a tranquil reply, bolstered by a truly Church Councilliatory mirth:

'And therefore we regret that we cannot determine with any certainty that your paternal grandfather was or was not a Protestant at the time of his birth. This forces us to withhold an *Ariernachweis*.'

Joseph Messing did not deliberate long. Had Herr Kietz given him hope of second thoughts, or was there something in the atmosphere of this venerable church that encouraged him to wager everything, just like his grandfather, a hundred years ago, in the same spot? Va banque.

With a shrug of his shoulders he exclaimed:

'I thank you for your kind and considerate investigation. Let us now regard the matter as closed.'

He half rose, raised his right arm for a final 'Heil Hitler' then sat down again and looked at the well satisfied Herr Kietz.

'You must be very proud of your splendid building, Herr Church Councillor. I saw, on my way to you, the appeal for help with the falling steeple. We - I cannot allow that to happen. Permit me . . .'

He put his hand to his inside pocket and said:

'Here is my modest contribution. And now I must take my leave, Heil Hitler!'

The Church Councillor, blissfully satisfied, answered:

'Yes. Wait a moment!'

But Joseph Messing had gone, leaving Herr Kietz with an envelope containing a thousand marks. The Councillor shook his now pensive head.

Meanwhile, Rolf Messing's organ recital had attracted quite a crowd into church. Having obtained permission from the chief warden to use the instrument, he started with a Bach fugue, continued via Telemann to end his short offering with a thundering transcription by Liszt. Now, surrounded by a few fellow well-wishers, he was meeting his father who took him by his hand, and smartly they made their way to the exit doors.

In the town they found an inviting looking restaurant for their evening meal. Little did they know of its history. 1850 was in the dim past. On such a night as this, heavy with the smell of lavender, did a gathering of friends and relations celebrate the union of Yossl Messing and Bettina Sommer, in the same wide-angled corner where father and son now were studying the menu.

'Tell me,' said Rolf.

His father gave an account of everything as he remembered it, including the absurdly jovial expression of the Church Councillor, and the father's final decision to play his trump card, the unmarked envelope with a thousand marks.

'Was that wise, father?'

'I do not know - yet. It may be Canossa. On the other hand, the post may bring the answer in one or two days.'

They decided to postpone further deliberations until then. Something strangely persuasive in the atmosphere of the restaurant, the church, the whole town made Rolf want to linger and explore. So he asked his father whether they could stay in Lübeck for another day.

'Sorry. I have some business at headquarters to attend. But by all means do stay a little longer. You are used to it, and your school is on half-term.'

Father booked a room for his son at the restaurant. It is there where Rolf, the great-grandson of Yossl and Bettina, slept that night, or wanted to sleep and could not. His thoughts went from his father's enigmatic account, mixed with organ sounds, to his ancestral kinsfolk, their potential achievements, their resistances, their - that is where slumber came, at last.

CHAPTER 4

Number ten, Kirchgasse. Rolf had made a note of his father's information. Now he had to find the place. He bought a guide to the town and consulted it. There was no Kirchgasse, but a Kirchstrasse. He would try this.

Number seven, eight, nine, ten. A tiny, ageing cottage door, remembering the past rather than enjoying modern comforts, opened to his hesitant use of the knocker. A little, white-haired lady looked at him with enquiring eyes.

'Excuse me, madam,' said Rolf. 'I am looking for someone who might have any intimation of my ancestors who used to live in this cottage.'

'And when would that have been?' enquired the little lady.

'O, some eighty or ninety years ago.'

'Jesus, Maria! Come inside. Come inside.'

She led up some steps, down some steps, along a winding passage into the sitting room, in which the sole occupant was perched on top of his cage. A parrot, who introduced himself with some gibberish.

'Come in. Come in. We have not lived here long. Actually, I am a widow now, you must know. But - Jesus Maria!'

'O, forgive me. Messing. Rolf Messing.'

He bowed to the little lady, who forgot to give her name. Or she did not want to.

'Messing. Messing? Messing! Jesus Maria!'

'Why? What do you know?'

The little lady spoke with a heavy accent. Rolf guessed her to be of Arab or Egyptian origin.

'Wait a moment,' she now said and disappeared.

When she returned, she carried a medium sized, very compact volume in her arms.

'This may - nay, it will interest you, young man. Messing! Messing! This is the diary of -'

She looked for and found her glasses, and haltingly read:

'*The Diary of Y Messing*'.

Rolf gasped. He slowly took the diary from the little lady, wiped the accumulated dust from the edges, the cover and the back, and said:

'My great-grandfather.'

CHAPTER 5

The postman delivered the letter from Lübeck on Tuesday morning. Joseph Messing had been confidently expecting its arrival. Now he read:

'Dear Herr Messing,
Your generous gift has been as unexpected as it was welcome. I can assure you that it will be put to good use. Your *Ariernachweis* is enclosed.
With friendly greetings.
Kietz.
Church Councillor.'

The slight trembling of Joseph Messing's manicured hands gave way to an amiable smile, as he put the letter and the document describing grandfather as a pure Aryan, into two separate envelopes which he placed in his inside pocket. Then he phoned his old classmate, Hans Eifer.

'Lunch at thirteen hours, usual place? I have the papers I needed.'

'Good. Any difficulties?'

'Difficulties? Why should there be any? Everything went smoothly. See you. Heil Hitler!'

The two SS men met at the appointed hour. They greeted each other heartily, forgetting the prescribed formula. But in their study of the menu they differed. While Joseph merely glanced at it, Hans Eifer made a lengthy perusal, turning the pages back several times, before deciding to ask for two different desserts in place of a main dish.

'Tell me the whole story. But don't leave out any details. Details are so important, you know.'

Hans Eifer pretended to be more interested in the choice of his sweets than in the details of his friend's story. He met Joseph's surprised glance with a nonchalant nod of his round head:

'I think, you can trust me, Joseph. But you know as well as I do, that we all live by details. With details you can either make or break a noose. Trust me,' he whinnied.

Inaudible alarm bells shrieked in Joseph's mind.

'Yes, of course.'

He invented some important touches to the story he had already told his classmate, finished his coffee and prepared to terminate the interview. Then came the parting shot from the other side:

'I am glad you bought - you obtained your *Ariernachweis*. Another of those bothersome details. But those curacao meringues! By the way, what was your great grandfather's name? Never mind. I must fly. Lovely meeting you. Lovely! Heil Hitler!'

Three stars, sit. Two stars, stand. That is how Hans Eifer had to report his luncheon betrayal to his immediate superior, Dr Greifer. The three-starred SS man had never liked Eifer. Today he loathed him.

'My dear Eifer,' he said. 'Splendid. You have helped discover a veritable hornet's net. Now, what do you recommend?'

'We arrest Kietz.'

'Yes. Why?'

'The Church Councillor has accepted a bribe.'

'Yes. How?'

'In the letter which Messing sent him.'

'Quite.'

Dr Greifer opened a file, extracted a letter and perused it. Then he passed it to the underling who suddenly felt rather ill. Was it the curacao meringues? Or Dr Greifer's ability to obtain a copy of that letter? The attention to detail.

'Perhaps you can help me, my dear Eifer. You spoke of a bribe. Please peruse this letter carefully, and point out where it alludes to a bribe.'

'Well. It is - it ought - I mean, it is self-evident -'

Dr Greifer was a changed man. He rose quickly, waved Eifer away, with:

'Dismissed!' leaving the perplexed Hans Eifer in considerable doubt as to the specific meaning of *dismissed*.

Had he seen the diary which Dr Greifer extracted from the safe and in which he scribbled, seated again at his desk, his uncertainty would have been lifted.

Eifer useless as information operator. Recommend desk job. Or work with new steeple in Lübeck. Leave Kietz alone. May be useful. Messing? Has son, aged 16 or so. Why is he not in Hitler Youth? Where Frau Messing? France? Spain? England?

It is on the third day, Wednesday, of the third week in the month, at three o'clock in the afternoon, that the *Trinity* forgather. They take their duty in turns. Today it is in school teacher Leni Eifer's cottage that they meet. Who are the other two? Psychologist Dr Magda Greifer and Eva Schleifer, housewife. Two hours of chatting about problems of the day, of their private lives, of haute couture, with attempted restraints as to the number of full-bodied pastries, absorbed with coffee in profusion.

Ten minutes to three. Leni took the framed photo of Joseph Messing from its hiding, and placed it on the mantelpiece.

Four o'clock. 'No slimming today.' 'Where do you get those gorgeous cream trifles?' 'And how is your husband?' Silence. 'Is it true that Joseph Messing has his manicurist call twice a week?' 'O, those eyes.' 'What a lucky thing you are, Leni.' 'His son is said to look even more fetching.' 'Speaking of his son, do you know anything about his mum?' 'I don't. And I don't care.' 'She is supposed to be abroad.' 'All that time?' 'Permanently.' 'In Spain.' 'No, England, I understand.' 'Have another cup, Magda.' 'You look fabulous again.' 'Where?' 'Kohnstamm?' 'You don't say!' Reproachful silence. 'They are being taken over at the end of the month. It's my last chance.' 'But, Eva, a - I mean, - a Jewish establishment?' 'The Führer proposes a solution.' 'Deportation?' Long silence. 'Or worse.' 'Have another.' 'Have a kirsch.'

5 o'clock. They have gone. Leni Eifer kissed the framed photo and locked it away. Safely.

Midnight. Peter Schleifer fights against fatigue. He manages to pen a few notes.

18.9.34. Spoke to Dr Greifer. Little comprehension. No point in stirring up matters. Even sleeping dogs can bark. Locate Frau Messing. Urgent! 'Christ, I am tired. Eva!'

CHAPTER 6

A year later, Rolf was crossing the channel on his first visit to his mother, since she had left Berlin for England.

His father, Joseph, had earned another silver star on his uniform. But what was that on the sixteen-year old boy's brown shirt? A swastika? Surely, this is some optical illusion, caused by the glittering waves and the heavy sun over the waters. Well, the ferry arrives at Harwich, and the swastika is still there. Has Rolf succumbed? Not he. Pressure had been applied, true. But Rolf joined the Hitler Youth, in order to exert influence on key members and persuade them to the value of their independent judgement. So when Hans-Joachim, the son of Dr Greifer, asked him last year to join, he readily agreed. What is more, his new comrade now accompanied him on the trip to England. He pleaded the boredom of their lengthy holidays, which was sufficient for Rolf to divine the real motive - a little spying.

They sat in their train.

'You must be looking forward to seeing your mother?' said Dr Greifer's son.

'Yes and no.'

'What do you mean?'

'I have not seen her for years, and she is my mother. So of course I am looking forward to meeting up with her again. But she left us rather abruptly.'

'When was that?'

'You mean, why, don't you?'

'It's the same thing.'

Rolf opened his briefcase.

'Here it is,' he said with a touch of pride, as he showed his comrade a large photo. 'Ursus Castle. Mother inherited it when her parents drowned. She turned it into a small school for about twenty children.'

'I am sorry. I did not know about the drowning.'

'It is one of those things we have resolved to keep to ourselves.'

'One?'

'One.'

'Not the only one?'

'Yes,' Rolf replied, with an air of finality. He gave his comrade the intriguing choice between Mrs Messing as secret agent for the Reich or a British snooper. Hans-Joachim fell silent. He was apparently beginning his reflections.

Their train came to a halt at Liverpool Street Station. They exchanged notes where they could reach each other. Hans-Joachim gave the German Embassy as forwarding address, and Rolf pencilled the location of Ursus Castle in the Lake District on a page from his notebook, promising his comrade not to be long with his invitation to the North.

The sun was scorching the Lakes after the habitual rain of the last few weeks. Rolf's arrival at Ursus Castle was greeted by one calm mother and nineteen tense children. Now Mrs Messing and her son were lolling outside, talking.

'I explained it all three years ago, when I decided it was in the best interest of everybody . . .' she said.

'Yes, but will you elaborate?'

'I simply could not put up with your father's smug opportunism. He incorporated for me all that is despicable about present day Germany. I see you have succumbed.'

'No, mother. I have decidedly not succumbed. We shall talk about that later. But tell me about yourself. Your school. Your plans for the future.'

'A small bunch of hopeful children from the continent. The youngest is ten, the oldest fifteen.'

'The girl with the sloe-coloured, sombre eyes?'

'Rahel Reimann, yes.'

'Who teaches them?'

I do, but I doubt whether the Board of Education would be quite amenable to our methods.'

'You make me curious, mother. Tell me.'

Frau Messing took her son along the path, which the gardener had established between the wilderness of rhododendrons, leaf-covered lakes and weedy undergrowth. Arm in arm they walked and talked.

'My special nineteen come from Germany, Austria, Soviet Russia and Czechoslovakia. They all learn to speak English sooner or later. But what is our plan, our philosophy? In simplistic terms, our goal is to help those children turn into adults who will know what they are about. They will have learnt to ask questions, to think for themselves, to query unsubstantiated commands, to scrutinise creeds based on tradition -'

'Hold on,' her son interrupted. 'Creeds based on tradition. I suppose this includes religion. Religions.'

'We probe everything that tries to by-pass our analytical sense of right or wrong. Especially religions. Though we leave that particular field, until the children are ready for it. That is, at about sixteen. Don't you see, Rolf, how much human misery exists, on account of our inability or unwillingness to delve and decide? Your dreadful order, *Führer, befiehl, wir folgen!* (command, we follow), is just one of many slogans, thoughtlessly adopted by an unthinking mass. This must not be.'

'You will have to battle against prejudices from all sides. Not only the educational world, but the whole of established society.'

Rolf's mother smiled. 'Don't I know it!'

'Then tell me how - where will you begin? I mean, where have you begun?'

'With Rahel Reimann. She is the eldest. Like all the children, she gets up at seven o'clock. What she does, the others do. She has a shower. She shampoos her hair. With *Alpine Glow*. We take a packet into the discussion room and examine it. It comes from Switzerland. That is the right moment for us to concern ourselves with Swiss customs, Swiss people, Swiss independence, cuckoo clocks, Schiller's *William Tell*, geographical conditions, historical growth and idiosyncrasies. So we shall go through the whole day of Rahel's life at Ursus Castle. We have arrived at her breakfast with eggs from Denmark, sausage from Germany, cheese from France, butter from Sweden and rolls, alas, from England. We shall finish her breakfast in about a year's time.'

'And when will you put her to bed?'

'She will never get there. Life is far too variegated and full of surprises. Besides, she will have left Ursus Castle long before bedtime. But that is not all. We teach, or we prefer to call it discover together the principles of citizenship, in as wide a sense of the word as possible. We start out with our own experiences. Why are we here, in England, in the time of mass expulsions from Europe? What made the rulers of the countries that bore us, turn against us? What lessons have we to learn from our experiences? Why is it not good enough to answer hate with hate? If we have lost valuable time, years perhaps, re-settling in a foreign country and learning a foreign language, can we turn this to our advantage by steeping ourselves in the new culture, learning new skills, widening our horizons? There are no textbooks as yet. We have to write our own. That will be part of the learning process.'

'Mother, what an undertaking!'

'Yes. Much depends on our books, on our materials for investigation. Nothing can be expected from Germany in the immediate future. But England and America have started to deliver the needs of a growing market, the market of the intelligent pupil, of the uncommon man. Hendrik van Loon, H G Wells, Bertrand Russell are the first. Others will follow. We have made their works available to our children. History, for example, becomes the study of man's evolution, rather than the battle story of kings and queens. There is no fixed timetable in our school. All lessons are *ad hoc*. Children report on what they have discovered in their investigations, with discussions, questions and answers. When they leave Ursus Castle as young men and women, we hope they will be more open to the challenges of our rapidly changing society, less bound by tradition, more able to think independently, less swayable by catch phrases. Our progress is and ever will be painfully slow, like going up a down escalator. There is another aspect, though. We must not underestimate our personal vulnerability. We shall be under attack, as we have already been attacked, by high and low.'

'Attacked?' Rolf asked.

'The Ministry wants to know why we do not offer examinations. Local schoolboys have thrown stones through windows. We are now looking for a PE instructor.'

Rolf sat up.

'Someone who can also teach the art of self-defence.'

'Mother, you are - no, words fail me. You are in a class by yourself.'

He rose and kissed her, when a commotion at the door diverted their attention.

'No need to knock. Come right in,' called Mrs Messing.

A black-eyed, black-haired girl, clad in a dress of Russian style, with high, dark collar reaching under her chin, had affected the room with a hint of raven perturbation.

'Rahel, meet my son, Rolf.'

The two looked at each other's eyes before shaking hands, then they averted them. Rahel thought, 'My god.' Rolf thought, 'My goddess.'

Next morning, the phone rang early in Mrs Messing's study. It was Hans-Joachim enquiring whether he could come for a day or two, to have a look at Ursus Castle, and to call for Rolf. Mrs Messing invited him to stay for a few days.

Six hours later their guest arrived, rather spectacularly, in a chauffeur-driven Mercedes. Since this visit was planned to be of an investigatory nature, the swastika pennant had vanished into the glove-box.

Hans-Joachim and Rolf were attending the afternoon session at one of the spacious sitting rooms at Ursus Castle. Practically the whole school had assembled here, except for Sigi, eleven, and Marie, twelve, from Austria. The former was engrossed in chopping apples and oranges for tonight's fruit salad. Since Ursus Castle had twenty-eight mouths to feed, including the personnel, this was no easy task. But Sigi preferred the odour of the kitchen to the ardour of learning. Whereas Marie simply went for a stroll.

Obviously the topic under discussion had been ongoing, when Mrs Messing called upon Jonathan, fourteen-year old former German, to take up the theme. The boy consulted his notebook:

'Why? When? How? Well, let's see. Why? My father and mother owned a small gentlemen's outfitters shop in Munich. In the last eighteen months we made ever diminishing sales. The reason was fear. Our non-Jewish customers stayed away, because they did not want to be photographed. My school had a new director who appeared in his brown uniform. So my parents decided I should leave Germany, because my future in Germany was too bleak. Father and mother would try to sell up and follow me. I applied for a visa to England, and in February I got it.'

Several children interrupted him.

'Have your parents come yet?'

'Why the photographs?'

'We had *Germans, don't buy from Jews* scribbled in large letters on our shop.'

The only reply Jonathan gave, was:

'They won't come now. My parents, I mean. When he tried to clear up the shop after the Nazis, they - they lashed out at him. He lost his right arm. No, they won't come any more.'

There was silence.

'Yes, Klara?' said Mrs Messing.

'I came over the day after it happened. It was the last straw, my mother declared. We had the visa for England at the beginning of the year. Then they burned down our synagogue. There were a lot of people, laughing. And then we had to clear up. It took us over a week. It was really quite funny. But the older people seemed to - I don't know - they didn't see the joke. Anyway. Next day they put me on the train.'

'Your parents?'

'O, father had died in the war. They gave him the Iron Cross. Second Class. Because he was half Jewish. But my mother will come as soon as she gets her visa.'

Hans-Joachim felt in need of fresh air and quietly slipped out. After a little while Rolf followed his comrade who was pacing up and down by the glasshouse, evidently deep in thought.

'Interesting?' Rolf said.

'I did not know,' came the answer.

'Quite.'

After their evening meal, some members of the household lit a campfire in the grounds of Ursus Castle. All the children and several grown-ups wanted to share this experience, which always seemed to undergo a strange progression from clamour to stillness, from many voices to one, reading, declaiming, asking questions.

Rolf asked Rahel whether he might borrow her guitar. Then he sang and taught the children one of the songs he had learnt in pre-Nazi times in his native youth movement, and had translated into English when he was told of the coming campfire. Now he stood in the centre, played and sang, and the children first hummed, then quickly joined him:

> *When the rain begins to fall, rook and finch no longer call,*
> *moth and glow-worm wing the air, star-swept winds caress*
> *your hair.*
>
> *Then goodnight, moon and stars have dimmed their light.*
> *Sleep in grace, till the sun will kiss your face.*
>
> *Sunlight sheds its parting gleam on the tent-roofs by the*
> *stream.*
> *Moth and glow-worm wing the air, star-swept winds caress*
> *your hair.*

Silence ensued. This speechlessness, whether engendered by the song, or whether it is part of the training, is the most precious moment of the evening. It lasts from one minute to ten, and it offers time for reflection, nostalgia, aspiration and feeling for not being alone when you are at your loneliest.

Then Mrs Messing spoke.

'Hanna. You have prepared a brief scene from Shakespeare's *Merchant of Venice*?'

'Yes, with Jonathan. He is Lorenzo, who has abducted Jessica, the Jewish daughter of Shylock, and wants to marry her. They sit together in the moonlight.

'How sweet the moonlight sleeps upon this bank,' Jonathan uttered.

'Here will we sit and let the sound of music creep in our ears.'

This was the moment for Hanna to turn the soliloquy into a duet. She began with her silver-toned voice to hum a sad, slow dance tune, which she had learnt from her Israeli mother.

'Sit, Jessica. There's not the smallest orb which thou beholdst but in his motion like an angel sings. Come ho, and wake Diana with a hymn.'

Jonathan's plain and Hanna's lovely voice made as unlikely a pair, as did the context. Lorenzo and Jessica. The Christian and the Jewess. How far were they apart? Literally, thousands of miles. In reality, they made a perfect match. As Frau Messing said, when at the end the children looked at her, as if they expected her comments:

'They loved each other.'

The fire had burnt down. Hans-Joachim approached Rolf.

'I am off in the morning. I need time. God, these kids, this campfire. How different everything is from back home. I need time.'

Rolf looked for Rahel. He wanted to return her guitar.

'O, Rolf,' she said. 'I wish I could play and sing like you. I am so ignorant. I know nothing. Will you teach me?'

'Rahel,' he muttered. 'Rahel. At this moment I do not know anything, but the sweetest sound: Rahel. The little I know, I'll gladly share with you. When will you be free, tomorrow?'

'In the afternoon, between four and six.'

'See you tomorrow at four.'

Rolf got up very early next morning. At seven Hans-Joachim knocked at his door.

'Give my regards and thanks to your mother from me. My train leaves in forty minutes. Heavens! I am confused, Rolf. But I will contact you within the week.'

'Don't forget.'

'If I forget thee, O Jerusalem, let my right hand forget her cunning. The nonsense they teach you at school. But - ah well - give me time. Good luck with Rahel.'

He forgot the obligatory salute, smiled at Rolf and was gone.

Midday, 'Mother, have you got a minute?'
'Of course.'
Rolf produced a thick, leather portfolio, the diary of his great-grandfather.
'Yossl!' his mother cried. 'How did you get hold of that?'
'I'll tell you the story some other time, if you don't mind. May I read you something?'
'I am listening.'
Rolf removed the bookmark. 'Today was the day that gives direction and good sense to all the coming days of my life. I asked Bettina whether she would consider spending our lives together, and she said she would. Then we sat, hand in hand, under the large oak tree outside little Lübeck, and watched the sunset. Neither of us spoke a word. This was the day of my nativity.'
Silence. Then Mrs Messing said:
'And this is the way you feel about Rahel?'
'How - did you know?'
'I am your mother.'

A bonny girl in her Russian blouse and a lissom boy in short trousers, which would have been as appropriate in his native country as they were odd in England, wondered how they got through the last four hours. Rahel paid no attention to *Gulliver*, while Rolf spent the same time scrutinizing the now inscrutable account of Yossl Messing's wooing of his young bride. But it was four o'clock at last, and one glowing and one colourless face bore witness of their eagerness for time to pass, for togetherness.
They cycled together along the winding road to Keswick. There they turned to the right and came to the large, still, solitary Lake Derwent. They now found themselves on a small path that skirted the banks of the water, and Rolf placed an arm on Rahel's shoulder, to keep her steady. She reciprocated the gesture, to prevent him from slipping. By a large willow-tree, whose leaves were mirrored, Monet-like, in the water, they dismounted. Without

looking at one another, Rolf lay in the shade of the tree, and Rahel dropped on the sandy mound opposite the willow. Then they caught each other's eyes, gave a coy smile, and decided to speak.

'I have here -', said Rahel. Simultaneously, 'I happen to have brought -', from Rolf. Then he added, 'You were going to say?'

The girl opened her sketch book and handed it wordlessly to Rolf. It contained several drawings with pencil, pen, or crayon. There were also a few watercolours. He slowly perused them passing by her last effort, yesterday's campfire, with Rolf at the centre, singing and playing her guitar. He felt tears welling up and suppressed them.

Rahel said, 'I fear that musical instruments are my weak spot. That is why I have hidden the body of the guitar in the smoke from the fire. But you are there.'

'I did not know you are an artist.'

'I am not. Far from it. At least not yet.'

'O Rahel. If you knew - let me see.'

He took her book and sat with it on her mound.

'You have made me look like - I do not know - yes, I have it. You made me look like the Greek god, Bacchus, who comes to take Ariadne on his boat.'

'Now you will have to teach me. Who is Bacchus? Who is Ariadne?'

'The ancient Greeks had a god they particularly liked. He was the young Bacchus, who heard that Ariadne was expecting him to carry her over on his ship, to the Isle of Oblivion. But he turned out to be her lover who took her into his own realm.'

'Hm.'

'Richard Strauss has written an opera, *Ariadne auf Naxos,* to the story of Hugo von Hofmannsthal,' he continued, while Rahel scribbled. 'Some members of the Hofmannsthal family have recently taken refuge in England, by the way. He had married a Jewess, you see.'

'Why can people not just live as people, Rolf? Instead of classifying each other as desirables and undesirables? So much misery. And such waste.'

He pondered over his reply. Then it happened. Both closed their eyes, and little by little their lips moved together. Her hands still held the sketch book, while his were implanted on the mound. But their lips belonged to each other. For ever, they thought.

'Bacchus,' she moaned.

He whispered, 'Ariadne.'

Then, as if no act of god, Greek or otherwise, had changed their lives, they continued discussing Hugo von Hofmannsthal and its festival. *Everyman* (Jedermann). And the magical moment, when the outdoor performance reaches its climax with repeated cries of 'Jedermann' reverberating from walls and by-ways of the town.

'Enough for the day,' Rolf exclaimed. 'Rahel. My Rahel.'

The girl wiped her eyes clear. Why did she always, when at her happiest, give the appearance of dejection? So she steered the talk to a topic that would justify her false front.

'It is a long time since I saw my parents,' she said.

'Tell me about them.'

'My father is a cantor at the synagogue in the Oranienburger Strasse in Berlin. He sings in Berlin. He sings at Friday evening and Saturday services and, of course, on all the holy days. He has a fine tenor voice. Like yours.'

'And your mother?'

'O, she is a stifled painter. She would spend the best part of each day and night at her easel. But she married an orthodox cantor, so she gave up painting.'

'And lived happily ever after.'

'No.'

'Will your parents try to join you?'

'I do not think so. Father will stay with his synagogue, as long as there is a synagogue.'

'And when there isn't one?'

'Then it will be too late.'

Stillness. Unspoken thoughts. Two small creatures caught up in one of the games the great powers like to play from time to time.

Rahel tore Rolf's picture out of her sketch book.

'A keepsake of the most bewildering, most sacred day of my life.'

Rolf bent over the girl and kissed her. Then he took Yossl's Diary from his pocket and removed the page that ends with:

Neither of us spoke word. This was the day of my nativity.

He handed it to her. She accepted it and cried:

'Heavens, it is time we went home. Promise me one thing, Rolf. That you will not forget me.'

He answered, solemnly.

'If I forget thee, let my tongue cleave to the roof of my mouth. If I prefer not you above my chief joy.' Lengthy silence. 'Psalm 137.'

They cycled back to Ursus Castle, their arms locked together, to shield their partner from mishaps on the road ahead.

CHAPTER 7

Hans-Joachim called for Rolf three days later. His appearance seemed somewhat altered. His lips were relaxed. His eyes, instead of scrutinizing, surveyed everything around him in a tranquil manner. He wore a blue shirt and white, short trousers. The two sauntered in the grounds of Ursus Castle, engrossed in discussing matters that they did not want to be overheard. Hence their periodical looking over their shoulders and sideways. And they spoke in German.

'I have decided, Rolf. Your mother's school here, the atmosphere of the place, the children, hunted but free, their forbearance - or is it resignation? - , all this has tormented me. Especially at night. I have reached a conclusion, Rolf, which I wished was unthinkable - *Odious, un-German injustice.*'

Rolf looked at him, weighing every word that has been spoken and that he was preparing in his reply, with care.

'I know the feeling. What are you - what are we going to do about it?'

Hans-Joachim laughed bitterly. 'That is another matter. What can we do? What can anyone do?'

'I do not know. Not yet. But we had better make a start with some thinking. Thinking for ourselves. Unaided by newspapers, family, church or party.'

'That is precisely what I have been trying to do these last few days. I am knocking against problem after problem. For instance, I am thinking about those children who had to leave their fatherland, and I ask why? Then I hear myself, with hundreds of others, repeating the formula of the oath we swore to our Führer.'

'I know,' said Rolf. 'Blind obedience. In other words, agree to be struck sightless, then follow any command, however hateful. But what, if the Führer who issues the order, is the blindest of all?'

'Rolf! Rolf!' Hans-Joachim gripped his companion's arm so hard that, entangled, they tripped each other up and landed on the ground. Rolf helped his comrade rise and let his hand remain in the other's.

'I would very much like to make the right decision now. Until recently I did not trust you. Now I play Va Banque. If you betray me, two lives will be lost. But I believe in your integrity. Be my friend.'

At such pivotal moments, two young Germans might be forgiven the appearance of theatricality, when they remember and quote Schiller's *William Tell*, as did Rolf and Hans-Joachim, facing one another.

'We shall remain a single bond of brothers.
nor fear the lion's mouth nor dragon's lair.
We shall prize freedom, as our fathers prized it,
and not be frightened by the might of men.'

After their evening meal Rahel approached Rolf. She held something in her hand, wrapped up in her handkerchief.

'Now I have something to teach you, teacher,' she said, and unpacked the hidden object. It vaguely looked like a bracelet and was made of metal.

'Do you know what it is?' she asked.

Rolf shook his head.

'Wait a minute, while you puzzle it out. It has to do with music.'

She left the room, and Rolf pondered. 'Too flat for a bracelet. Too insignificant for some kind of ornament.'

When Rahel returned, she held her guitar triumphantly aloft.

'Which is your favourite key for playing?'

'The ones that are easiest to finger. I suppose D, E and G.'

'Ah! But what do you do, if you want to play something in D-flat, or in E-flat, or F-sharp?'

'I play it in the nearest key I have learnt to finger.'

'You mean, you fake it. Well, here is something that will help you not to fake it, and still to use one key only, say D. This is a Capo. A little latch you slip over the neck of the guitar and fasten it with this lock, like this. And now you will play everything written in E-flat with the fingering of D.'

'Ingenious,' he praised her. 'What is its name? Capo? Well, it offers you a chance to be only half an imposter, when you play E-flat with the easy fingering of D.'

31

'Will you try it out?' she asked.

Half an hour later the school assembled in the large sitting room, waiting for the class to begin. Rahel announced that they would have a short singsong first. Rolf, with Capo on Guitar, began:
'My hat, it has three corners, three corners has my hat.
And had it not three corners, I'd give it to the cat.'

The class repeated it. 'Now we leave out the word *hat*, and mime it instead.' They sang:

'My - (*point at head*) it has three corners, three corners
has my - (*point*)
And had it not three corners, I'd give it to the cat.'

Rolf called, 'Leave out *my*, and point at yourself instead like this:
' - (*point*) - (*point*) it has three corners,
three corners has - (*point*) - (*point*).
And had it not three corners, I'd give it to the cat.'

Rolf next asked for *three* to be mimed, then *corners*, followed by *not and* so forth, until the children, notwithstanding occasional errors, mimed every word of their song, except the last, *cat*. This was expressed by twenty one melodious *meeeeououooouws:*
(My) (hat) (it) (has) (three) (corners)
(three) (corners) (has) (my) (hat).
(And) (had) (it) (not) (three) (corners),
(I'd (give) (it) (to) (the) meeeeououououw.

Next day a worried looking Rolf had to face three delicate, critical interviews. The first was with Hans-Joachim, who stated that he was going to leave for Berlin, since he had a phone call from his father, asking or ordering him back. The two shook hands, after Hans-Joachim assured his friend that nothing had or ever would change. The oath they swore was in his heart. Rolf informed him that he himself could only stay a few more days, as school was to begin shortly.

Then he approached his mother.

'You probably are aware of what I am going to ask you?'

'Speak. I am listening.'

'It concerns Rahel. I mean Rahel and me. I have only known her for a few days. But she is in my thoughts day and night. And Yossl and Bettina knew they belonged to one another, from the first encounter. I shall have to leave here in a week's time. Will you –'

'Look after her, comfort and cherish her?', interrupted his mother and took him in her arms. 'You may rely on it. Whatever happens.'

The third interview would take longer. As it was the end of the week, he obtained leave for Rahel to accompany him on his attempted ascent of Mount Skiddaw tomorrow.

It was one of those nights that will never end. They wanted to leave at seven o'clock, and at four o'clock he was still awake, shifting, remembering what she said, changing, speculating on what to say to her, stifling, frozen, floating at last, with two hours to sleep. Then the alarm at six, a shower, and at seven they met, outside the house.

They cycled to the foot of the mountain. Then they began the ascent. Half way up the snaky path they had a rest. Rolf had rehearsed his utterance last night, for hours. Now he did not remember.

They huddled together. Against the cold, and for their mutual benefit.

'What are you thinking?' she asked.

'Nietzsche,' he answered. 'He was a German philosopher. 19th century. He also wrote poetry. *Denn jede Zeit will Ewigkeit.* He wanted to arrest time to make it stand still. As I do now.'

They held hands. They caressed. They hugged, they clung to each other, as if to challenge the world to tear them apart. Then Rolf, instead of telling her that he would soon leave Ursus Castle, confided to her:

'Whatever the immediate future brings, Rahel, we belong to one another. A whole life together. Does this keep you awake at night, as it does me?'

She looked at him. 'It does.'

They wandered on, upwards towards the summit, arm in arm where the path allowed, and the girl ahead when it was too perilous for two. At last, exhausted and open-mouthed, they reached the bare plateau at the top. The wide view offered vistas of smaller mountains, hillsides with sheep or goats, slopes grassy, slopes woody, slopes desolate. This was an occasion for gasping, not for speaking, except in whispers. After a lengthy time, they sat close together and unpacked their lunches. Then Rahel said:

'You are not Jewish, Rolf. Do you mind my being a Jewess?'

'My dearest,' he replied. 'Whether you are a Hindu, Muslim, Buddhist, Mormon or Jew, is a matter of complete indifference to me. Your religion has no bearing on my love for you. And as for my religion, I hold it with Faust.'

'With whom?'

'O, Goethe's *Faust*. Yes, you have heard of it. You have? Fine. But you have not read it. Never mind. Faust is with Gretchen. She asks him about his religion. He answers, *All-upholding, all-enfolding, does he not hold you, me, himself? Name it, as you will. Happiness? Heart? Love? God? I have no word for it. Intuition is all. Names are meaningless.*'

'And Germany? Will you - shall we live there? Or here, in England?'

'Germany will be free one day. What matters is not where but when.'

'You speak of Goethe. From the sublime - I have here -' She searched her possessions. 'Here it is. It is nothing, really. But you may peruse it.'

He unfolded the sheet of paper. A poem. By Rahel. He read it. The sheet dropped from his hand.

'Will you read it aloud? For me.'

'Who might you be, that violets grow
where nothing ever grew before,

and nothing will tomorrow;
that golden waves roll to my shore,
where gold was never seen before.
For halcyon days? For sorrow?
You curlew cry,
over and over.
You lullaby.
You four-leafed clover.

It has your features. Your serenity. Your beauty. Golden waves. Gold? Is that hair? My hair? O Rahel. May I keep it? I may? It will be with me all the days of my life. Here.' He pointed to the pocket, nearest his heart.

They had two hours at their summit that neither of them would ever forget. Endearments. Holding hands. Silences. Chaste kisses. Togetherness.

They decided to walk slowly, as one, all the way down, notwithstanding perils of the path. Any minute now he would tell her of his imminent departure. But not yet. Then it happened. Rahel gave a cry, as she fell to the ground, clutching her left foot. She had tripped over and evidently tore something, for she could not stand. Rolf picked her up gently, and carried her on his shoulders, all the way down to their bicycles. They agreed to telephone Mrs Messing for help.

'Mother, we need your assistance. Rahel had a little accident. Her foot. She cannot walk or cycle. Can you send someone to help?'

Mother agreed. And that is why Rolf did not tell Rahel what he wanted to tell her.

Solicitations all round. Doctor's call. Examination. Verdict: strain of tendon. Healing time? Four weeks. Maybe six. Walking? Yes with stick.

Mrs Messing visited Rahel in her room.

'I find it remarkable that you made it to the top in such a short time. Your poor foot will remind you.'

Rahel looked at her interlocutor, wondering. The woman continued:

'Rolf has told me. I think you should know that. And I am happy and proud that you have accepted him.'

Since any show of feelings were not her strongest points, she deviated from the topic, lest it deteriorate into mawkishness.

'Now we will have to learn to do without him, till the next holidays. You and I. Come and see me, whenever you like, Rahel. Auf Wiedersehen, my dear.'

To Rahel's astonishment, and to the greater one of Rolf's mother, she received a kiss on the forehead. Then she slipped out.

The girl sat motionless. 'We will have to learn to do without him,' she repeated to herself. But then she said, 'Till the next holidays,' over and over. Like the curlew's cry.

CHAPTER 8

These were the parting presents which Rolf and Rahel gave to each other, on the evening before his departure from Ursus Castle. She had prepared hers in a flat parcel, wrapped in several layers of special gift paper, and tied with two ribbons, black and gold. His keepsake for her was plainly a voluminous book, encased in a very large envelope.

Seated in Rolf's room, one of the guest-rooms in Ursus Castle, they were eager for the other to open theirs first. At last they agreed to unwrap the offerings simultaneously. Hers took much longer than his. They held in their hands a painting and a book. The painting was a ship leaving port and steaming across the sea, to the other shore which could be seen in the distance. The striking aspect was the colouring. Almost black in the foreground, where the ship was seen, then getting brighter in the middle distance, the water, and crowning everything, a golden coastline by the far horizon. A closer look revealed the back of a girl in black, looking in the direction of a fair-haired young man among the passengers on the ship. Neither gave a sign of recognition. They simply stood there.

'This is the saddest picture I have ever seen,' Rolf said. 'At the same time it is full of hope, of assurance. Look at that rainbow! How can I thank you?'

Rahel smiled. 'Just remember me.' Then she added, 'Can you read the ship's name? No? Here is a magnifying glass.'

He read, slowly, deciphering the inscription on the side of the boat: *Covenant*.

Before Rahel could open her large envelope, Rolf spoke:

'This is of all my possessions the most precious. *Yossl's Diary*. It is full of wisdom and humour. It contains intimations of a marriage that was always illuminated by love. Like ours, I trust. I want you to look after it, read it, treasure it.'

Rahel cautiously freed it from its wrapper and held in her hands the book with the missing page, the one he had torn out to give her, on the summit of Mount Skiddaw.

'Who is Yossl?' she asked.

'He was my great-grandfather,' he answered. 'You will love him. And his wife, Bettina. So much like you.'

'Will you read me a page or so from the diary,' she begged him. He nodded, searched and found an entry, marked 25.3.1853:

'Today was the first time since our marriage a few years ago, that I had to leave Bettina alone. I am writing this in the post chaise, on the first leg of my lengthy journey from Lübeck in the north to Coburg in the south-east of this great country, Germany. Bettina knows how important that town might be for me, and possibly for her. So she agreed to the trip, and to my staying away for possibly half a year, like Mozart when he had to leave his beloved Constanze, with one tearful and one joyous eye.'

Next morning he was gone. When would he be back? At the end of term. Earlier, if he could. And she? She would not allow herself to be depressed. She would work, she was certain of his return, she had *Yossl's Diary*. Why did Yossl travel to Coburg?

CHAPTER 9

Rolf was on his way home. Home? In the train from Hook van Holland to Berlin he strangely found that he had left home behind. How could he deny the potent claims of the hills and valleys, the still lakes and their shores, of the aura of Ursus Castle and all it contained, as a second motherland?

In Berlin, he walked the moderate distance to his home in the Potsdamer Strasse, appreciating the cleanliness of the streets and resenting the displays of swastika flags from many shops and windows. Thankfully, the only decoration of his own house were the trailing geraniums in the balcony boxes. He inserted the key by the note: *Joseph Messing, Senior Broadcaster, Radio Berlin.*

His father was not at home yet. It was dark by now, and Rolf unpacked and settled in an armchair, to peruse the painting, his keepsake. He thought only a few minutes had elapsed, when a quick glance at his watch taught him the truth - he had devoted an hour to contemplation, before his father's entry.

'Hello, Rolf. It is good to have you at home.'

'Hello, Father,' Rolf replied. 'How is Berlin?'

Joseph Messing pointed to the additional silver star on his uniform, and added:

'It could not be better, especially now you are back.'

Rolf gazed at his father. Slick. Polished. Bland. Smooth. He suddenly felt sorry for him. Here was a man with hundreds of acquaintances, but no friends. A well-groomed opportunist, whose span will not be limitless. What then? Will he have the necessary resolution, to deny his past for a second time?

'How is Yvonne?' his father asked.

'Mother is wonderfully well. She - wishes to be remembered to you. Her school is an extraordinary place. The children? Most of them Jewish. All of them forced to leave their homes in Germany and some adjoining countries. Why?'

'Why indeed? Who forced them to leave? You must not believe everything the unfriendly media report. I know some matters need to be attended to, but on the whole -'

'Let be, father. Let be.'

Rolf turned the black and golden picture over to its other side. Joseph Messing, with his well-tuned voice that secured his job at the Radio Station, really sounded hurt innocence.

'Have you made up your mind yet about your future?' he asked. 'You have one more year at school. What then?'

'I shall train to become either a teacher or a musician. Where? There is a fine Teachers' Training College here in Berlin. And if music will be my life, there is supposed to be no better place than Coburg.'

'Hm,' his father replied cautiously. 'Meanwhile, you may be pleased to hear that tomorrow night we shall entertain the doctors Greifer and their son, Hans-Joachim. I am told the father is partial to Franconian wine. Bring three bottles up from the cellar, please. And his wife commented on the smoked salmon we offered her last year.' Joseph Messing addressed the last sentence to himself, while looking at his pleasing reflection in the large wall mirror.

The bell was rung next evening, punctually at twenty hours. After their greeting which was 'Heil Hitler' with subsequent handshakes of the elders, and an exchange of 'Hans-Joachim' and 'Rolf', but without the ritual of their parents who entered the lounge, while the young men were vanishing into Rolf's room.

'Rahel?' asked Hans-Joachim.

Rolf smiled and nodded. He unfolded the black and golden painting. His friend studied it for a considerable time. Then he said:

'I have never seen a sadder picture. But what an artist.'

'At the same time - it does not lack - it has confidence, it has reassurance. Don't you think?'

'I know you will not fail her, Rolf.'

Both wanted to take up their brief exchange of views, which ended with the oath in *Wilhelm Tell*, 'We shall remain one single bond of brothers', but they did not find it easy. At last Rolf said:

'It is at home that charity begins. I shall have a go at my father, and you - well, seeing what your father represents -'

'I shall try my luck with mother. Yes. I think that is a feasible proposition. She is a doctor of psychology. A bit of thinking for herself should not hurt her.'

The dinner bell was rung, and both hurried to join their elders.

By the third bottle of the Franconian, conversation had become more relaxed. Hans-Joachim was asked by Herr Messing what his plans for the future were. On receiving the answer:

'I have not quite decided yet. At present the police and the teaching profession have an equal chance to be enriched by my affiliation.' Mrs Greifer enquired similarly from Rolf, who said:

'It will depend on the general situation. If things remain calm, I shall want to become a teacher. But if they - get out of hand, I shall study music.'

The general consternation was diverted by Joseph Messing's proposal for the dinner party to adjourn to the salon, where coffee was being served by Selma, their occasional maid.

Dr Greifer took up the interrupted theme. 'Police or teaching. Both fine callings. Music is out, I believe, as things will certainly not - what was it you called them - get out of hand.'

'Thank you, sir. This is a great relief, coming from you, sir,' Rolf dissembled. But he spoke with such moral certainty, that Dr Greifer was convinced he had saved a lamb from the lion of doubt.

He now turned to Joseph. 'My dear Messing. I hear your wife is still in England at this so vital time for our own country. When can we expect her back?'

'I would love her to come home tomorrow. So would Rolf,' who nodded sadly his assent. 'But to tell you the truth, she left me a few years ago, of her own accord. I have lost any hold on her. Sad.'

'I see. I did not know. And one wonders how the upper echelons of the SS would react, if they came to hear of one of their stalwarts not being able to control -'

Here his wife interrupted him. 'They need not know, dearest.'

'Of course they need not. What business is it of theirs?' Hans-Joachim put in, to the surprise of the doctors Greifer. Even

Joseph Messing raised his eyebrows, which he had trimmed and moisturized only two hours ago.

'You are quite right,' said Dr Greifer, now all bonhomie. 'Nobody has the right to snoop into other people's intimate affairs. Especially not Schleifer.'

'I do not know who this Schleifer is,' Hans-Joachim put in, 'but would you apply this right at a higher level, too?'

Dr Greifer, ill at ease, looked from wife to son.

'What do you mean?'

'The head of SS, for instance. Or Dr Goebbels. Or even - Adolf -'

Dr Greifer let his fist fall on the coffee table with such venom, that the tablecloth bore visible witness to his rage. At the same time he shouted:

'Stop it, you hear! Please forgive me.' The last words were meant as an apology to Mr Messing, who on his part trilled:

'Sunt pueri pueri. Or in the vernacular, boys will be boys. You are excused, you two.'

They disappeared, with Hans-Joachim smiling at his mother, but not at his father.

A mouse inhabiting the space between the salon and the upstairs sanctuary, provided it had mastered the human language, would have heard the following snatches of conversation:

'O Christ, I went too far.'

'Confounded kid. What did he mean with Himmler and Goebbels and Hitler?'

'It was only a bit of fun, dearest. He has the greatest respect for Adolf Hitler - and the others.'

'A bit perhaps. I did not do much better with my warning that the situation might get out of hand.'

'Anyway, I am sorry for the nice cup. The saucer is still alright.'

'Selma!'

'We'll have to learn. Refine. Know how far to go, to avoid suspicion. Civilize. Mature.'

'Considering all aspects, I shall make another attempt to persuade my wife - she is still my wife, you know - to think again.'

'Excellent, my dear Messing. Excellent.'

'I must be cruel, only to be kind,' says Hamlet. That is how I plan to make my father think.'

'I am - we all are glad, that your son has joined the Hitler Youth at last. Later he can link up with us. It is good for everybody to have a fixed place where he belongs and serves.'

'My mother is quite decent. I doubt whether she would be a Nazi if she had not married my father. I shall begin by asking her comments on one of the principal features of academic tuition, the necessity for free and independent thinking.'

'There is one aspect, my dear Messing, that has been troubling me just a little. A copy of the letter which you sent to a Church Councillor in Lübeck, has found its way to headquarters. I have not the slightest idea how, have you?'

'It is getting late, dearest. The world will proceed without your help in clearing up the mystery of a letter from a Church Councillor in Lübeck. Let us call the young.'

'It was a lovely evening.'

'It was. It was.'

CHAPTER 10

Three days later. The small, discreet hotel by the shores of the Wannsee, a little outside Berlin, harboured in one of their luxuriously furnished apartments two people in post-coital tranquillity. Neither was ashamed of the other's nakedness.

'Two whole days and nights together,' said Leni Eifer, lighting a cigarette.

'It is really quite paradoxical, that so well-informed an informer as your husband, is quite in the dark when it comes to matters that ought to concern him, don't you think?'

'How did you manage to escape the manoeuvres?'

'A convenient heavy cold. Extremely infectious you know. And you?'

'O, a womanly thing,' Leni snuggled up to him.

'What does that mean?'

'I told the head on the phone that I was suffering from pre-natal depression.'

'But you don't - you haven't -' Joseph propelled himself to an upright position out of Leni's arms. 'Tell me the truth!'

'You heard me, pet lamb.'

Joseph was by now in an uncharacteristic rage. He stamped through the room, his vexation deflated by his state of nudity, and demanded:

'You assured me.'

'I forgot.'

'How can you? I mean, it is incredible -'

'It is incredible, don't you think, that so well-informed a radio informant should be so innocent when it comes to matters that ought to concern him a little, my pet lamb.'

She reached in the drawer of her bedside table and removed her diary. She looked up the page *Favourable days for fertiliation,* and found under the current month: 22nd, 23rd, 24th. Today was the 23rd.

Rolf had never seen his father unshaved in the afternoon. But as he returned early from his manoeuvres, he greeted his son with:

'I could feel better. Damned exercises. I think the rest will do me good. Take any phone calls for me, will you? You can say I am asleep.'

Rolf told his father that he expected his Piano teacher any moment, but he would attend to his wishes.

Herr Dickstein arrived five minutes later. He was a tall, white-haired, upright gentleman, who answered Rolf's enquiry after his physical well-being, with:

'All right, thank you. But what has this to do with Beethoven?'

So Rolf began to play this month's assignment, the Sonata Pathetique in C-minor, by his beloved Beethoven. Halfway through the first movement, his teacher sprang up.

'You play well. You play correctly. All the notes, all the soft and loud passages. But it is not Beethoven. To come to grips with him, to find out what he wants you to feel about music, you have to play the invisible notes.'

'Invisible notes?'

'Yes. Play what lies behind the notes. Allow me.'

The teacher took his place at the Piano. He closed his eyes, waited a little, raised his hands slowly, and brought them down on the keys with a shattering clang. A pause ensued, followed by a short figure of four imploring chords, from piano to forte, but the fifth chord sank back. resigned, but not defeated. So he went on, through the whole movement, through man's struggle with his destiny when he, Jacob-like, cries out: *I shall not let go of you, unless you bless me first.*

Herr Dickstein wiped his face and said to Rolf:

'Your turn.'

Rolf played. And thought. Of his past struggles with people, with the system. Of exertions to come, which threatened his liberty. Of Hans-Joachim, of his father, of England and his mother, and above all of Rahel. And all the while his music, Beethoven's music, illuminated his pondering. After the last chord there was silence. Rolf had never known such giddiness, such exhaustion, such breakthrough before. His teacher remarked:

'Rolf, I think you are a musician. For your next assignment, you can tackle the second movement. Think, perhaps, of a song at night, with somebody answering it. On this answer much will depend. Goodbye.'

When his teacher had left, Rolf sat at the Piano for a long time, listening to he knew not what. Then he began to play dry, mechanical scales. Scales in major and minor, in thirds and sixths, in contrary motion, in octaves crescendo and diminuendo. He was still playing, with his eyes closed, without noticing that his father had slipped in.

'Practising?'

'Nasty word. Training.'

'Ah.'

Father looked better than before. He appeared to be considering how to broach the topic on his mind. At last he spoke:

'You know, when you practise - forgive me, train after lunch, and I sleep on the couch? Well I don't really sleep. I listen to your playing scales and arpeggios. And they make utter sense to me. Much more than a Beethoven sonata. They are regular, every note is where it belongs. I love it.'

This was the moment when Rolf ought to have got up from his position at the Piano and grabbed his father's hand or his shoulder or God forbid! should have kissed him. Instead of his churlish reply:

'Like soldiers on manoeuvres.'

Rolf would regret that missed opportunity, when it was too late, with a keen sense of loss.

He tried to make his father feel at ease, and said:

'I missed you last night. The moon was full, the nightingales were singing. It was a good evening for talking.'

Father strode through the room attended to his chair with a pocket comb, struck a few notes on the Piano, and finally spoke:

'The moon is veiled, the blackbirds are not to be heard, but let us talk, just the same. You are seventeen, and I need a man-to-man talk.'

Heavens, thought Rolf, we have been through the bees and the birds five years ago, when mother was still with us. He replied:

'I would like that very much.'

Father stretched out on the sofa, while Rolf took possession of the leather rocking chair, in his favourite position, with his long legs across the arms at ninety degrees to the rest of him.

'I am not a convincing liar, Rolf. I was not at the Spandau manoeuvres. No, I did not mean to keep it from you, but from the others. I was with Leni Eifer. Her husband is my equal in rank, but my inferior in affairs of the heart. Until last night. We were staying in a hotel by the Wannsee where we had booked for two days.'

'So, what made you come back after the first night?'

'I - it - well, when it was over, it was all over.'

Rolf looked at his father. 'Would you like to explain?'

'She *forgot* to take precautions. And now we are in the charming situation of expecting - a possible new arrival. That is why I cut short our ill-advised manoeuvres. That is why it is all over.'

'Father, Leni Eifer could become dangerous. She has been found out and she might want revenge. Has she got any documents that could prove where and with whom she has been?'

'None, as far as I know. Hang on! She signed the hotel register for both of us, I think as Herr and Frau Kraus or Krause. I was busy with our luggage at the time. And I believe she put the receipt into her hotel guide, damn it.'

Rolf considered. Wicked father. Poor father. 'I shall see what can be done.'

Joseph Messing was glad he had summoned up sufficient courage for this talk with his son. He knew he would find Rolf ready to listen, to understand, to forgive. Therefore he answered:

'What shall I - what shall we do? If I leave it to you, will you keep me informed?'

Rolf nodded his head, thinking. 'Leni Eifer is a school teacher. Where?'

'In the Bismarck Gymnasium. Why?'

'Something must be done, to free you from this nightmare. We shall do that.'

'We?'

'Hans-Joachim and I. He happens to be a student at the Bismark Gymnasium.'

Next evening, after supper, Rolf met Hans-Joachim under the Kolonnaden, a walk protected by columns in the antique style, which formed part of the Kleistpark.

The attraction of this unique location was their cloistered isolation from the rest of the metropolis, while only a minute's walk away was the fence that separated the park from its clamorous neighbours, the fairground, whose centrepiece for all, including Rolf and friend, was the *Ringerbude*, the wrestlers' booth. This night, the first of many, was dedicated to pacing up and down, like two new Athenians, discussing the state of the world and its inhabitants.

'Trouble!' said Rolf. 'Father, perhaps understandably, thought it was time to experiment with one of those arrangements listed in Holy Writ under the heading *Sins*. It involved a discreet hotel and one of your teachers, Leni Eifer.'

After ten minutes, Hans-Joachim knew everything. He shook his head several times, and remarked:

'Leni Eifer is really a harmless creature. Her tragedy is being tied to the wrong husband. He would not hesitate to sell his grandmother, if that bought him another stripe. It is to him that we must look for danger. First things first. Destroy the evidence.'

'How?'

'I owe you - quite a lot. You will have it tomorrow night, or the Bismarck Gymnasium will ditch a relegated student.'

Two ways are open, one to the ordinary customer and the other to the entrepreneur of visiting the fairground. One involves expense, the other climbing the fence. Rolf and Hans-Joachim chose the latter. They made straight for the wrestlers' booth. Six starved specimens, shadows of their former selves, were in action, their tame bouts interrupted by occasional announcements, like the following:

'Ladies and gentlemen! We now come to one of the highlights of this evening's entertainment. Our youngest professional here will wrestle with any fearless member of the public who will receive five marks, if he survives for three minutes without being pinned to the floor for the customary count of three seconds.'

The youngest professional, at least fifty and of sad countenance and bearing, was waiting for his challenger. Hans-Joachim stripped to the waist, before Rolf could either stop or encourage him, and made his way into the sandy arena, where in the centre stood the ring, its rather irregular square marked by sagging ropes. Hans-Joachim towered over the wrestler who was overcome with fear, or so it seemed. But when the bout began, he put a half-nelson on his opponent's back, turned him to the front and gently laid him down, as one would put a baby to sleep. He held him flat on his back for the count of three seconds, his former miserable bearing now changed to a sympathetic demeanour. He helped Hans-Joachim to his feet, gave him a playful slap on his back and disappeared inside the back of the booth.

'Let's go,' Hans-Joachim said to his friend, as he put his shirt and his shoes back.

Rolf put his arm around Hans-Joachim's shoulder. 'That should teach us not to meddle with professionals.'

Using the exit for paying customers, they walked northwards.

'Actually, I was considering taking up the challenge myself, but you beat me to it. My turn next.'

'He will put you down,' Hans-Joachim smiled ambiguously.

When they arrived at Rolf's house, Hans-Joachim collected his bicycle and before riding away, whispered:

'Fingers and eyebrows crossed for tomorrow. So long.'

His father was asleep. Rolf unfolded Rahel's painting, stared long at it and proceeded to write her his first letter. After the sixth page he fell asleep, dressed and unwashed.

He dreamed of a little wrestler, who had found a new opponent in Rolf, whom he put similarly to sleep. But when he proceeded to do the same to Rahel, Rolf woke up, stared about him amazed that he was not in bed. He decided to finish his letter in the morning, got undressed and washed, and was asleep immediately.

Hans-Joachim, on the other hand, had a sleepless night. He considered several scenarios, one more daring than the other, for his planned rescue action on the next day. Finally, with just three hours left before rising, he had it - the key!

At his school, they had reached the end of their Geography lesson, in which Mrs Eifer held splendidly forth about the rainforests in Bolivia. At the sound of the bell, she put her capacious bag in the cupboard which she locked. She put the key into her desk drawer, as she was wont to do. Hans-Joachim knew that she invariably would spend the next ten minutes in the toilet, two floors down, attending to whatever ladies needed to attend to.

Hans-Joachim gave himself seven minutes. His classmates left - one minute. Get hold of the key and unlock the cupboard door - two minutes. Open her bag and rummage - three minutes. At the bottom he found and retrieved the discreet hotel brochure and, indeed, inside it was what he searched for, the voucher for Mr and Mrs Krause - five minutes. He hid it in his inside pocket, went to the door, looked carefully right and left and was gone, with one minute to spare.

Rolf's day was the opposite to his friend's. He had to content himself with waiting for Hans-Joachim's visit, fixed for the afternoon. Then he would learn what the plans were and if and how he could assist. First, he finished his letter to Rahel. Then he added a postcript:

'I did not want to say this in a letter, but it is such a long time till we see each other at the end of term, so here it is. My father has got himself into trouble. He has been to a hotel with a married woman who fancies him. For all sorts of reasons which I cannot go into in a letter, this may have serious consequences for him, if it is discovered. I fear it will be. My father can be rather foolish at times. But mother left him five years ago. Never leave me. Unless I deserve to be left.'

Then school. Double Maths. They discussed the law of averages. Did they know that every year eleven people would be murdered in Berlin. They did not. Well, it might be nine in one year and thirteen in the next, and the total might slowly fall or rise, but it would remain in the vicinity of eleven. The class might like to indulge in an experiment. The teacher distributed twenty-two dice among the class, and asked them to throw the dice a hundred times, keeping a record of their scores. They did, amongst laughter that gave way to concentration. Then the teacher asked them to add up, and divide the total by one hundred, to arrive at the average. The result was 3.5 in every case. Why? The vast majority of the class were mathematicians and they nodded their heads wisely. They did not expect anything else. But Rolf was disturbed. He decided to broach the matter, next time he met Hans-Joachim under the Kolonnaden. And he looked forward to discussing this with Rahel. Who guided the dice? And why is every single throw haphazard, while the total remains average?

At two o'clock the phone rang in Mr Messing's room. Rolf, who had just returned from school, answered it. A breathless voice tried to shout, but could only whisper:

'I - have got it! I am on my way.'

A cyclist, disregarding police regulations, raced up the Potsdamer Strasse, up to Rolf's room, and sank exhausted on his bed. He handed his friend a large envelope. Rolf opened it, and found inside a smaller envelope with a scribbled message:

'It is due to you that I found my life. So this little return is due to you.'

Rolf looked at Hans-Joachim. He discovered inside what he wanted - the receipted bill for Mr and Mrs Krause, issued by the discreet hotel at the Wannsee, for a stay of two nights. They put their hands together, each reinforcing the shake with their left hands cupped over the other's right. No words were spoken. Before Hans-Joachim left, he reminded Rolf:

'At eight under the Kolonnaden.'

When Mr Messing returned from his duties at the Radio Station, he found by his glass of whisky provided by his son, the note stolen by Hans-Joachim. He was incredulous. This gave way to elation. But then he said:

'You said you would keep me informed?'

'I was prevented. He got there first.'

'Who?'

51

'Hans-Joachim. The Greifers' son. Do not ask me how he obtained the note. I do not know - yet. When I do, I will explain.'

'Why? What has Dr Greifer's son - I just do not understand.'

'While we were in England, we had time to talk. And I persuaded him, that much of what the Nazis stand for is wrong. Yes - please let me have my say first. It is deeply offensive and un-German to persecute people for no other reason than their race. To humiliate them. To smash their shops. To take them to concentration camps and to torture them.'

'All this is done without our Führer's knowledge.'

'What sort of all-powerful Führer have we got, who does not see what happens behind his back. Father, one day - I trust - you will see how rotten we are, how deep we have sunk in the estimation of many thinking people.'

Mr Messing took his reading glasses from their case and polished them meticulously. Then he proclaimed in his radio voice:

'That day will never come. Instead, we are all going together into a glorious future, under our beloved Führer.'

'Or into the Dark Ages. But father -' He pointed at the sheet.

'Does this ease the burden?'

'It does. God, it does!'

Evening under the Kolonnaden. The two arrived almost simultaneously. They began their walk, up and down, from light of the evening sun to darkness of the shades of the columns, from light to dark, from dark to light, up and down.

Hans-Joachim answered all of Rolf's hasty questions about his morning's exploits, with Rolf's final observation:

'If there will be a little Eifer, I suppose Leni will congratulate her husband.'

Up and down. Their talk had arrived at Rolf's mathematics topic, at the theory of the law of averages. He explained the experiment with the dice, and the result.

'What did you expect?' asked Hans-Joachim.

'I know,' Rolf replied. 'But do understand my scepticism. Suppose you throw just one die. It might be any number between one and six. The die and the thrower are firmly in command. Agreed?'

'Yes.'

'But you realize, don't you, that if you were to continue throwing the dice, you would with the growing number of throws, also increase the probability of obtaining the average, namely 3.5?'

'I suppose so.'

'And that means none of the throws was a matter of chance. Each one was subject to an independent law?'

'Er - yes, I suppose so.'

'Now, in the light of this our establishment of the fact that the cumulative throwing of the dice is subject to the law of averages, let us return to the first throw, the haphazard one. Is that single throw not also under the command of the unseen power?'

'You are leaving Mathematics,' said Hans-Joachim, 'for Philosophy.'

'No. I am trying to build a bridge from the one to the other. There comes a time when Mathematics alone will not suffice, does not comfort. Suppose you discover that the law of averages does not apply any more, that the dice you throw comes up with a weird cumulative result, say 2 or 5 and they do this consistently. Then the law has been cancelled. Why? By whom? Surely, this would merit your stupendous surprise?'

Hans-Joachim laughed. 'That will never happen. Mathematics and all its rules dominate our lives.'

'I wish I could share your conviction.'

They left it at that.

CHAPTER 11

'It is Saturday evening, and I am at leisure to write to you, and to tell you about the most extraordinary discovery I made in Yossl's Diary. But first let me inform you that my foot is much better, and that I walk without a stick now. Though its support reminded me of our day on the fells.' This is how Rahel's letter to Rolf began.

She next mentioned her school work. 'Shakespeare! His comedy, *As You Like It*. We have to write an appraisal of the first act. How strange that even in his time he had to face the argument (?) why two innocent young girls were turned away from their country, for no other reason than they displeased the tyrannical father of the household.'

But now she approaches the main part of her letter. 'You told me that you have not read beyond the chapter in which Yossl tells of his first visit to Coburg. Well, I shall have to copy several pages for you, and I wonder what you will make of them. He starts in the coach. It is his second visit to Coburg, and he is now thirty:

'Today I left my beloved Bettina and my little cherub behind for the second, and hopefully the last time. For if our blossoming dreams ripen, we will all be united in this part of the world.'

Here the Diary breaks for two hours. One of the horses had put his leading leg into a hole in the road, and hurt his knee. The coachman, with Yossl's assistance, gave him first aid, and after a while the beast was ready for the shifting of his load.

After this little adversity, he describes the results of his previous visit to Coburg and his expectations of the future. How he had founded his first String Quartet. And now I shall continue with my copying:

'It was a weird but exciting experience. Pierre, the Frenchman, played the first Violin, and how! with me on the second. Ben from New York was a most sensitive Viola player, and the Russian Mischa was *married to his Cello,* as he put it. Would they still be there? And would they be prepared to work with me, to travel around, with concerts in large and small halls, in schools, hospitals, and outdoors, as they did willingly and enthusiastically a

54

couple of years ago? What a surprise was awaiting me on my arrival in Coburg. Pierre and Mischa greeted me with bear hugs, and informed me that Ben was on his way from overseas. And they had acquired a newcomer, Silke from Sweden, as their Pianist. The first rehearsal was scheduled for the next day. O, the youth today! They are so immersed in themselves, that they forget to keep in touch with their elders. None of them is over twenty. They are scruffy. They forget to shave. But they have an enormous appetite for their music. And that is what counts.'

'Now, Rolf dearest, comes the bombshell. Yossl sees a newspaper account that appeared shortly before his arrival in Coburg:

'A Composer's Wire Studio'

Our reporter gained insight into the mysterious ways a modern composer plies his trade in Coburg. Yossl Messing, who has earned some considerable attention with is *Amici String Quartet* and with his own compositions, has devised and constructed his own studio which served him to compose in a new and totally different way from masters, such as Haydn, Mozart or Beethoven. Messing maintains that the music is there already (he points at the space above and around him), and that his task is to catch the invisible notes. Thus, says Messing, the office of the composer can be likened to that of the sculptor. To realize his ideas, Messing had hired two rooms in Coburg, which he has combined into a very long studio, whose sides he had strung with wires, on the ends of which he had assembled clusters of small, black discs. These, I am informed, constitute the notes. The process of composing involves constant reaching up, crouching down and stepping on to the benches which have been placed at the disposal of the composer. The curator of the studio tells me that he expects Messing to arrive in Coburg next week, and that he has agreed to a public demonstration of his novel way of composing in his wire studio.'

'Well, well! What do you say? Is not this extraordinary? But now see what happens next (I transpose some of the sheets for the sake of dramatic interest):

'When I finally made it to Coburg, I was greeted by Mischa, who introduced his recently acquired pianist, blond and lanky Silke from Sweden to me. He told me that she had proved a most valuable addition to their trio. They now had the option of performing Piano Quartets, like the new one by Robert Schumann, or Piano Trios like Schubert's and the more recent one by Felix Mendelssohn.'

He mentions, with slight amusement, his coming demonstration at the wire studio, and goes on:

'They expect Ben to arrive shortly from New York. I do not know where he will land, and how he will make his way to Coburg, but these Yankees seem to have answers for everything.'

There follows a description of the staid life in Coburg, of some excursions they had made into the breathtaking countryside, and eventually of his demonstration recital:

'I wanted the evening to begin at eight o'clock, but at half past seven the studio was packed, so that I started twenty minutes early. I told the listeners I would try for the beginning of a new Piano Quintet. I do not know how to put on paper the events of the next half hour, so I enclose Silke's report for the Coburg Gazette:

7.40 at the packed Wire Studio. Yossl Messing is to demonstrate his new method of composing. He has a piano, several sheets of manuscript paper, and lots of notes bundled together on countless wires that stretch from one end of the long room to the other. For the opening, he moves seven black discs from right (their resting place) to left (the beginning) at eye level (denoting the piano). He checks this with his own piano, jumps up again to alter the position of one of the black balls, checks it, is satisfied, adjusts the note lengths, and proceeds from there. To reach the wires allotted to the first violin, he jumps up on one of the benches placed alongside the wires. But now a transformation overcomes the composer. His movements become hastier, his eyes are fixed like in a trance, and his lips - is he smiling or is he agonizing? He jumps down, he crouches, he races to the piano, he hurries back to his wires, to the little black balls, and in the space of half an hour he comes to an end, utterly exhausted. Then, after a pause for refreshment, he plays the first forty eight bars of his new work, a masterpiece in the making.

O, I am tired, Bettina. Sleep well, you and our little cherub, and open the window wide to admit the lulling, protective rustling of the lilac tree. And when you wake in the morning, tell little Emanuel he will soon be travelling south, to his father, who needs to share his newly acquired prestige with people of sanity, who know right from wrong.'

We shall have much to talk about. In addition to Yossl's method of composition, there is also the strange nocturnal brawl between two of his friends, the quartet's leader Pierre, and Mischa, the cellist. They discussed the war, some fifty years ago, in which Napoleon invaded Russia. Mischa alluded to General Winter, his country's finest warrior, who was never defeated, but regularly he packed his country's enemies in his icy grip, until they retreated miserably or died of starvation and cold. Pierre called General Winter a coward who preferred soulless, natural consequences to manful battle. I quote from Yossl's Diary:

'I let them have their say. Next day I spoke to them, separately. I told Mischa that discussions of that nature were demeaning for the participants. How could they ever think of truly doing justice to a Beethoven quartet, with General Winter hovering in the background? And to Pierre, the one whose violin could bring tears to a hardened professional reviewer, I just spoke two words, *Noblesse oblige*.'

CHAPTER 12

The 1936 Olympic Games included, as a humanitarian by-product, a close season for stags, foxes, grouse, rabbits and Jews. Not that the latter were admitted as spectators, but for the sake of many foreigners present in Berlin they were ignored for a precious fortnight.

To celebrate Rolf's seventeenth birthday and the confidently expected defeat of the racially inferior Jesse Owens by a pure Aryan, a party was held at the home of Peter and Eva Schleifer. The other guests were the doctors Greifer and their son, Hans and Leni Eifer, and Joseph Messing and son.

Amongst the brisk Heil Hitlers on arrival, there was some secret surprise at Leni Eifer's maternity outfit, and the unuttered comment *O, I could if I would, but I shan't as I can't.*

Rolf received several presents, relevant to a seventeen year old. Serviette rings with swastika emblems, a copy of *Mein Kampf*, and a case for collar studs, particularly useful for a young man.

After the meal, the party assembled around the radio, to listen to the sprint duel between the plebeian nigger and the prototype of the master race. A pity television had not arrived to show the Führer's face, distorted with frustration and anger, as the German superman Germer was outdistanced by the Negro.

The ladies took their liqueur and coffee in the salon, while the men withdrew for their talks about the fundamental facts of life to the library, where the smoke of their cigars mingled with the vapour of their drinks, strong coffee and whisky.

'Shame about Germer,' said Eifer. 'I wonder if he trained hard enough?'

'Matter for investigation?' enquired Dr Greifer.

'Do you want to reconstitute the medieval witch hunt, with the obligatory burning at the stake?' asked Peter Schleifer.

Eifer ventured. 'Not a bad idea altogether. I would not mind conducting an investigation. Let us have the man in and see what he is made of.'

Embarrassed laughter, as Peter Schleifer added, 'And don't forget to call in the Führer's aunt and search her shopping basket.'

Dr Greifer wanted to steer the banter into respectable debate. 'I saw the other day a report about the various techniques of interrogation. I was particularly struck by the *two opposites* ploy. There you have one particularly rough questioner, who is alone with the suspect, and is followed by his opposite, the nice, comfortable man. Whereas the first interrogator wants to extract information, the second one needs your help. No wonder, he wins every time.'

Joseph Messing, who has not spoken a word yet, wiped his glasses, then his forehead with a different tissue, and spoke:

'I find all this most absorbing, although I have no first-hand experience of enquiries or questionings. But I can say that I have studied the literature covering the field, and I know the theory. All I need is some practical experience. Would it be possible?' he turned to Peter Schleifer, 'to be present at some such event? Perhaps behind a screen?'

'Glad to oblige,' answered Schleifer. 'Phone me tomorrow to arrange dates.'

As the discussion seemed to fizzle out, Hans-Joachim's father took Peter Schleifer aside and whispered:

'O, by the way, my son has news for you from England. He wonders whether it would be convenient -'

'Convenient? It will be a pleasure and a privilege to hear the young man. Tell him to meet me in the billiard room in five minutes.'

'- and there I met Frau Messing. She runs a school, most efficiently, in the North West corner of the country, near the Scottish border. They call it The Lake District, and the school's name is Ursus Castle. She has about forty pupils, taught along old-fashioned lines, with strict discipline. I visited the place with her son, Rolf, who is willing to answer any questions you may have. I understand that Frau Messing leads something of a double life. For the natives she is the wealthy Englishwoman whose marriage to a German was a mistake, for which she atones by living and working in her country. Her heart, however, belongs to Germany, to which she sends regular information through the second press attaché of the German Embassy. That's about it.'

'Splendid, my boy. Splendid. Couldn't have done it better myself. I'll see that your Battalion Leader comes to hear of it. Time for promotion, eh?'

Hans-Joachim joined Rolf and said 'He swallowed it all. One wonders what it is, that makes such people a Colonel in the SS?'

Rolf showed caution mixed with elation. 'A lovely snare for those who are being caught. But a hell to get out of, if things go wrong.'

'That's what life is in 1936, isn't it?'

Eva Schleifer rose from the sofa and made sure that the doors to the salon were safely shut. The room was full of smoke from their cigarettes, goodwill on account of Leni Eifer's altered shape, and bad will for the same reason.

'When is the happy event, Leni?' - 'Two months from now, I believe.' - (Aside) 'I wonder whose nose the baby will have? His or his?' - 'Lucky girl, Leni!' - 'Have another rum truffle. They are the last ones from Kohnstamm. They have sold up.' - 'Well, we all have to make sacrifices these days.' - 'How much longer do you expect to work, Leni?' - 'A fortnight.' - (Aside) 'I wouldn't like to be her, if it turns out to be Joseph's brat.' - (Aside) 'In that case I wouldn't like to be him, either.' - 'What do you think about Jesse Owens?' - 'He has won two gold medals, the 100 metres and the 200 metres.' - 'You are behind the times. The long jump and the 4 by 100 metres makes four golds.' - 'And he is the only winner whose hands Adolf Hitler did not shake.' 'Of course not. A black man.' - (aside) 'A champion.' - 'What do you make of the Rhineland situation? Were we right to march in?' 'Historically, it is ours. It is due to the Locarno treaty that we had to renounce it, temporarily.' - 'I should have liked to see our troops free the Rhinelanders.' - (Aside) ' And lay the foundations for a new war.'

Two days later, Joseph Messing appeared at the Prinz Albrecht Strasse headquarters of the Gestapo (Secret State Police) for his debut in the methods of squeezing information out of the unwilling. They provided him with a desk and chair, and a screen, as arranged. Today's philanthropic carnage was the former editor-in-chief of a widely read journal. He was greeted by his persecutor:

'Your name, swine. I am waiting, but not too long.'

The man, a shrivelled caricature of his former self, was too sick to answer, or even to understand what was wanted of him.

'Swine. Your name.' A heavy blow landed in the victim's face. 'Let us try persuasion.'

He nodded to one of his two assistants, who tore the victim's pants off his shrunken body, and began to squeeze his testicles with both his hands. The tortured man was either too sick to scream, or was beyond the barrier of pain. But his face was one of indescribable agony, with his mouth formed in a howl too painful to be heard. The foreplay being over, the first persecutor left the room. The second one entered. He surveyed the situation, ordered the two henchmen to help the victim to his feet and his trousers, and offered him a drink of water. Then he addressed him, in a friendly, fatherly voice:

'I am sorry. There must have been a mistake. I shall find out whose fault it was, and punish the perpetrator. Meanwhile, let me say that we shall not keep you much longer, Herr von Ossietzky. Yes, I recognise you, of course, though your face is - somewhat - altered. You can go now.' The last four words were directed to the two henchmen. 'If you will just sign this document which secures your freedom, and guarantees your further immunity.'

Joseph Messing, who during the ordeal of the author had his eyes firmly closed, now adjusted his cravat, brushed his lapels, and left without a word.

CHAPTER 13

Rolf's second visit to Ursus Castle stood under an inauspicious star. Before crossing into Holland, his train had to undergo the usual passport examination, which turned out to be most unusual. While all the other passengers obtained clearance without much delay. they were kept waiting, together with Rolf, for the return of his travel documents. A suspicious controlleur checked his passport against a list with photos, and decided to obtain further assistance. He handed Rolf's passport to his superior who, after five minutes called him over into his room. There he asked him for the purpose of his journey, for the length of his stay in England and - for his luggage. A thorough examination followed, during which Rolf was grateful that Yossl's Diary was in safekeeping. At last, after half an hour's delay, he obtained his clearance.

On the channel steamer from Hook van Holland to Harwich he experienced, for the first time, a storm that tossed the ship about in a most unsailorly fashion, with consequential damage to the organs of orientation. The results were all over the boat, in the shape of copious traces of sea-sickness. When the passengers disembarked, after a long journey, it was night, and many wished, though just for the moment, they might be allowed to curl up and die.

Rolf decided to stay in Harwich during the night. Next day he faced another two train journeys, one to London, the other to the Lakes, from where he took a bus that went twice a day and brought him, very late, but fully recovered to Ursus Castle.

His mother's room was the only one still showing light. She had been expecting her son since early afternoon.

'Mother.' They exchanged kisses of welcome.

'Are you well? How is the school? How are the children? How is Rahel?'

'The answer is three times splendid, but -'

'What is the *but*?'

'We missed you. Some of us more than you can imagine.'

Next morning he knocked at Rahel's door, which opened forthwith. Neither spoke. Slowly they walked towards each other.

Sunday. Their second ascent of Mount Skiddaw. A few sharp rainfalls tempered the broiling slopes with welcoming ease. They sat, hand in hand.

'Yossl' and 'The Diary' they said simultaneously. He let go her hands and jumped up.

'It is incredible really. I find it incredible. It is - I mean - incredible.'

She pulled him down and took him by the hand. 'Would you like to explain?'

'Yes. I read about his wire study. And - words still fail me - while I was reading. I felt - somehow - that those were not Yossl's words, but mine. That I was Yossl. Can you understand that?'

'I can.'

He got to his feet again and made a few steps into the heather.

'Listen, Rahel! For several months now I have been thinking about music, about composing, about my way of composing. And I imagined the ideal way to tackle it, would be - well the way I described it, no, Yossl described it, in his our Diary.'

He grew more agitated, while he emphasized his points by underlining them with much waving of his arms.

'I came to the conclusion that composing, for me at least, is a far too elemental an undertaking for the armchair. It needs space for the composer - no for the receiver - for that is what you really are, a receiver of notes that exist all around you. You collect them. Then you bring them into a system of order, of consequence, of correlation, until everything is in its place, where it should be. You are obsessed to the core, while you are composing. Even while talking about it, I feel this weird bewitchment taking hold of me. Composing is like sculpting. Just as the sculptor senses the real shape hidden in the stone or the marble, and liberates it, chiselling away, until it is there, liberated as he alone foresaw it - yes, Rahel, that is the way we shall, we must compose. And to help us achieve this state, we must be on the move. Indoors or outdoors. We must construct a studio for ourselves, that serves as a microcosm which offers us a semblance of the macrocosm. O, I do not know whether this makes sense.'

Rolf had curbed his wild demeanour and whispered to her:

'Do you know how truly wonderful it is, talking to you about this?'

Rahel rejoiced.

Sunday night. Mrs Messing had asked her son into her office. 'You must be tired. Rolf. But I need your advice. Read this.'

I am pleased to confirm that the inspection of your school at Ursus Castle will take place on July 28th, the penultimate day of your term.

'You received this letter a fortnight ago.'

'Yes. So we had ample time -'

'Where is the difficulty?'

'The authorities won't like our free and easy tone, together with the voluntary attendance of lessons and homework. And we need to have more than one teacher.'

'Well, the last point is easily settled. Count me as one of your auxiliaries. Assistant instructor of music, drama and maths. As such I need no registration, if I do not teach longer than one term.'

'Precisely what I thought.'

'As for the rest, let us play a little, harmless charade. You turn yourself into a benevolent authoritarian. There can be no question of voluntary attendance or freedom from homework, of course. And as a precautionary measure, the continental background of our children is to be played down for the day.'

'Thank you Rolf. It is in a good cause.'

'The best.'

The inspection team consisted of one elderly gentleman who looked like being happier sitting in his back garden under the apple tree, smoking his pipe than undergoing the arduous office of climbing the stairs, walking from one end of Ursus Castle to the other, keeping track of what was going on, what was omitted, what needed improving, what was to be recommended, and what was better not commented upon.

'I am sorry' Sir Brian Braithwaite introduced himself to Mrs Messing. 'My colleague has been called away to London, so I shall be on my own. I hope you do not mind.'

'Not at all, Sir Brian. Shall we start with our classes in mathematics? I see we are thirteen minutes behind our time. Let us hope the children are not too restless.'

On entering the classroom, they found the pupils seated in three separate units. One for under-elevenses, supervised by Jonathan. One for the elevens to thirteens under Rahel, and one for the top age range under Rolf. All rose at the entrance of their headmistress, who introduced their visitor.

'Good morning, Mrs Messing. Good morning, Sir Brian!', in two parts, nineteen trebles and one tenor.

There were thirty minutes left, and the three groups displayed extraordinary zeal in mixing earlier learned material with newly absorbed techniques. The youngest had to solve the question: Exactly how old am I on 31st of December of this year? The older pupils had to determine the approximate number of words on a page of a book, while the top were given the task of arriving at the *average* number of *words* in a book. The headmistress walked from group to group, available for guidance. She looked at her watch, announced the homework, and rang the sonorous handbell which she had brought with her. The children, surprised by the unfamiliar sound, had a smile on their faces, as they filed out for their next lesson, much to the satisfaction of a greatly impressed Sir Brian.

Due to the fact that the next lesson was to take place at the other side of the building, class and teacher arrived there well before the adults. Rolf had Rahel's Guitar, with Capo, in his hand, as he stood in the centre of the large room, surrounded by his pupils, who were looking forward to their music lesson. Nearest to him, in a circle, stood four small pupils on their chairs, with placards held high, each depicting a section of the song. The class had learnt this last week, but the pictures were new to them, although they were painted by members of the class:

In the forest stands an inn,
and a deer is lodged therein,
when a rabbit pays a call,
knocking on the wall.
> *Help me, help me, let me in,*
> *or the hunter's gun will win.*
> *Dearest rabbit, come to me,*
> *here you shall be free.*

This is what the class sang, with the four placards illustrating the eight lines. But now the message of the song overcame the class, as they had to illustrate the illustrations. Could it be that, God forbid! the one thing Rolf intended everybody to play down, - the children's refugee status - was here emphasized?'

In the forest stands an inn,
And a deer is lodged therein.

**When a rabbit pays a call,
Knocking at the wall**

**Help me, help me, let me in,
or the hunter's gun will win**

Dearest rabbit, come to me
Here you shall be free.

The class accompanied by Rolf and his guitar, gave an affecting rendition of the simple song, with animations of the deer in distress, the hunted rabbit, and the final shelter, with everybody throwing their arms up with the joy of freedom.

Other songs followed, including their favourite, *My hat it has three corners.* Then, as a contrast, Rolf wound up the gramophone with its large, funnel-shaped speaker, sharpened a wooden needle, and played the *Nimrod* section from Elgar's *Enigma Variations.* Some children listened with closed eyes, others scribbled or drew in their exercise books. Sir Brian rose and looked at them and their work. When the record came to its end, there was silence. Then Mrs Messing's bell announced playtime.

The final lesson before lunch was English. Mrs Messing shepherded the class into their original room, in which they had to sit on benches, an unconventional enterprise. Sir Brian arrived, and Mrs Messing addressed the class:

'Your assignment was the fifth act of Shakespeare's *As You Like it*.

Which is your favourite scene, and why? Yes, Marion?'

'The wedding feast, with Hymen proclaiming the four couples. What I like is the clever rhyming, like *good Duke, receive thy daughter, Hymen from heaven brought her.*'

'And you, Sigi?'

'The end. It goes on a bit, but on the whole I understand it. I like the way he charges the women, to love the play and the men. And then he charges the men to do the same. That is good. Especially at the end.'

'Yes, that is a fair proposal,' said Mrs Messing. 'And now will you open your books on page 127. Klara, will you be Phebe? She is foolishly in love with Ganymede, who is really Rosalind. Jonathan, you are Silvius, her poor suitor. Rolf, you are Orlando, and you, Rahel, take the part of Rosalind.'

Phebe:	Good shepherd, tell this youth what 'tis to love.
Silvius:	It is to be all made of sighs and tears; and so am I for Phebe.
Phebe:	And I for Ganymede.
Orlando:	And I for Rosalind.
Rosalind:	And I for no woman.
Silvius:	It is to be all made of faith and service: and so am I for Phebe.
Phebe:	And I for Ganymede.
Orlando:	And I for Rosalind.
Rosalind:	And I for no woman.
Silvius:	It is to be all made of fantasy, all made of passion, and all made of wishes; all adoration, duty and observance, all humbleness, all patience and impatience, all purity, all trial, all obedience, and so am I for Phebe.
Phebe:	And so am I for Ganymede.
Orlando:	And so am I for Rosalind.
Rosalind:	And I for no woman.

Mrs Messing held up her hand. A sign for the discontinuation of the reading. After a brief silence she asked:

'And what is the outcome of this brief scene?'

Rahel answered. 'Phebe will learn that infatuation is not love, but duty and adoration and observation is.'

'It is lovely, how the same words are repeated by the same characters,' said Jonathan. 'It makes you want to sing them.'

'Yes. That's it!' Hanna insisted. 'It should have music. Shakespeare used it often, why not here? It cries out to be sung!'

Mrs Messing smiled, then she announced:

'That is your homework for tomorrow. Write your thoughts about the music you are going to give this scene. Consider a different tune for the different characters, and consider how to set the lines. *And so am I -*'

She caught herself being more progressive than she intended, and made up for it by banging her bell twice, with the declaration - new to her pupils - to walk down the stairs in a single file.

During lunch, Sir Brian, seated next to Mrs Messing, spoke to her in undertones. 'You are running a highly efficient school here, dear Madam, A veritable island of sanity in a vast ocean of good, mediocre and the downright shabby. My written report will follow. Allow me to congratulate you.' He stretched out his hand. 'You will pass my words to your pupils, I hope. Being forced to leave their countries, they have found freedom here.'

Who could have told the lovers that their elastic month, their expanding holiday together, would be the briefest month of their lives? They spent it at Ursus Castle, with Yvonne Messing, eighteen pupils and the domestic staff as familiar background to their intensive searching into their affinities, their positives and negatives, their temperaments, their very core. And they saw that it was full of promise. They roved through their environs, sometimes with the pupils, sometimes with Yvonne Messing, sometimes by themselves. When they were alone, they talked about their past separate lives, and the future, their golden time.

Rahel asked, 'Does your heart ache as mine, when you think of Germany?'

'It is near to breaking point, Rahel. One can do so little amid all this stupidity, this organised cruelty and self-destruction. I have written a poem called *Historia*. Do you want to hear it?'

'You know I do.'

> *A new drilled well. We drunk, until*
> *we had our much-beholden fill.*
> *The water sprung from unplumbed deeps*
> *where noble vine with gentle poppy sleeps,*
> *where vine and poppy liquefy each other,*
> *while up above man liquidates his brother.*
> *Spite Errant Knight and Death, spite Bach and Goethe,*
> *spite Ode to Joy, spite Zauberflöte,*
> *a nation hurled itself into the well*
> *which made it drunk with heaven and with hell.*

Rahel demanded to hear it again. Then she asked, 'Will you explain?'

'You see, the tragedy of Germany is their surrender to the dark forces. They thought they could snatch whatever they wanted, unpunished. *Vine and poppy* make you drunk and make you sleep, thus allowing the hordes to roam the streets and kill.'

'I think I understand. What or who is the *Errant Knight and Death?*'

'A drawing by Albrecht Dürer, one of the most wonderful artists produced by Germany.'

'Yes. And now you must hold me enthralled for a third time.'

When Rolf had finished, Rahel whispered:

'Which made it drunk with heaven and with hell.'

Her eyes were bathed in tears. Rolf kissed them away, one by one. After a while she spoke:

71

'It has nothing - o yes, it has to do with Germany. I had post this morning. My Mutti is ill. I think it is the former trouble - her heart. That and your noble poem, the suffering, the attempted building of bridges.'

'We must continue. No matter, what. If we do not,. who will?'

'My break in the clouds,' Rahel replied. 'My solace in adversity, my pain killer.'

She opened her sketch book and stared at Rolf, who was rooted to his chair.

'Please Rolf, do not move. Just sit and look at me, if you can bear it. You may talk, or change your position. I want to catch you in various moods. Sketching - for me - means studying the object - throughout.'

'Head over heels?'

'Very funny.'

Rahel made several initial pencil strokes, that captured the outline of his head. From there she proceeded to delineate Rolf's hair. She murmured, while working:

'Where is my tawny colour? I need it for your mane. It falls so naturally into place, in spite of its - massiveness. The parting - on the left. Yes.'

She continued, until she had mirrored the top section to her satisfaction.

'Now for the difficult bit. The forehead. Its thought lines.' How I shall love them, she thought, when age will have turned them into furrows. A twin suggestion of a probable future. And those two short notches between the eyebrows, that became prominent when he was deliberating.

'Please Rahel. I have no wish to upset you. But is there anything we can do to help your mother?'

'Nothing. Her doctor is knowledgeable. He is a friend of the family.'

She searched for a pencil sharpener to repair the broken point.

Rolf resolved to see what could be done, on his return to Berlin.

'Now to the eyes,' said Rahel. She looked deeply into those mirrors of Rolf's being and searched for a colour to fit them. She chose aquamarine. 'O, why must you be so difficult? Your eyes change their colour all the time. Now they are close to azure. Heaven knows what they will be like in five minutes.'

'Sorry,' said Rolf. 'Call them plain blue, and blame the changing light for the difference of shadings. Incidentally, Rahel.'

'Hm?'

'Do you know the pretty tale of Achilles and the tortoise?'

'No. Do you?'

'Well, you might bring it up in one of your Mathematics periods. Achilles, the Greek hero who almost lost his countrymen the Trojan War, was challenged by the tortoise to a 100 metres dash. Achilles is ten times as fast as the tortoise. So he gave the slowcoach a generous ten metres start. By the time he had traversed those ten metres, the tortoise had managed one metre. By the time he had traversed one metre, the tortoise had managed one tenth of a metre. By the time he had traversed one tenth of a metre -'

'The tortoise had managed one hundredth of a metre,' put in Rahel. 'And therefore the tortoise will never be caught by Achilles. You said Achilles almost lost his countrymen the Trojan War. He was surely a born loser. A pretty tale. But meanwhile your eyes have become forget-me-not.'

'Forget-me-nots.'

'What?'

'Forget-me-nots. It is the plural of Forget-me-not.'

'Strange language. The plural of *me* is *us*, but who has heard of the plural of *not*? Anyway, your eyes are finished. Do you like them?'

He rose from his chair, inspected the sketch book, and shook his head.

'Insofar as they are my eyes, I am attached to them, but I have no particular liking for them. Insofar as it is you who has sketched them, I love them.'

He gave her a kiss and returned to his former position.

'Now I have got to come to terms with your outstanding, most perplexing aspect, the aquiline nose. You may have noticed that the slight swelling at the side of the holes is the one feature that would disqualify you from becoming a film hero?'

'One could rectify that. A small operation perhaps.'

'You dare. Hand me the rubber.'

'Please!'

The greater the artistic involvement, the more cavalier the banter. A rule that could probably apply to most painters and sculptors from Dürer to Epstein, and from Dürer's great-aunt to Rahel. And thus, her artistic mind in total control, the sketch was finished in less than an hour, ready for brush and water-colouring, which, she decided would be attended to later, alone.

Both put their heads together in looking at her work, pondering, judging, and finally pronouncing on its merits. Rahel said, 'Possible,' But Rolf declared, 'You are a true artist.'

She put her sketch book away and said 'What were we talking about before I tried to draw you?'

'Germany.'

'And your poem. *A nation hurled itself into the well which made it drunk with heaven and with hell.*'

'Where do you - did you live in Berlin?'

'Oranienburger Strasse 14. Father has a short walk to his synagogue. But our flat on the third floor is slightly smaller than Ursus Castle. I wish I could stay here forever, Rolf. The school, Mount Skiddaw, your mother - it all has become a real home to me. I cannot envisage living anywhere but here. And yet, I know that I must leave, when the time comes. Where do I go?'

'Wherever you go, I go. Wherever I go, you go.'

'Rolf.'

'Yes, dearest?'

'Nothing. Just Rolf.'

CHAPTER 14

1857. A small boy with wheaten-coloured hair streaming uncontrolled over his shoulders, jumped from the steps of the theatre at Coburg down to the street, where his mother took him in her arms.

'Yossl,' this is what he called him. 'will be coming soon from his re - rebursal.'

'Rehearsal,' put in Bettina. 'Say it. Re-hear-sal.'

'Re-hear-sal,' repeated Emanuel, fixing an important new word in his vocabulary.

After ten minutes Yossl came out of the building, tired but elated. He hoisted his son high up, flung him several times around, kissed him and left him to his mother. He said:

'Sorry, I could not take you into the theatre, Manny. They do not allow spectators to rehearsals. But you can come tonight, to the performance.'

'Hurrah,' shouted Emanuel.

They walked together to the small first floor flat they had rented a few months ago.

After their meal, the three spent the afternoon sleeping (Emanuel) drawing (Bettina) and preparing for his performance (Yossl). At six o'clock they walked the short distance to the theatre. A brightly coloured streamer was running across the entrance:

Wagner Evening
With
Yossl Messing

Richard Wagner and his 'music of the future' had lately been sweeping and conquering the country. The *Ring of the Nibelung,* that gigantic work in four operas, was half finished. The composer had just returned from a triumphant tour of eight concerts in London. But his own countrymen had banished him into exile, due to his involvement in the 1849 Dresden revolt. Here was a composer who was worthy of people's attention for more than his composing.

Yossl began by playing two short pieces, the *Fantasia* and the *Polka for Mathilde Wesendonck,* on the Grand Piano. Then he addressed the audience:

'Wagner forswears advice. His teachers', his family's. Why? Because he knew better. That did not make him popular, but it made him a fine composer.' He held aloft, for the audience to inspect, a capacious bundle of some two or three hundred foolscap pages of manuscript paper.

'This is Beethoven's masterpiece, his Ninth Symphony. When Wagner was seventeen years old he copied the full score, note by note, against the advice of his teacher of harmony, in order to learn from the master. Imagine what that means, and what he learnt. It meant hours and hours, days and nights, weeks and weeks of painstaking candlelit labour. And when he finished, he had learnt how high and how low each instrument could go. What instruments blend with others, which combination had better be avoided, what to do with your original ideas, how to vary them, how to combine voices with the orchestra, how to handle harmony and counterpoint, and thousands of other vital aspects. And when he had finished copying, he had turned himself into a composer. To seal his achievement, he made a piano arrangement of the whole symphony.'

Yossl walked to the piano and played the beginning of the work.

'But this is not the whole story,' he continued. 'Wagner now packs up this piano arrangement and sends it to Schotts in Mainz, the respected music publisher. With it goes this letter.

I am sending you herewith my piano arrangement of Beethoven's Ninth Symphony. I require no fee, but I should be much obliged if in return you were to make me a gift of music, namely Beethoven's *Missa Solemnis,* Beethoven's *Ninth Symphony, full score,* Beethoven's *Two Quartets,* and *All Beethoven's Symphonies arranged by Hummel.*

Schott obliges, and Wagner gets about ten times more than Schotts would have paid for an unknown beginner's effort.'

He paused for the giggles and whispered conversations among the audience to subside. Then he continued:

'But his method of persuading people to part with large sums *for nothing* needed refinement. By our own time, in the 'fifties' he has succeeded. Take this letter he wrote a few years ago to his friend, the piano teacher Baumgartner in Zurich:

Dear brother, I worry about your future. In winter you have a steady income which you use up as you go, while in summer you earn very little and have to go short. I herewith offer you to open a credit account with me. If you will send me 300 francs (£300) now, I shall return this amount without fail in July. Just think how pleasant it will be for you to receive, all of a sudden, an unexpected windfall. You see how I care for the future of my friends.'

The giggles turned to guffaws and downright laughter, just at the appropriate time for Yossl to announce the interval.

Bettina and little Emanuel were the first to storm into Yossl's dressing room.

'How is it going so far?' Yossl asked.

'It is interesting. Some of the spectators seem to be spellbound. I think you are convincing them.'

'And you, cherub?'

'O, Yossl. The peppermint chocolates Bettina gave me at the beginning, have lasted me until now. They were - yummy.'

'Good. See you at the end.'

Others wanting to meet Yossl Messing were the Burgomaster, a newspaper reporter and the director of a school. The former exchanged polite trifles in a minute, but the next two were invited to speak to him after the performance, since Yossl had to prepare himself for the second half.

What the expectant audience saw, was the curtain, and three men, pacing up and down, or sitting on the edge of their chairs. The three were identified by the spectators, through their dresses and demeanour, as a banker (Pierre) a tailor (Misha) and a rabbi (Yossl). Behind the curtain, unseen was Wagner who owed sums of money to all three of them.

Banker	*We are agreed then, gentlemen?*
Tailor	*I go along with you, sir.*
Rabbi	*I vote with the majority.*

Banker	Very well. I'll go in first. Rabbi, have the goodness to look after this, while I settle my accounts with Herr Wagner.

The Banker passes a book to the Rabbi, and rings a tinkling bell. A sonorous gong answers. He disappears behind the curtain. Meanwhile, the tailor uncoils a narrow paper roll from which he reads aloud:

Tailor	One dressing gown, pink. One ditto, blue. Jackets, one pink, one pale yellow. Trousers, one pink, one pale yellow. One snow-white pantaloons. And I shall not leave here, until I'm paid. In toto!

The Banker returns, elated.

Banker	Success, gentlemen! It was far easier than any of us could have foreseen. Success all along the line!
Tailor	My compliments, Herr Banquier.
Rabbi	Mazzel tov! He paid your bill?
Banker	Bill? Nothing bill. Billet! Gentlemen, billet. Wilhelmine Schröder-Devrient, the finest dramatic soprano in the world, is to be billeted for four weeks in my villa! An honour of this kind, gentlemen, comes once in a lifetime. What is an overdraft of a few hundred - a few thousand marks, compared with such a prestigious personage?

He paces up and down, then stops abruptly. He has realised that he has been bamboozled.

Tailor	Try and hoodwink a master tailor. Nobody has ever made an ass of me.

He rings a tinkling bell, answered by a sonorous gong.

Rabbi	Here is your book, sir. Chinese philosophy. That should provide some comfort.

Banker	It does. (He opens the book) Take this old magistrate, the harshest judge in ancient China. He sent minor offenders, manacled and chained, to the dungeons or the torture chamber. Then one day he had a vision. Some sort of angelic messenger whispered something in his ear. Next day, the magistrate committed himself to a month in prison. He wanted to see what it was like. After his release, he became known as the mildest, the most understanding judge in China.
Rabbi	Of course. He had seen the bottomless pit.
Banker	And the futility of all human endeavour. And the hunger for redemption.
Rabbi	The stuff that ignites Wagner's operas.
Banker	That Chinese judge, dear Rabbi. - he had glimpsed the bottomless pit. Wagner is its permanent lodger.

The Tailor returns. He avoids eye contact.

Rabbi	Well?
Banker	Well?

The Tailor uncoils his paper roll and adds:

Tailor	Sky-blue tail coat, with gold buttons. Very tall top hat with narrow silver rim, and sulphur yellow kid gloves. By - next - Friday.
Tailor	It's not funny at all, gentlemen. Those garments escalate his reputation, promote his persona. Gold buttons, people will say. On a sky-blue tail coat. Yellow gloves, they will say. No wonder he is famous. And then they'll try and find out who made that tail coat. And that, gentlemen, escalates my reputation. (to

79

	Banker) Just as Madam Schröder -
	Devrient escalates yours.
Banker	*Yes, yes. But did you get paid?*
Tailor(hesitates)	*No.*

The banker shakes his head. The Rabbi gives him a sad smile.

Banker	*You're next Rabbi. And may the god of your fathers be with you.*
Rabbi	*I don't think so.*
Tailor	*What do you mean?*
Rabbi	*I shan't go in to see him, after all. I'm not afraid of him. But I am afraid for myself. I don't want to mar my memory. Seeing him, always sets me back. I don't want to remember the impossible man. I want to remember the real Wagner. Yes, I have given him a lot of money. He hardly said thank you. I told him I couldn't help being a Jew. He called me Shylock. You see, my friends, the world is full of people who borrow and don't repay. Who steal other men's wives, daughters and sweethearts. But only one of them wrote Tannhäuser and Lohengrin. And if he needs velvet and silk and sulphur yellow gloves to help him create his miracles, so be it. I only hope my children and their children will not listen to me, when old age might make me bitter, but will listen to his music. They will enter a world of wonder. A world of excitement and of real truth. It is there they will find the strength, as I did, to face the dangers, the ghettos of this life. It is there they will find comfort -*
	wisdom - and joy.

The three actors slowly disappeared behind the curtain, amid silence from the audience. Then an increasing applause showed that the spectators were responding with a fellow feeling of involvement.

It took Yossl the best part of an hour to say thank you to all the wellwishers, participants and theatre personnel. Then a small troop of five made their way home, to a late bite and coffee - Yossl, Bettina, Emanuel, the Reporter and the Director of the school.

'This is exactly what our pupils need,' said the headmaster. 'An introduction to worthwhile music, intelligently and skilfully presented, together with a thought-provoking scene, that shows us the working of the mind of a great composer who is also a vainglorious man, and the reaction of three totally different characters to the shabbiness and the glory. We have a hundred boys and girls, aged fourteen to eighteen. Will you come and enlighten us?'

'It will be a privilege,' Yossl Messing replied.

The reporter had been scribbling in his notebook. Now he shut it and looked at Yossl:

'Herr Messing. You showed us three characters in your last scene. But your sympathy seemed largely - dare it say it, inordinately - devoted to one of them, the rabbi. Do I detect more than - do I detect some consanguinity here?'

'What do you mean, consanguinity?'

'Well, some blood relationship?'

'Have another cup of coffee,' answered Yossl.

Small wonder that two days later he read this in the local paper:

Should Jews be allowed to judge our culture?

In an otherwise unexceptional performance of music and scenes from the life of Richard Wagner, composer Yossl Messing put a protective mantle over a veritable hornet's nest, by refusing to answer the vital question whether he was a Jew.

In the following twelve months, Yossl repeated his performance, always with suitable variations, ten times in the local theatre, four times in schools, while visits to the neighbouring towns of Bamberg and Schweinfurt were planned for the near future. But the centre of his attention was his composition. In his wire study he created several works which were performed by leading ensembles throughout Germany. He gave them intriguing names. His first string quartet was entitled *Roaring Mouse*. His first piano quintet became *Girl Chases Boy*. And his second string quartet was printed as *Softly Softly Catches Carelessness*.

When asked why, he replied:

'I try to compose honestly and to the best of my ability. Is there anything wrong with guiding the prospective listener towards a glimpse of what he is going to hear? *First String Quartet in C-major* buys the bread. *Roaring Mouse* provides the butter.'

CHAPTER 15

The day after his return from Ursus Castle, Rolf made his way to the Oranienburger Strasse. This was a new world to him. The street was crowded, amongst others with men in black, their long locks flowing over their ears. On their heads they wore bowler hats with wide rims. They walked slowly, usually in twos and threes, talking in undertones with one another. The scene could have been a ghetto at any time, anywhere.

Rolf dared not look too inquisitively at those strange folk, lest they took him for an informer. He walked up one side of the wide road and down the other. Then he found the house, Rahel's house. It was a tall building, consisting of many flats, grouped around square courtyards. He had the number of the house, but not the number of the flat. So he entered the junk shop that opened out from the entrance.

'Excuse me,' he said politely. 'I am looking for a family named Reimann. Can you help me?'

Consternation. A foreigner amongst them, a German looking one, who was enquiring after one of them. They played for time.

'Just a moment. If you will allow me,' said the junk dealer, while he disappeared behind the shop. When he came back, he announced:

'Young sir, we believe they have moved away.'

'Have you got a forwarding address?'

'Unfortunately, no.'

Rolf tried several other people in the flats. Not one of them was at home. Or they pretended not to be there, for he heard whispered sounds from within. He went out into the street, to accost one of the men in black. They had vanished. Rolf felt like the anti-hero in the old tale of the forest, where deer and foxes, squirrels and hedgehogs, linnets and chaffinch went after their business of searching for food and relaxation. Suddenly they all disappeared, one by one, for a man had entered the forest.

The merry merry-go-round began the day Herr Droppenbrick was installed as the German Ambassador to Great Britain. It resulted in an invisible, yet omnipresent red line dividing parts of the Embassy building, indeed single rooms therein, separated into armchairs for the Anglophobes (Heil Hitler) and armchairs for Anglophiles (it's raining).

It started with a phone call, taken by a representative of the latter kind.

'Heil Hitler! SS headquarters, Berlin. Schleifer speaking. Can you help me? Does the name Yvonne Messing ring a bell?'

'Ring a bell? What do you mean?'

'She runs a school in the Lake District, Ursus Castle. Is anything known about her?'

'What should we know about her?'

'Well, anything.'

'Anything that could conceivably be of interest to people listening into our conversation?'

'No. Yes. No.'

'Wait a moment, while I hand you over.'

After a considerable time the other kind of representative took over the conversation.

'Heil Hitler.'

'Heil Hitler. SS headquarters, Berlin. Schleifer speaking. I am wondering whether you have anything adverse or positive, on Yvonne Messing, who runs a school in the Lake District. The school's name is Ursus Castle.'

'How do you spell that?'

'U-r-s-u-s C-a-s-t-l-e.'

'No. I need the lady's name.'

'Y-v-o-n-n-e M-e-s-s-i-n-g.'

'Hold on.'

This time it took ten minutes, before the Anglophobe continued. 'We shall require more time. How much? I think about a week. Is that satisfactory? It is not? You wish to speak to someone higher up? Very well. Hold on. Heil Hitler.'

'Heil Hitler.'

This time Colonel Schleifer had to wait fourteen minutes, while calculating the rapidly mounting cost to the SS budget, of a phone call at peak time.

'Good morning. Terrible weather here. Is it raining in Berlin, too?' enquired the Anglophile.

'Heil Hitler. Schleifer here, Colonel Schleifer, SS headquarters. I am wondering whether you -'

'Yes, yes, I know. You need not repeat. Telephones cost money. Yvonne Messing is well known to us. She is doing fine work.'

'How am I to understand this?'

'What?'

'Fine work.'

'Do you want me to spell it? No? I can try Herr Droppenbrick, if you wish. The Ambassador can't take the call just now, but -'

'No, thank you. Heil Hitler.'

Within a ten minute walk of the SS headquarters in Berlin was the *Tanzschule* (dancing school) *Degenscheidt*. It was here that Rolf, whenever he found time, played the piano to the awkward attempts at correct dance floor behaviour of rows of middle class boys, affected by clumsiness and acne, and girls aching for the right partner.

Mr and Mrs Degenscheidt were simply perfect. They guided their charges through their first encounters with the opposite sex, an encounter that was hitherto denied them by their schools, which strictly separated them and promoted a mystique of extravagant romanticism that was at the same time wonderful and fallacious.

'The theme today, young ladies and gentlemen, is the Tango. A slow dance, which packs a still, but persistent rhythm. We shall demonstrate. Pianist, please.'

Rolf played four bars introduction. Then he launched one of his own *Schlager* (hit songs i.e. the melodious equivalents to today's pop music). *Pomp* pom   pomp *pomp*   pom - the persistent rhythm galvanized dancers and beholders into two opposing parties.

The greater the enthusiasm of the learners, the more restrained the conduct of the demonstrators.

'Now, the young gentlemen put their gloves on and select their partners. Whoa!' remonstrated Mr Degenscheidt. 'I think the word was *select*, not *attack*.'

After a minute or two, the former three species - wild enthusiasm, propriety and iceberg mentality - became one row of even-paced young gentlemen.

Pomp pomp   pomp *pomp*   pom.
Pomp pomp   pomp *pomp*   pom

Claus Moritz, a school friend of Joseph Messing and Hans Eifer, remembered them after all these years, and invited the two to his newly built villa outside Munich. They should decide the time of their arrival, according to their priorities, and bring their families, if they wished to be included. Now, in early 1937, the time has arrived.

Hans Eifer, his heavily pregnant wife, Joseph Messing and his son, were the small party alighting from the train. Claus Moritz met them with his Mercedes.

'My god! - Twenty years! - You have hardly changed - Do you remember - What has become - You don't say - in Australia? Why? - O, I see - Those were the days - Don't say that - I mean, the bad old days - Is it going to be a boy or a girl? - Welcome to Munich. This is where it all began.'

After a short drive they arrived at the white-washed, modern villa. They were shown their rooms, since they were asked for two days. Both had balconies, which offered delightful views of the southern German countryside, with birches swaying in the breeze and willows taking a dip in the stream. After an hour, the dinner bell chimed.

By the time the Zwetschgenkuchen (plum cake) arrived, the conversation flowed. 'How come - plums at this time of year?' Leni Eifer wanted to know.

'We fly them over from Africa,' said Claus Moritz, as though he had bought them this morning at the grocer's round the corner.

'Claus. You allow me to call you what I used to call you.' Joseph tried to steer the conversation into deeper channels. 'You mentioned Munich, *where it all began*. Refresh my memory.'

'Where our Führer and Ludendorff marched through the streets. Where he was taken to court and to detention. Not to prison. They did not dare. He wrote *Mein Kampf* there. Incidentally, on paper provided by Winifred Wagner, the composer's English daughter-in-law.'

'Astonishing,' said Joseph.

'Exact and to the point. I like details,' answered Hans Eifer.

'Just you wait,' thought Leni.

'So that is where it all started,' remarked Rolf, wondering where it would end, and whether he would be there to see it.

'Claus, would you mind if I had another of your delicious Zwetschgenkuchen? It is irresistible,' said Hans Eifer.

After dinner they inspected the villa, which Claus Moritz had built for himself only two months ago. They all found it cosy, though modern, and while the absence of a woman would be in other circles a drawback - Claus Moritz was a confirmed bachelor - it had immense charm. On being asked what he did for a living, he answered:

'I am in charge of everybody and everything here.'

They mentioned the slightly puzzling feature of all windows to the west being free of shutters, shades or blinds, while throughout the villa every window to the east was heavily curtained and roller shuttered.

Claus Moritz spent several minutes in freeing one window from all obstructions, including sound-proofing material. Close by they saw dozens of men in pyjamas standing to attention and shivering. Further away there were hundreds of creatures, clad likewise, attempting to haul a gigantic load up a hill. They heard the cries of the feeble, the old and the sick who were flogged for being feeble, old or sick.

And they heard the sounds of a band playing selections from operettas. They were dressed exactly like the rest. Over the entrance fluttered a blithe banner:

Labour Liberates
Concentration Camp Dachau

Two days later, Rolf met Hans-Joachim under the Kolonnaden. Their mood was initially not the jauntiest.

'I am worried about Rahel's parents,' said Rolf, and he told his friend about the strange happenings in the Oranienburger Strasse, the men in black, and their disappearance.

'I shall have to write to Rahel and ask her for exact directions to their flat. Trouble is, she does not want me to go there. Bother. And last weekend did not improve matters. We went to Munich. That is father, Leni and Hans Eifer. To see Dachau Concentration Camp. It is under Claus Moritz, a school fellow of my father's. What a place, Hans-Joachim. I was too flabbergasted to say anything. Moritz had a villa built by the inmates, which is hermetically sealed from the world outside. Over the entrance to the camp is a banner, with the inscription *Labour Liberates.*'

'I did not fare much better,' said Hans-Joachim. 'Just when I sowed some political seeds of doubt into Leni Eifer's constitution, she stopped teaching on account of her coming happy event. But I did succeed in persuading a few former *Trucht* members (anti-Nazi youth movement, dismantled in 1933) to meet us, if you agree.'

'Is that wise?'

'The time is out of joint. To set it right, we must - what did you say? - play Va Banque.'

Rolf was silent for a long time. Then, as if packed by a sudden illumination of his senses, he announced:

'I have it! I have it now!'

He stood still, leaning against a pillar, and spoke in hasty undertones to his friend:

'Why did we not think of this before? It is so clear and logical. And relatively safe. Listen, Hans-Joachim. We must abandon all plans of influencing key people directly. It is far too dangerous. There is a better and safer way. Religion. Any religion. Query the unthinking surrender of otherwise sane people to this immense force. Query the instinctive blasphemy, inherent in repeating parrot-fashion formulas like the prayers that begin with *Remember O Lord.* As if God suffered from amnesia. Think of the Crusades, of any war at any time, and the unspeakable horrors that were - and are - perpetrated by both sides in the name of God. A thinking person must take God seriously. That means a recognition of our restricted organs of research and discovery, when dealing with such an unrestricted phenomenon. If we were triangular shaped, we would give our God three sides. As Empedocles said, *The nature of God is a circle, of which the centre is everywhere, and the circumference is nowhere.'*

'You are right,' said Hans-Joachim. 'Especially since the church has been pronounced fair game by the authorities. Marvellous. That is our avenue in future. Step by step approach. And then such thorny questions as *Religious persecution* - if you do not believe in it, why does the state? O, I can see it. Yes, let us work it out.'

'Careful, Hans-Joachim. We must not write a single thing down. We shall train our memory and trust it. There must not be a scrap of evidence.'

'Shall we meet the Trucht members?'

'How about tomorrow night?'

'Under the Kolonnaden.'

CHAPTER 16

Telegram from Rolf to Ursus Castle - 'Easter holidays soon. Want to see you and Rahel. Hans-Joachim and important friend also. Can they stay two nights? Myself one week. Love Rolf.'

The answer arrived the same night. 'All welcome. Rahel (17b) and I send best love.'

The nocturnal meeting under the Kolonnaden was marked by openness, and boded well for the future. Only two of the former *Trucht* members were free to attend this first meeting. They talked almost in whispers. They did not take any notes. They approved the plan to influence key persons via the religious route. And now they wanted an experienced adult to be their mentor. Rolf's mother seemed to be the obvious candidate for the job.

It was early Spring in Berlin. The cherry trees lining the roads were in flower. Hawkers offered their bundles of blooms at street corners. Secondhand booksellers trundled their wares on carts to their favourite positions. And Wilhelm Gustloff, leader of the Swiss Nazi Party, was murdered in Davos by a Jew, with dire consequences.

Rolf felt listless. A change had occurred in his relations with his school, that made him spend his afternoons in an uncontrolled way of starting with one book, turning it aside, taking up another for a few minutes, before discarding it, wandering through his room, staring at the growing heaps of gramophone records, pamphlets, letters that waited to be sorted out. He was always an alert, clever pupil. But since the beginning of the year Dr Schönbrunn had been replaced as director of the school by Herr Deipert, a plebeian looking, plebeian mannered man in a brown uniform, who had taken an instant dislike to Rolf, as the churlish ever suspect the intellectual.

On receipt of the telegram from Ursus Castle, Rolf made his way to the Oranienburger Strasse once again. This time he had better luck, as he was in possession of the number 17b, the number of Rahel's parents' flat. It was an unassuming address, in an unassuming neighbourhood, designed as much for seclusion as for guarded foregathering. When Rolf rang the bell, it took some time before he could hear a response. Keys were turned, the spyglass revealed a searching glance, and the door, secured by a chain, was opened fractionally.

'Yes?' enquired a sprightly, middle-aged woman.

'Messing,' came the reply. 'Rolf Messing.'

The chain was pushed back, the door flung open, and Frau Reimann cried:

'Rolf. Come in. Come in. You are very welcome.'

When they were settled in the lounge, Frau Reimann explained that her husband was detained at the synagogue, but he would be back in half an hour. Meanwhile, would Rolf please tell her everything, including tiny details, about Rahel, about her work at Ursus Castle, about her proposals when leaving in a year's time or two and, of course, about the two of them.

'I willingly answer your questions,' said Rolf, 'But allow me, first of all, to ask after your health. Rahel is in some distress about it.'

'O, that. It is the old heart trouble, reminding me that I am getting on, that I ought to take things easier, that I should do this and should not do that. The pills that Dr Cohen prescribes make me feel worse. But it comes and it goes. The main thing on which medical opinion and my own common sense agree, is a relatively quiet life. Avoidance of excitement. Tell that to a Jew in 1937?'

'Frau Reimann, I wonder if I can persuade you - my father works for Radio Berlin - we have many friends, amongst them first-rate doctors -'

'No. No. But thank you. I have told Rahel in my letters, that she is not to fret. I shall follow my doctor's advice, and as long as I have not to worry about her, I shall be fine. But, Rolf,' and here she put her hand above his. 'I cannot help being concerned. Day and night.'

'About Rahel?'

'About the two of you. Rahel has her religion, and you have yours.'

'Frau Reimann, I herewith promise you that, if Rahel wishes it, I shall convert to Judaism before we marry. That is, if we have your and Herr Reimann's blessing.'

There ensued a lengthy silence. Frau Reimann still held Rolf's hand in hers. She gave it an affectionate squeeze, as they heard the key in the front door turning.

Frau Reimann and Rolf rose, to greet Rahel's father. 'Look, who has come to see us,' she exclaimed. 'Rolf Messing.'

Moshe Reimann was a stocky, bearded man, with a bald head, and eyes that alerted the reader of physiognomies to search for rocks ahead after the initial impression of kindliness.

'Pray, be seated, Herr Messing,' said Rahel's father, with an agreeable voice that hinted at years of training.

'Please call me Rolf. I am only seventeen.'

'Well, Rolf. What is the news in England? And at Ursus Castle in particular?'

'I have quite different things to report from the country on the whole and from the school. The country, alas, shows little signs of awareness of the peril posed by the German power and German ruthlessness. They think that as long as they do not see it with their own eyes, it does not exist. The ostrich mentality. Ursus Castle, on the other hand, is a real jewel. It believes in true education, in contrast to traditional learning. It has, of course, all the advantages of a small, friendly place, with like-minded children of a similar background or fate. And -', here Rolf paused, and it took all his courage to speak these words, 'it is privileged to house someone whose price is above rubies, one that is dearer to me than anybody in the world, your daughter Rahel.'

'Tell me,' her father put in, 'how on earth do you imagine you can propose such a - liaison, under present circumstances?'

Rolf rose from his seat and went over where Rahel's father sat. 'I know, the whole thing must look absurd in your eyes. But I assure you that I shall do my utmost to secure Rahel's safety and happiness. We shall live in England at first, and later, when the system has changed, perhaps in Germany. I beg you to consider this and give your consent.'

'Consent to what?'

'To our marriage, when we are old enough.'

'Herr Messing. Yes I use this form of address, because I see you have worldly wisdom beyond your years. Do you realize what you are asking me to do? You have just delivered my death certificate. While I would expect this from the present rulers at any time, it is strange that it comes from someone who professes to love my daughter. How could I continue to be a cantor at my synagogue, with my daughter Rahel married to a Christian, whose father is an officer in the SS? If I cannot sing any more the praises of God, the entreaties to God, the request for fulfilment of his ancient promise to his chosen race, then I am nothing, I am dead.'

'Moshe, consider,' put in his wife.

An angry but controlled glance from Herr Reimann's eyes was sufficient to stifle her intended pleading. He continued:

'The day I give consent to your plans, shall be my last. This I swear. And now no more about this March madness. Have the goodness to share our modest meal with us, Herr Messing.'

Rolf looked at Rahel's mother. She indicated, by slowly lifting the insides of her hands to the height of her shoulders, her inability, not her unwillingness, to help against such doom dedication. She went to the kitchen.

Rahel's father took a notebook from his pocket. He opened it and perused several pages covered with Hebrew letters.

'I have here,' he said, 'an inventory of your country's measures against my race. It gives you an interesting picture of a plan of a gradual reduction of power to live, until the sewer rat has far better chances of survival than we.

1.4.33.   *Boycott of Jewish doctors, lawyers and businesses.*
12.4.33 *Jewish students refused admission to Universities.*
22.4.33 *Jewish doctors can no longer work for health insurance.*
4.5.33   *Dismissal of Jewish civil servants and employees in public services.*
5.2.34   *Jews may not take exams as doctors or dentists.*
28.7.35 *Jews excluded from many municipal baths.*

18.8.35 Marriage between Aryans and non-Aryans forbidden.

15.9.35 Jews may not employ females under 45 in their homes.

24.3.36 Jewish families with many children lose their state benefit.

26.3.36 Jewish apothecaries declared illegal.

This is just the beginning, Herr Messing. But, our God is a God who does not forget. He is a God of vengeance, who will exact retribution, measure for measure, on the day of reckoning.'

Here Rahel's mother brought in the soup.

Rolf did not know what he was doing, whether he was eating or not, since his head was full of conflicting tales of hostile races, of the Nazis and the orthodox Jews. His bridge building, where was it now? Who was the worse imbecile in the uneven battle between the two? He thought of the richly bejewelled Jewesses he had seen, flaunting their Persian fur coats in the restaurants on the Kurfürstendamm. He remembered the uncommonly high percentage of Jewish doctors, lawyers, writers, actors, musicians and chess players. He used to explain this. Jews, he would say, had only fairly recently been given the same rights as their hosts, and that was their way of celebrating their freedom, in common with the high numbers of doctors, lawyers, writers, actors, musicians and chess players, who displayed their intelligence, honed to near perfection in the long ghetto years.

When Rahel's mother served the fish dish, Rolf said at last:

'This is a terrible indictment, Herr Reimann. I can only hope the system that is responsible for those totally unjustifiable rules and laws, will not survive much longer, and that you will soon regain all your rights as German citizens.'

As nobody responded to this, Rolf continued:

'When the time comes, we shall have to rebuild, reclaim, heal. All of us. You and I, Herr Reimann.'

Rahel's father looked at his watch. 'I must hurry. The Barmitzvah class starts in quarter of an hour.' He laid into his carp more quickly than was good for his digestion, but at least it dispensed him from continuing the conversation.

Before leaving his dinner, Rahel's father took Rolf aside:

'You are a sensible young man, Herr Messing. I am sorry we find ourselves diametrically opposed, given the time and particularly the space. When you see Rahel next, give her our love. I cannot stop you, but I should find it more appropriate, if you would turn your relationship into one of pure friendship. Remember, she is but a female.'

Rahel's mother, who from the moment of her husband's arrival had been timidly kept in the background, now looked at Rolf with her big, black eyes full of sympathy.

'Do not judge him too severely, Rolf. He has so many things on his mind. As cantor, he regards his voice as a link between God and his people. He sees and hears of many atrocities committed against members of his dwindling congregation. And now Rahel. He always wanted a son, of course. But God gave us just one daughter. For me she is indeed a pearl of great price. He thinks of her, with pity, as but a female.'

'Do I understand that you approve your husband's injunction, for Rahel and me to -'

'No, Rolf. As Rahel's mother, I bid you - let your heart be your conscience.'

On his way home, Rolf went along the Oranienburger Strasse, until he came to the junction with the August Strasse. He halted at the tall, modern building, from which the sound of singing, of particularly fine singing emanated. It was a girls' school, with the choir practising after school hours. He went as close as he could towards the entrancing sound. What was it he heard? German folk songs. *Ade nun zur guten Nacht* (Marie, it's good night to you) in three parts. And *Hoch auf dem gelben Wagen* (High on the yellow wagon). And *Lustig ist das Zigeunerleben* (Merry is the gypsy's life). And *Drüben am Wiesenrand* (Yonder in the meadow). Rolf looked up to read the large letters across the outer wall: *Jewish School For Girls.* Surely, he thought, here is the key to survival. At a time when the sounds officially preferred were marching tunes, this choir practised German folk songs, with innocence and dedication. They were, without knowing it, hurling a bridge into the future.

CHAPTER 17

Rolf neglected his school work at a nonchalant speed. He found it irrelevant and a waste of time. But he discovered a new entertainment that was neither. Six day racing had lately taken over Berlin. It came from America, and now Berliners could revel in its excitement throughout the night. Hans-Joachim, a seasoned and knowledgeable follower, was the right partner for Rolf. They met under the Kolonnaden, from where it was just five minutes to the *Sportpalast.*

Inside, they marvelled at the transformation this theatrically designed building had undergone. Surrounded by a good many rows of seats for the spectators was the cycle track, constructed with two equidistant, long straights, linked to each other with two hair raising, double curves, which swept high up, giving the cyclist who had climbed and then swooped down, a tremendous speed.

'There are twelve teams of two,' explained Hans-Joachim, 'and they cycle uninterruptedly for six days and nights, one of each team, until he is relieved by his partner's hand touching his shoulder. Between the hours of early morning to mid-afternoon the race is neutralised, that is you can cycle as slowly as you will, as long as you keep going. The partners meanwhile snooze in those cabins you see in the centre, marked 1 to 12.'

The arena was packed with enthusiasts. There was a constant movement of spectators from their seats to the refreshment stalls and toilets, and a mass of sound coming from thousands of throats, animating their favourites, mixed with the noisy brass band.

The two friends sat in their seats and studied the programme. Hans-Joachim explained:

'In five minutes, at eight o'clock, we have the Chase for Points. It lasts for one hour and features a number of races within the overall race, each with five points for the winner, four points for the second, and so on. You swap partners after each race. Watch the team in white and black, the number three. Ehmer-Kroschel, my favourites. They are Berliners.'

A clamorous bell commanded a sudden hush. The announcer explained over the public address system that the Chase for Points was about to begin. When he had finished the spectators answered with a redoubled burst of sound.

'Twelve rounds to go,' said Hans-Joachim.

'Where is your Ehmer or Kroschel?' asked Rolf.

'Right amongst the rear. But don't worry. It's Ehmer. He is a terrific finisher.'

Hans-Joachim was right. By the tenth round, Ehmer was in the middle, by round eleven he had joined the leaders, and when the bell went to announce the final round, he climbed high into the curve, and from there unleashed an irresistible finish, to cross the line several metres before the rest.

Rolf agreed that here was an exceptional sprinter. But would he have the staying power for six days and nights?

By the end of the hour, Ehmer had won three sprints, came third once, and his partner, Kroschel, won two and came second once. Their total in this particular chase was 32 points.

'The eventual winners of the six day race will be the winner of the most sprints?' asked Rolf.

'No, it's not that simple. Let us look at the programme. Here is the position after the fourth day. Van Kempen-Rutt lead by 2 laps.'

'Now you have lost me,' said Rolf.

'We shall see.'

Hans-Joachim took his friend to the sandwich bar. 'At eleven o'clock an hour's Free-For-All will take place. That is the climax of the whole night, when the winning or the losing of a complete lap may decide the eventual winner.'

Rolf let his eyes wander up and down the whole arena. Below sat the select. Film stars, leaders of commerce, high party functionaries. Suddenly he gripped his friend's arm:

'Look! Leni. Five rows below. At the third table from the left. With - no, it is not my father. It's an SA man. A come-down. She must have had her baby. There is a champagne bottle on their table.'

At that moment, the bell summoned silence for the announcement over the public address:

'My lords, ladies and gentlemen. In five minutes you will hear the siren sound. That means, the Free-For-All is about to begin.'

Rolf asked, 'Shall we meet her? Exchange some pleasantries? We might tell her how good she looks, and enquire after the baby.'

'Better no. In any case, the next hour will be too exciting for chit-chat.'

And it was. Right at the outset, one of the bottom teams tried to win back one of their seven laps they had lost to the leaders. They were a young pair, having their first Six Day experience. After an initial dash, they had gained three quarters of a lap on the rest of the field, who showed little interest in stopping them. But they took turns too often. In every round their change-over cost them slight, but vital delays. After five minutes they were so exhausted, that they were caught by the rest and promptly fell back, losing another lap.

Hans-Joachim explained, 'Whoever gains the highest number of laps, will be the overall winner. After that, the number of points won will decide the final position of the teams who are on equal laps.'

A yellow streak flashed by. Piet van Kempen, the flying Dutchman, had come from far behind, climbed high into the curve, and swept down the track. Single-handed he overhauled the field, before giving way to his partner.

'A canny customer,' remarked Rolf. 'He is not interested in points. But he has gained three laps on the field.'

Midnight. An hour to go before the next feature, the Devil-take-the-Hindmost.

'I'll explain when it starts,' said Hans-Joachim, when the band struck up the crowd's favourite, the *Sportpalast Waltz*. In the front row, above the finishing straight, sat *Krücke* (The Crutch), a small, rotund invalid, who attended every Six-Day race in Berlin, always at the same seat. He was the official mascot of the spectators, and now, in the Waltz played by the band, you learned why. He had a most mellifluous whistle, with unfailing intonation and immense carrying power. Indeed, he was the band's finest instrument. And now, during the next three minutes, there was silence in the vast spaces of the arena, while Krücke, assisted by his band, gave his prize performance. Roaring applause accompanied the collection of silver and banknotes, presented to him in several buckets from both sides of the house.

Devil-take-the Hindmost. This turned out the most exciting entertainment of the night. They competed in ten times ten rounds. The last of the twelve riders in each lap was eliminated, until only two were left. The flying Dutchman was the first to quit. Voluntarily. He knew better, for he reserved his energies for the decisive battles to come, for preservation of this three laps' advantage. In the final ten rounds the field consisted of Kaufmann and Ehmer. The young Swiss led by a quarter of a lap, until the eighth lap, when Ehmer began his devastating spurt and beat his opponent by the merest whisker. Premium: 100 points.

When the night advanced towards the next morning, prominent guests were introduced to the spectators. Willy Fritsch and Lilian Harvey, the stars of the big screen. They chatted amiable for three minutes over the tannoy, gave details of their next immortal creation, and finally offered a thousand marks to the next competitor who gained a lap.

After they witnessed Piet van Kempen earning his acclaimed windfall, Rolf and his friend made their way to the exit. They passed Leni's table, where she and her friend were far too engrossed in each other, to take much notice of what was happening around them.

Outside, the early editions of the morning papers were sold. What a good thing that Rolf did not buy one. He would have been greatly troubled by the headline:

Church Councillor Kietz Arrested.

On the first day of the Easter holidays, three young men made their ways separately from London to Ursus Castle. Hans-Joachim travelled on the morning boat to Harwich. The representative of the *Trucht* made his way via Paris and Calais, while Rolf, warned by his experiences on the previous journey, took a later Calais steamer. The three rendezvoused at Penrith, in the Lakes, and phoned the school for transport.

At the gates of Ursus Castle stood Mrs Messing and Rahel. When the landrover arrived, she raced towards it and flung her arms around Rolf. Silently they went inside.

After dinner Mrs Messing and her three guests assembled for their first meeting, which was followed by several more. The purpose of their discussions was to establish a fairly safe route of arguing with anybody who was willing to argue, about religious aspects, such as the existence of God, immortality, free will, persecution in the name of the deity, civil liberty under the church, papal infallibility, punishment of infidels. At the end of the third evening Mrs Messing announced:

'We have established two layers of debate. Firstly, nothing is ever to be written down. No memory aides. No drawings. Nothing at all. Secondly, the line of argument. Concentrate entirely on the religious aspect which is also the Nazi-line. Never mention the present leaders or their way of thinking. Let it appear that you wish to support their line. In reality you make them think, and eventually they will ask questions and, hopefully, rebel. Happy with that?'

The three indicated that it was a fair summary. Only Rolf was dejected about Rahel's absence from their discussions, which was due to his own insistence. Rahel, he thought, had enough to worry about, and her religion was at least something to cling to.

Rolf sat on Rahel's sofa, with the girl stretched out and her head cradled in his lap. He had been telling her about his encounter with her mother and father.

'Poor mother,' sighed Rahel. 'It would not be fair to expect any assistance from her, in her present state of health. Father has always been a difficult man to understand. I do not know whether his religion is real or imaginative. He bases his belief in the inferiority of women on the bible. How can one?'

'Let us just agree that he is set in his ways, and leave the bible out of it.'

'What shall we - what can we do?' asked Rahel, tears surging. 'First let us tackle her health problems. She says she does not want any assistance. How can we get round that? We cannot send an *Ayran* doctor to the Oranienburger Strasse, - - - I have it! We must somehow persuade her to go and see the *enemy*.'

Rahel and Rolf thought long and hard. Then she spoke:

'Two problems must be solved. Who and how. Who is the medical adviser who would agree to the unusual proposal to treat a Jewish patient? And secondly, how can we persuade mother to undertake such hazards, without her husband's knowledge?'

'Leave both to me. To us. We have faced more difficult tasks in the past. We shall manage.'

On their last evening at Ursus Castle, three young guardian angels assembled in Rolf's room. They were Hans-Joachim, the newly won Sven, and Rolf himself, all convinced not only that they were right in what they intended to do, but that it could be done.

The first problem to be discussed was that of Rahel's mother. Hans-Joachim said:

'My mother has told me of a doctor who treats several Jewish patients. Privately. No fuss. Nobody needs to know.'

Sven said:

'I have a classmate. He is a friend. Jewish. He could help. He would help.'

Rolf summed up:

'All right. Sven's friend persuades Frau Reimann to see the doctor secured by Hans-Joachim. I ascertain the most favourable time for the visit. A whole morning or a whole afternoon, when the Cantor is not at home. Agreed?'

'Agreed,' the three declared in unison. Their deliberation of the second problem took the best part of the night. In the morning, they departed, with Rahel looking after the station wagon, long after it had disappeared behind the bend in the road. In her head was Rolf's parting message:

'*Let us be sober, putting on the breastplate of faith and love*'.

CHAPTER 18

1862. Bettina was feeding the young. Under her careful nurture, three fine specimens had grown to be ten, four and three years old. Yossl composed. Yossl gave demonstrations and lectures. Yossl cultivated all the arts, in his effort to learn from practitioners both friendly and opposed to his own ideas. Yossl tried to build bridges, to connect his art with theirs. One such was a man some twenty years older than himself.

'Call me Carl,' said the man.

'Thank you, Carl, I will. You mentioned Paris yesterday. When did you see this wonderful, this cruel city?'

'Last year. I agree with your first description. But cruel, Yossl?'

'You must have heard of Wagner. No? Richard Wagner, whose shoelaces none of us is worthy to tie. He had his *Tannhäuser* whistled off the stage in that unpredictable town.'

Carl Spitzweg, wealthy painter, shook his head.

'Tell me, what did you make of the freaks? My freaks? Did they mean anything to you? Did they speak?'

'Did they speak? A whole fortnight I listened to them, and then I wrote down what they told me. Do you want to see and hear?'

The Sunday Excursion

Can anyone tell me why we must? Sunday after blessed Sunday?

Just now, I should be lighting my pipe in my garden.

Rover would be snoring in my onion bed, while the children were playing in the next-but-one meadow.

Instead? Sweat, sore feet, giggling and fretting, and terrified butterflies. Another four and a half miles.

My God. My God. My God. Tomorrow is Monday. What a comfort!

The Eternal Bridegroom

Ears and eyes in every doorway, everybody makes a fuss.
Neighbour's milkmaids titter, twitter, and your mother
watches us.
There it happened in your chamber,
Where we two together lay,
And your bed began to creak, love,
That it took your breath away.
All the moonlight night we snuggled,
And your teeth have left their mark.
Tomcat howled and screech owl hooted.
Mother too, was in the dark.
Time has come for moderation
Hence this bashful floral show.
Let my honeysuckle tell you,
What the world must never know.

The Love Letter

Highly esteemed Madame, Open this letter while I watch you from above. Heavens, how slender and youthful you are! One might take you for your Demoiselle daughter. Permit me to be brief, time is short. They are performing the delightful *Till Eulenspiegel* in the Residenz Theatre around the corner. Please accept the enclosed ticket and go in my place. Why? Because you look so entrancing in your yellow spring creation. To return the favour, dearest lady, kindly ask your Demoiselle daughter, to favour me with a cup of her delicious lime blossom tea, up here, in my attic room. But please hurry. The performance begins in a few minutes.

Embarrassing Scrutiny

Greetings, dear father! Are you going hunting? I? I was just strolling in the meadows, picking flowers. Yes, this is where I must have fallen asleep. That's why the corn is a little squashed. My hair? Dishevelled? No wonder. It's so very windy today. And before you ask me father, the top hat - well, I found it - in the road. You know where the post chaise always takes that corner too fast. Yes, some fine gentleman must have lost it. You see what the wind is up to today. And now the scarecrow can lose its old hat, and get a noble, shiny one instead. Adieu, father, and good hunting!

What a good thing he did not notice the walking stick!

Carl Spitzweg read and re-read. Then he gave the four poems with their pictures back to Yossl, folded his hands and leaned back in his grandfather chair. A lengthy silence ensued. When at last he spoke, he had to clear his voice several times before he could speak effortlessly. 'Why could we not have met earlier? You understand me. Better and more fully than anyone. They would have flocked to my atelier. They would have bought my pictures. Together we would have introduced them to the quiet merit of the non-conformist - We would have? We can still do it! Yossl, let us plan. You could give Spitzweg presentations, with your texts and my pictures. I shall be there, if possible. We shall sell programmes with some reproductions. There will be Spitzweg/Messing almanacs on offer. Where is the limit?'

Yossl listened to the outpourings of the older man and comrade with a mixture of incredulity and admiration. He had experienced the uncertainty of staged spectacles. He was aware of the immense preparation, the follow-ups, the whole apparatus which needed a cool manager's head. He would discuss this with Bettina. Perhaps one of his old Coburg friends would be interested?

Carl Spitzweg opened a bottle of *Urzheimer Auslese*.

'Here is to us, Yossl!'

The wine was wonderful. During the following hour they emptied two bottles, with their cheers growing more extravagant, but their pronunciation somewhat risky. Yossl said:

'Here is to the oddities on this earth.'

'Bohemians, unite. No, bohemians would not. Just, bohemians!' said Carl Spitzweg.

'The eccentrics! May they flourish!' said Yossl.

And the painter added, before slumber closed in:

'Here - is - to the - *Originals*. The only originals. Carl Spitzweg and Yossl Messing.'

Their dreams were of fame, fortune and how to find a true place in the world for the world's most puzzling inhabitant, the free spirit.

CHAPTER 19

Did Hans Eifer, with all his meticulous care for detail, overlook the baby's, his baby's tendency for forming an aquiline nose? Did he agree to Leni's outrageous suggestion to christen the newcomer *Josefene*? The more he grew indifferent to domestic irregularities, the greater his attention to the promotional machinations within the SS. Now he had reached the natural limit to his ambitions, equality with Peter Schleifer. Above him? The untouchables. To break in there, was given only to those who were on speaking terms with the bullet or the poison bottle.

The interrogation room was ready. A desk. An armchair. A high stool. An adjustable, powerful spotlight. No other illumination. No windows.

An exhausted elderly man with white hair was half dragged, half carried in by two wardens. They deposited him on the stool. The spotlight was turned full on his eyes. As he tried to shade them with his hands, they were roughly wrenched backwards and tied behind him.

'Kietz?' asked Eifer.

'Church Councillor Hieronymus Kietz,' came the weary reply.

'You know why you are here?'

'I have not the faintest idea, I confess.' came the weary reply from the Church Councillor's lips.

'So, you confess.'

'I what?'

'You have just admitted your guilt.'

'I did nothing of the kind. I said, to the best of my recollection, that I confessed to having no idea why I have been arrested. But I wish to protest against my detention as well as my bondage and my prevention of sleep. When the Bishop of Hamburg - -'

Hans Eifer gave a command to the two attendants to untie the Church Councillor's hands. He tried a different approach, the one recommended by the book, modified into a one-man-with-two-faces operation. Also, mention of the Bishop helped his sudden humanity:

'Let us be sensible. After all, we are after the simple truth. Tell me just one thing. What happened to the donation you received from Joseph Messing, the day he came to Lübeck three years ago?'

'Joseph Messing? Messing? - Let me see. Do turn that absurd spotlight off, will you?'

The Church Councillor took his notebook from his pocket and perused it. The light was swivelled away from his face, illuminating the reading area. Several minutes passed.

'Yes. Joseph Messing called for a certificate of his grandfather's birth, which I issued in due course. And here is a codicil. 'Spire donation 1000 marks by J Messing'. I thanked him in my letter which advised him of his grandfather's birth and christening. Herr Messing's bank should have proof of the transaction, if needed.'

'I see,' said Hans Eifer, now truly chastened, as he realized that the arrest had been a mistake. To ingratiate himself, he added:

'I must admit, we seem to have slipped up in your case. I shall investigate the circumstances of your regrettable detention and shall take personal responsibility for punishing those responsible. Meanwhile, please accept my apologies for this regrettable little interlude. I hope to be able to make up for it in the future.'

'Perhaps a donation for the restoration of our church spire? It is nearly finished, but every bit is important to us.'

Hans Eifer reached for his cheque book and handed the Church Councillor 500 marks.

'May we arrange transport for you to the station?'

'No, thank you. The Bishop's car is waiting outside.'

Hans-Joachim, his head full of plans for the coming, more salubrious state of the world, was alone with his mother. Eva Schleifer, his mother, kept an open mind about the Jewish question, but concealed such treacherous tendencies from her husband.

On his return from Ursus Castle, with Dr Schleifer away on official duty, mother and son shared dinner at home. Eva wanted to know more about Mrs Messing's school.

'Mother, it is a peerless place. It lacks our discipline and state propaganda, but it plants the seeds of thinking for yourself in the minds of the young. If it were not treacherous, I should say it is the place for me.' 'Steady, Hans-Joachim' said his mother. She looked over her shoulder, for in 1938 you could not be sure whether your *Hauswart* (house monitor) was on listening duty outside.

'I have a risky question, mother,' said Hans-Joachim, putting her in the picture about Rahel and Rolf, about Rahel's father and mother, and about the treatment she needed. His appeal to Eva Schleifer's heart was counter-balanced by the perils its realization would entail. After some hesitation she picked up the phone and made an appointment with Dr Fischer.

Heinz Benjamin, Sven's classmate, was knocking at the door of Oranienburger Strasse 17b. Frau Reimann looked through the spy glass, and on recognizing the unknown but unmistakable facial characteristics of her own people, she opened the door.

'I am sent by Rolf Messing,' he said. 'My name is Benjamin. Heinz Benjamin. Is your husband at home?'

'No, but come inside.'

Settling in the chair that was offered, he began:

'Your daughter Rahel and her friend Rolf beseech you to take the medical counsel which has been arranged for you. There are no costs. Everything has been prepared for an initial consultation with the leading man in the field. Transport is ready. All you need is to decide when you are free for, say, three hours. For Rahel's sake, please say yes.'

Several minutes elapsed, spent in thinking, consulting notebooks, and finally Frau Reimann said, with a heavy heart.

'Yes, I will.'

Three days later, when her husband attended his half-day classes at the Synagogue, Frau Reimann went to the West End by car, to see Dr Fischer. She was not shown into the waiting room, but straight into the surgery. The next forty minutes were spent with exhaustive tests, questions and investigations. At the end Dr Fischer pronounced his patient's health as precarious though stable. He prescribed medication and wanted to see her again in four weeks. Frau Reimann left the way she came in, with the car waiting for her.

The *Trucht* was an exclusive, small organisation within the German youth movement, which consisted of the finest, the fittest and the most intelligent young men. It was, therefore, forbidden to exist in 1933. But a former member of the *Trucht* is one for life, however long or short. Sven was one of them. His older brother, Erich, however never belonged. He was a Battalion Leader in the Hitler Youth.

'Erich, do you believe in God?' Sven asked him one evening, apropos of nothing.

'How much do you want?'

'No. Seriously. Do you believe God exists? And is he all-powerful?'

'Yes. Of course. And he is omnipotent.'

'I think so, too. But if he is omnipotent, can he create a stone that is too heavy for him to lift?'

'Silly question. Of course he can.'

'If the stone is too heavy for him to lift, then he is not omnipotent.'

Silence. Erich pondered. Then he said:

'There is something wrong with the mathematics of your proposition. I was never any good with figures, with plus and minus, when at school, but I know there is something not quite proper with your question. I know someone who gets it right. I'll consult him. You will have your answer by tomorrow.'

'I can give you the right answer now,' said Sven. 'Being omnipotent includes the ability to perform the unperformable. To bridge the chasm that separates one fact from its opposite. Omnipotence is something profound and breathtaking. It includes the ability to see all sides of an argument. It suffers no clear answer. It never says Yes or No. It always says Yes. And then it goes on to say why. It is breathtaking.'

'Sven, old boy. Thinking is all right. But speculating? Next time you feel like talking about omnipotence, take a cold shower instead.'

Rolf was awaiting his father's return from the radio station. This gave him the opportunity for writing a letter to Rahel. In it he informed her of her mother's visit to a doctor. He omitted names and other details, in case the letter was intercepted. But he expressed his satisfaction about the outcome, and hoped that she, too, felt easier about her mother now. He ended with:

'I have just obtained my school leaving certificate. A pass, with Satisfactory in most subjects. That will do. What next? Expect me at Ursus Castle in a fortnight, when we shall discuss this, and much else besides. Best love, Rolf.'

He re-read this a few times. Then he scribbled at the bottom:

'Rahel. My Rahel.'

Joseph Messing entered. He put his coat on a coat hanger, the umbrella in the umbrella stand, his hat on the hat shelf, and took his reading glasses, and the polishing cloth from the spectacle case with the engraved initials *JM*. The evening paper featured the mistaken arrest and the subsequent apology of Hans Eifer.

'I suppose we must be grateful that this cup has passed us by' he remarked. 'As for Eifer, he has earned this setback. I must admit some satisfaction. Have you heard from your school yet?'

'Yes, with the midday post. Satisfactory. All I wanted. Or deserved.'

'You have left the question of your study undecided far too long, Rolf. What will you do?'

'I wish it were an easy matter to decide. But I still do not know. Basically there are two possibilities. Coburg, with its ideal places for studying music, and the return to my roots, to my great-grandfather. Or England, with Ursus Castle.'

'And Rahel,' observed his father.

'Yes. She is constantly on my mind. She is seventeen now and has another year at Ursus Catle. Resettling in Germany is out of the question, of course. That means - you can see my dilemma, father, can't you?'

'O Rolf, Rolf. If you were not my son. I would do anything to keep you here. But - my own flesh and blood. No.'

Rolf rose slowly, walked over to his father and kissed him silently on the forehead. Mr Messing looked bewildered at his son.

'I know that you believe in the coming war and unspecified catastrophies. I believe in Adolf Hitler, his basic goodness and sense of decency.'

It occurred to Rolf that here was an opportunity, for doing his father a good turn, by broaching the topic that might make him think and rethink.

'You make it sound as if Hitler were a god, with his sense of decency and goodness.'

'That is my belief.'

'Is God really good and does He have a sense of decency? In the face of untold human misery, destruction by disease, catastrophes, hunger and premature death, can we truly call this power God?'

'What would you call it?'

'Devil?'

'Rolf. Hush, Rolf!'

'No. I do not mean it. I only want to show you that the one is as inapplicable as the other. A god with a sense of decency, a god who listens to prayer, to cajolings, or to sacrifices, does not exist. A power, call it God, call it what you will, that is totally immune, totally indifferent to our troubles, is the only feasibility.'

'You have picked up those ungodly notions from your ungodly mother, haven't you?'

'I simply repeat the official party line, father. After a hundred years, Darwin is in, and the bible is out.'

Joseph Messing shook his head, while he contemplated life without God, who surely had his place in a receptacle that could be opened on Sundays, for a few minutes of private consultation. He was not aware of Darwin having supplanted the New Testament. The Old one, perhaps. Anyway, it was much more comfortable to continue believing in God as practically everybody did. It involved no extra expense, no commitment. As for Darwin, Joseph Messing decided to continue leaving him at the outer periphery of his thoughts. His theories were not proven. Just theories.

'Father,' said Rolf, hinting that the argument had run its course. 'Will you support my stay at Ursus Castle for an open-ended period? It may be a week, it may be a month.'

'No need to ask. Rolf. My compliments to your mother. And -' here he looked at the entrance door and continued sotto voice, 'and - love to Rahel.'

CHAPTER 20

It was almost summer, in 1938, when Rolf set out on his third visit to Ursus Castle. This time he took the old, familiar route via Hook van Holland and Harwich. He wanted to test the border control, whether the last incident was just that, or whether the authorities planned something sinister. His suspicions proved illusory. and he enjoyed a trouble-free journey. The German rulers seemed to indicate their readiness for peace and orderliness, in a state wholly devoted to the greatest happiness for the greatest number of its citizens.

Twenty-four hours later he arrived at Ursus Castle. As it was past midnight, only his mother was awake to greet him.

'Welcome, Rolf. It is good to have you here with us. I wish it could be for ever.'

'That is why I want your advice - how is Rahel?'

Before his mother could answer, the door to Mrs Messing's study was flung open, simultaneously, with three or four knocks. They rested in each other's arms.

In the morning, Rolf took some time to take in all the new features of the school. Mrs Messing had doubled its size. There were now forty-two children, between eight and seventeen. A new mistress had been engaged. Two rooms Rolf did not know existed, were opened for educational purposes.

Hanna and Sigi, now thirteen or fourteen, greeted Rolf with joy.

'I remember your singing as Jessica,' said Rolf. 'Your Israeli tune, that blended so unexpectedly with Sigi's - I mean with Lorenzo's nocturnal lines.'

'I have not got so much time for Shakespeare now. They have made me chief assistant to the cook.'

To the six-foot boy who had joined them, Rolf said:

'You must be Nathan.'

'Jonathan,' he replied. 'You won't believe this, but I am training with the England squad to become a useful long jumper.

116

They actually say I might make the Olympics. If not the 1940, then the 1944.'

'Terrific,' Rolf proposed. 'How about joining the teaching staff at Ursus Castle, later on?'

'Exactly what I have in mind. Sports, Self-Defence, Swimming.'

After school hours, Rolf and Rahel met for a walk in the neighbouring lanes.

'My mother,' said Rahel.

'I know,' Rolf answered. 'The first step has been taken. The fact that she actually went out to consult Dr Fischer -'

'Who paid for it all? The tests, the medicaments, the taxi?'

'Please do not ask. There are plenty of decent people left in Germany. If too many questions are asked, they risk losing their lives. But now we have to encourage your mother to take an interest again in her art. We must encourage her to paint. Will her husband object?'

'Father is stubborn. He has not always been. But now he has decided on the best way - the only way to survive. And that is seclusion from the outside world, both for himself and for his wife. And the wife's place is the kitchen.'

'Why not ask her opinion on some matters connected with your own efforts? Can you send her some drawing or painting and ask what she thinks of it?'

They declared the matter closed for the present. In a gently rising field, they sank into the oats, and gave themselves over to innocent oblivion.

'Mother, what is to become of me?'

Mrs Messing thought for a while, before she responded:

'That will depend on several circumstances, some of them out of our control. The present nightmare in Germany - when will it terminate? What do you see yourself doing in, say, five years' time, if a fairy fulfilled your innermost wishes? Is it independence as a composer, or teaching in our school? How does Rahel fit in?'

'Yes. It is a trauma. Let us start with your final point. I cannot and will not entertain the idea of a lengthy separation from

Rahel. As for the situation in Germany, an early collapse of the regime must be questionable, in spite of the opposition which is restricted, alas, to internal forces alone. We cannot count on help from abroad. Peace at any price - that is the magic slogan there. That seems to leave me with Ursus Castle. Much as I would like to, is that practicable? I mean, how can I study to become a teacher?'

'Several obstacles stand in the way. However, they could be overcome. You would need a special dispensation from the Ministry of Labour, to enable you to study in this country. Then we would have to apply for permission to employ you, showing that your qualifications are better than those of native competitors.'

'Say no more, mother. I want to discuss this with Rahel. But I feel, she would agree that our future lies in England, at your school.'

Afternoon class at Ursus Castle. All forty-two pupils assembled in the gym for this, since the combined classes had reached Rahel's daily routine of her Swiss Day with the evening, the time for her leisure, for reading about the Swiss hero, William Tell. That involved geographical facts, social conditions, freedom as a matter of life or death, the world of Friedrich Schiller, and the names of the Austrian oppressors.

It started with a presentation of a scene from Schiller's play, *Wilhelm Tell*, which the students had been preparing for several weeks.

Mrs Messing, book in hand, stood before her pupils.

'You have read the third act of this drama, in which Gessler forces Tell to shoot the apple from his child's head. To Gessler's dismay, Tell has been successful. Now let us see, how he reacts. Sigi, will you be Gessler? And you, Paul, are Tell.'

Sigi (Gessler)	*A word, Tell.*
Paul (Tell)	*Sir, your pleasure?*
Sigi (Gessler)	*Thou didst place a second arrow in thy belt. I saw it well. Thy purpose with it? Speak!*
Paul (Tell)	*It is a custom with all archers.*

Sigi (Gessler)	*No, Tell, I cannot let that answer pass.* *There was some other motive, well I* *know.* *Frankly and cheerfully confess the truth.* *What'er it be. I promise thee thy life.* *Wherefore the second arrow?*
Paul (Tell)	*Since you have promised not to take my* *life, I will, without reserve, declare the* *truth. If that my hand had struck my* *darling child, this second arrow I had* *aimed at you. And, be assured, I should* *not then have missed.*
Sigi (Gessler)	*Well, Tell, I promised thou shouldst have* *thy life. Yet, as I know the malice of thy* *thoughts, I'll have thee carried hence,* *and safely penned, where neither sun nor* *moon shall reach thine eyes.* *Thus from thy arrows I shall be secure.* *Seize on him, guards, and bind him!*

Silence. Then murmuring. Then clamouring voices.

'Just as it is in Germany today.' - 'When did he write this?' - 'Schiller. 1759 to 1805.' - 'Why Austria?' - 'Think who was born there.' - 'Can we have it again?' - 'Yes. But give Gessler more bonhomie. To enhance his wickedness. And Tell: try for a little more innocent revelation of the truth, which promotes his downfall.'

The second, improved reading of the scene took place. This time the silence at the end was prolonged. Then, first one pair of hands began to clap, then others followed, until all were united in their ringing approbation.

Rolf and Rahel made for the same field that gave them shelter yesterday. Only this time they went up to its highest part. Under the branches of an oak tree they sat down, prepared to share its amenities with a flock a gently bleating sheep.

'Rahel, I want your advice. This is a question that concerns us both. I have left school. I am eighteen. I do not know what to do.'

119

'Have you asked your mother?'

'She suggests seeking permission for staying in England, for studying to become a teacher, and for eventually working here, at Ursus Castle. That would include you, and my dreams would come to fruition.'

'Is there an alternative?'

'Yes, there is. There is. We would go to Coburg, where Yossl spent those exciting years. I would study music, and you would study art. There we would fulfil ourselves.'

'Wait a moment. Haven't you forgotten something? Who has heard of a Jewess going back to Germany in 1938?'

'Forgive me, Rahel. I quite forgot. So Coburg will be postponed until the situation in Germany has changed.'

'Dearest, that will not be for a long time. Perhaps not in our lifetime. No. I can see just two possible careers for you. One in England. And one in Germany.'

'You mean, one with you, and the other without you.'

'Yes, dearest.'

'It is settled then,' said Rolf.

'Is it?'

'Sheep!'

They kissed. They were together. Baa. Baa.

'Rolf.'

'Yes?'

'I was wrong. You must go to Coburg. Your heart is already there. Composing. Conducting. Becoming what you were meant to be. Think about the chances you would have to influence people, to build bridges.'

Rolf interrupted her. 'Not without you!'

'I shall wait for you. Possibly at Ursus Castle. I shall - we shall talk to your mother about this. Tonight.'

Sigi walked into the open room. They had left the door ajar, because they expected him, carrying his culinary masterpiece for three. Now his moment had arrived when, with a grin, he planted his large tray and three covered dishes before his diners, Mrs Messing, Rahel and Rolf. The three rose simultaneously, as was the custom at Ursus Castle, put their hands on the covers, and synchronized their uncovering of the dishes. Fruit salad, prepared with care and imagination and lashings of Swiss cream. Apples, Oranges, Bananas, Mangoes, Blackberries, Apricots, Peaches, Sultanas and Walnuts. Sigi, still smiling, bowed out. His future at Ursus Castle seemed assured.

Half an hour later, they discussed a serious matter. Was Rolf to study in Germany or in England? Rahel put the case for Coburg, for Rolf's roots, for his great-grandfather, Yossl, for his true destiny. She added that she would be waiting for him, no matter how long.

Rolf objected. He would not abandon Rahel. A change of regime in Germany was unlikely, at least in the foreseeable future. Teaching at Ursus Castle would suit him fine.

Mrs Messing weighed, wondered, meditated. Then she spoke:

'Why don't we take the preliminary steps for both careers in the same way we took our fruit salad? There is no harm in finding out, what is possible and what is not. I shall make enquiries from the relevant authorities about permissions to stay in the country, where to study, how to apply for a teaching post at my school. And you, Rolf, investigate the position in Coburg. Just in case. Things might change. As for Rahel, she will remain my responsibility, until you can set up house, wherever. Coburg or no.'

Rolf stayed another fortnight at Ursus Castle. He made music with the two classes, played the guitar and the piano, chatted with the students whenever he could, had many wonderful hours alone with Rahel, reading to her, listening to her, admiring her drawings, and going on many rambles, three to Mount Skiddaw.

They resolved that Rolf would undertake another trip to the Oranienburger Strasse, to see whether he could help in building up Frau Reimann's independence. And, with mixed emotions, he agreed on a fact-finding visit to Coburg.

CHAPTER 21

Rolf's passion for Richard Wagner was of recent origin, but it swept its compulsive way into his reading habits like a tornado. During the past few months, he had accumulated a small library of his writings, letters, diaries and monographs. He had a few of them at Ursus Castle, but he did not mention them to Rahel yet. That would have to wait until he knew more about this mysterious man. But he read voraciously, on the train, on the boat, and at home.

On his way to Frau Reimann, about two hundred metres from her door, Rolf was startled by the screeching sound of a car, which had slewn halfway across the road, in an effort to avoid some obstacle. It turned out that a careless pedestrian had crossed the road, without looking left or right, and was saved only by the motorist's prompt action. Unconcerned, the reckless man went on his way, followed by fierce comments from the driver.

Rolf looked surprised, as he found the near-victim a young man of about his own age.

'Pardon me,' he said. 'Are you new to Berlin? Can I help you?'

It turned out that he was indeed not used to the traffic of a metropolis, and that he was unaware of the commotion he had caused. They exchanged names. Rolf Messing and Herschel Grynspan.

'Actually, I was going to find my way to the Synagogue in the Orianesburger Strasse.'

Rolf said he was going past the place, and the two walked the short distance together, chatting.

'I certainly need some advice, and I think I can obtain it from someone at the Synagogue. We live in Hanover, and my parents who came a long time ago from Poland, forgot or wanted to forget to obtain German nationality. Now they are threatened with losing their Polish nationality as well. That would be a catastrophe.'

'I hope you find someone who can help you. If you do not, feel free to contact me.' Rolf gave his address. 'And in future, look out, before you cross roads or other obstacles. Here is your temple. Goodbye.'

Five minutes later Rolf was with Rahel's mother. He was correct in his calculation that the Cantor would be at his Synagogue at this time.

'Tell me Rolf. Is Rahel cheerful? Does she eat regular meals? Does she get enough exercise? Is she coping with her school work? What will she do when she is eighteen? Forgive me. I am anxious.'

'Rahel is coping wonderfully well, Frau Reimann. We do not know yet what she will do when she leaves school. My mother has promised us to look after her and take responsibility for her well-being. But, tell me, are you feeling better now?'

Rahel's mother smiled. 'I would not have believed it. I can do things I did not dream were in my range, before I saw Dr Fischer. His prescription really worked. I get a spray for my angina that makes it possible for me to stretch the radius of my activities by several kilometres. And the other drugs, all new and unknown to my previous medical advisers, seem to produce pleasant results as well. I have seen Dr Fischer twice now, and I am truly grateful - if it were not for -'

'I know what you are going to say. Please, Frau Reimann, let this be of no concern to you. Dr Fischer is indebted to you, and not you to him. It is his chance to make up, by a tiny fraction, for the terrible injustice everywhere. As long as you do not tell a soul, we shall be safe.'

'Rolf. I wish -'

'What is it, Frau Reimann?'

'I wish I could give you Rahel.'

Rolf nodded his head, sadly. 'I know you would. I know you will.'

He took Rahel's gold and black sketch out of his breast pocket, unfolded it and laid it before her.

'Look at this, please. Then tell me what your thoughts are.'

Frau Reimann glanced at the watercolour. Then she put her reading glasses on for a closer inspection. At last she spoke:

'It is by Rahel. She has made progress. Fine, thoughtful work. Correct perspective. Confident brushwork. Let me show you - -'

She disappeared into the next room. After a while she emerged, carrying a dusty portfolio. She inspected several sheets, then removed one and said:

'I was twenty then.'

She gave it to Rolf, who held in his hand the pen-and-ink drawing of a young man, dressed in black, who cradled in his arms a Torah (Hebrew Old Testament), which he looked at as a mother would regard her baby. His eyes were beatific, his mouth wide open as he sang, perhaps of his privilege to carry the holy relic. But he was not standing or walking. He was flying. Flying into the arms of an unseen beloved.

'Yes, this was my husband, as he wooed me almost thirty years ago.'

'Extraordinary,' declared Rolf, 'quite, quite extraordinary. I have never seen anything like this before. It is a wonderful, original picture. Who could resist such wooing?'

Then he became very quiet. His eyes were closed, as he seemed to consider something grave, something he may have never considered before.

'Why is it,' he said at last, 'that people who are so fervently close to each other when young, can grow into relative strangers to each other, when old?'

'I love my husband, Rolf. The older he gets, the more life ensnares him, the greater my love. And he feels the same about me. It is only the unseeing, the forgetful, who fret about their bodies which begin to shrink and are subject to the adversities of age. But with age comes the discovery that none of your qualities have disappeared. They have only crept inside.'

That gave Rolf more food for thought.

'Frau Reimann, why do you not take up your drawing and painting again? You are so immensely gifted.'

'Actually, I have started already. What has so long been dormant, has finally clamoured so loudly, that I could no longer

124

resist. Next time you come to see me, I will show you something that may surprise you.'

The Schleifers had invited the Messings and the Greifers for an evening meal and a discussion about their sons' further career in the SS, now they had outgrown the Hitler Youth.

'Seventeen thousand?' asked Magda Greifer, on their way in the Mercedes.

'That is the latest figure I was given,' said her husband.

'I know it is in the interest of the state but - the poor souls.'

'Magda, they are Polish Jews. Many of them have kept their Polish nationality. Others have renounced their former homeland and have lived here, without bothering to apply for naturalization.'

'So, what are you going to do with them?'

'We are going to transport them to the border. After that, it will be up to the Poles what will happen next.'

'They can't all be scoundrels. Yet you treat them like cattle. There must be mothers with children. There must be -'

'Whose side are you on, Magda? A nation, encircled by enemies, wants to survive. Do you know what that means? You have to be hard and unbending like steel.'

At that moment, their argument was cut short by the arrival of the Mercedes.

After their sumptuous meal, which was preceded by Champagne and finished by Tokay and assorted gateaux, the gentlemen withdrew to the study, and the ladies to the salon.

'Hans-Joachim,' Peter Schleifer called. 'A word. There seems to be a little confusion over your assessment of Ursus Castle.' He dropped his voice. 'The director - is she - reliable - a good German?'

'From everything I have seen and heard, yes.'

'The Embassy gave us conflicting answers to this question.'

'No wonder, sir. That is to be expected, is it not?'

'Is it?'

'I should have thought Embassies must take particular care in appearing neutral. So we should not be surprised at conflicting answers.'

'I suppose you are right,' Peter Schleifer allowed himself a brief chortle. Then, with his normal voice, he called Dr Greifer, Joseph and his son:

'We are ready. On with the motley!'

When the five men, but not the ladies, had assembled, Peter Schleifer began:

'Our purpose is to help these two young hopefuls to take their rightful places in the structure of our fatherland. We shall begin with you, Hans-Joachim.'

Rolf had debated this matter with his friend on many nocturnal walks under the Kolonnaden. Where would they find the right people to influence. Where would they be able to do most damage-and-good. Now Hans-Joachim was ready with his reply:

'I would like to join the Waffen-SS. That way I would have the opportunity to serve my country's security in peace, and its strength in war.'

'Splendid,' exclaimed Peter Greifer. 'The three signatories needed are here, I take it? Good. Then there is the interview. You will have to show that you know the history of National Socialism, together with all relevant laws since the seizure of power in 1933. I take it you have read *Mein Kampf?'*

'It has a permanent place on my bedside table,' said Hans-Joachim.

'And you, Rolf?'

'I too wish to serve my country to the best of my ability. And that ability seems to be - music. I already play the piano, the organ, the guitar, and I sing in a choral society. I want to study all these, together with composition and conducting. When I have finished, I see myself taking a band or an orchestra on travels, and playing to people who want to hear our music. They will experience strength through joy.'

'In that case,' said Peter Schleifer, 'you will need an exemption from the usual duties expected from a school leaver.'

'That should not prove impossible,' Joseph Messing put in, and Dr Greifer added, 'Two clearance applications for non-liability regarding post-Hitler Youth and military service are required. But five people have to vouch for his character and his probable success in his career, and the interview is rather stiff. About fifty per cent fail.'

'That means fifty per cent succeed,' countered Joseph Messing.

And Rolf rejoiced in the knowledge, that if he could not go to Coburg, he would slip out of the country and live with Rahel at Ursus Castle -?

Rolf spent the following two months, September and October 1938 in Coburg. He called it his fact-finding research. He got thoroughly acquainted with the character of the town and its people. He stumbled on reminders of his great-grandfather's time in that part of the world. And he read Richard Wagner's letters. Greedily. Every evening, before going to bed, he wrote to Rahel, giving an account of his daily ventures, his achievements and his failures.

Amongst his successes was the presentation of a Wagner programme, in the same place where Yossl Messing once had given his own. He calculated that the Wagner Festival in the neighbouring town of Bayreuth would supply him with enough interested visitors, if he could hire the theatre for one night on which there was no performance at Bayreuth. He was correct. The small place was packed.

Rolf had made up his mind to adapt Yossl's plan for the Wagner presentation. So he persuaded two young members of the local theatre to help him out by playing along with him. Madeleine and Max were a French-German couple, who went into ecstasies when it came to Richard Wagner.

The first part of the evening was devoted to a rebirth of the story of the Bayreuth Festival, starting with Wagner, not yet forty years old, dreaming of it.

Rolf

A performance is unthinkable before the revolution. I shall send out invitations to a great dramatic festival. There will be one year's preliminary work, and then I shall stage the whole ring cycle in the course of four days. With this work I shall acquaint the children of the revolution with the meaning of the revolution, with its lofty and great-hearted ideals.

He opts for Bayreuth, a small town, but blessed with shrewd councillors and townspeople, who open their hearts and purses to him.

Rolf

Singers and orchestral players will only get expenses, not fees. Anyone who will not come to me for the honour of being asked, can stay where he is.

The story continues with the building of the Festival Theatre and its key feature, the invisible orchestra.

Madeleine

Imagine an orchestra which produces a clear, pure sound, free from those extraneous noises which necessarily accompany the production of an instrumental tone. Imagine the advantageous position of a singer who can establish personal contact with the audience. Imagine also how comfortably the singer will be able to enunciate, and you will agree with the efficiency of the invisible orchestra.

In 1875, the year before the opening of the Festival Theatre, the rehearsals are in full swing. The three Rhinemaidens, frolicking in the river, had to use specially constructed swimming machines.

Madeleine

Squeezed into tight corsets, it needed a good deal of physical effort, quite apart from our musical performances. We fastened our belts, and the journey began. Even Lilli, who has just risen from her sick-

bed, became quite intrepid. We all swam and laughed. Wagner had placed flower bouquets in the swimming cradles.

Even before the first performance, however, the Festival had to endure calumnies from ill-wishers, like this missile from a clerical journal that specialised in divination:

Max
Adversity which is held by all Christian believers to be the rod of God Almighty, will plague Bavaria, threatening ordeal by fire and water. It is in a town that a dreadful calamity will occur. A huge structure will be erected, and countless onlookers will hurry there from far and wide. Music, song and vain, glittering pomp will beguile the senses of the curious. But one day fire will break out at a time when the building is filled with thousands of people. Where a moment before sinful song and music had rung out, the despairing shrieks of the damned will resound. But the place where the ill-fated building had stood will serve the sinful indulgences of the sinful no longer. A temple dedicated to God Almighty will be built there, as a memorial to the lost souls.

Long after the first Festival was over, newspapers published articles and advertisements containing news or non-news. Such as this piece of gorgeous gibberish from the Illustrierte Zeitung.

Madeleine
'Wagalaweia, waving waters' - how many times have we admired those joyful Rhinemaidens' ditties? We ourselves have to go to the sea and let the invigorating spray splash over us. A costly and time-consuming exercise. All this has now been remedied. With the help of only a few buckets of water you can easily produce the wildest tidal flow, by gripping the upper end of the bathtub and making it rock back and forth. Amidst the rushing and splashing of water you seem to hear Wagnerian chords. The complete appliance costs just forty marks.

Hermann Levi was the conductor of *Parsifal,* Wagner's final work. He was in charge of the performances at Bayreuth in 1882. To his father, the Chief Rabbi, he wrote at the end of the year.

Rolf

It was wonderful in Venice. I went daily to him in the Palazzo Vendramin, joined in the gondola outings, had all meals with them, and every day we visited a different church. I was intoxicated with sheer joy. Therefore I refuse even to consider whether I deserve a decoration for Parsifal. The Order of Merit is the appropriate award of the Bavarian crown, but that might be rather awkward, considering my name is Levi.

With this last item, carefully chosen and presented by Rolf, he split the audience into two hostile camps. They clapped and they whistled. They stood cheering and they booed. Two men were seen scribbling in their notebooks, and rushing to the telephone in the interval.

Before they could begin with the second part, Rolf, Madeleine and Max had to apply sufficient stage make-up to make them look twenty years older and, in Rolf's case, establish at least a passing similarity to Richard Wagner.

Rolf = Wagner

He faces the audience, is about to address them, but first he takes his gloves off, ceremoniously. He shows his hands to the audience.

Wicked, wicked, wicked journalists. Are these hands capable of setting fire to my beloved Dresden opera? In assuring you, ladies and gentlemen, I assure posterity. Queen Victoria will bear me out. She received me when I conducted a whole series of concerts in London.

Light on Queen Victoria, seated on throne, stage right.

Madeleine = Queen Victoria

Kommen Sie, Herr Wagner.

Rolf = Wagner

(bows low) *Majestät.*

Madeleine = Queen Victoria

Actually, my dear Wagner, we had better converse in English. I ordered my Master of Ceremonies to ask you for an audience with me. The dunce misunderstood, and provided an audience for me. He comes from Berchtesgaden. Now tell me, Herr Wagner. How is Papo?

Rolf = Wagner

Your Majesty are goodness itself. I am deeply honoured. My parrot is extremely well!

Madeleine = Queen Victoria

And Peps. Is he as well behaved as ever?

Rolf = Wagner

The only time he barks is when I come home. Your Majesty displays a finely honed sense of priorities, if I may be so bold . . .

Madeleine = Queen Victoria

You may, and we know, dear Wagner. Now to less esoteric matters. Are you writing another opera?

Rolf = Wagner

Four, Your Majesty. A whole cycle. Der Ring des Nibelungen.

Madeleine = Queen Victoria

(makes a note) *Der Ring des Nibelungen. Dear Albert will be delighted. I hope you will have it translated into Italian, so that we can hear it at Covent Garden. My husband and I particularly like the Tannhäuser Overture. Dear Albert was so impressed with -* (consults her notes) *the first violins cascading* (sotto voce) *whatever that means. You will encore it for us, my dear Wagner, won't you?*

Rolf = Wagner

Your wish is my privilege, Gracious Majesty.

Light off Queen Victoria. Light on Reporter's desk, stage left. Reporter dictates to (unseen) secretary. (NB. All quotes are authentic).

Max = Reporter

(dictates) *The Overture to Tannhäuser, repeated for the advantage of His Royal Highness Prince Albert, does not improve on closer acquaintance. So much incessant noise, so uninterrupted an exhibition of pure cacophony. We sincerely hope that no performance will ever make such senseless discord pass, in England, for a manifestation of art.*

Music: Tannhäuser Overture, bars 320 to 351, then fade.

The more we see and hear of Herr Richard Wagner, the more are we convinced that music is not his special birthgift. Full stop. Please dispatch to The Times.

Light on Wagner, seated in armchair. Reporter is beckoned by Wagner to sit on chair facing him.

Max = Reporter

(notebook in hand) *Herr Wagner, you have had time to get accustomed to our way of living, to our public, our cuisine* (Wagner winces), *our artistic life. What do you think of the English?*

Rolf = Wagner

Your typical Englishman is your typical sheep.

Max = Reporter

(scribbles, murmurs) typical sheep.

Rolf = Wagner

They both have a practical mind which makes them find their fodder in the meadow.

Max = Reporter

(scribbles, murmurs) *fodder in the meadow.*

Rolf = Wagner

But the beautiful meadow and the sky above do not exist for your typical Englishman. I can see both sky and meadow, but can't get at the fodder.

Max = Reporter

My readers will be nonplussed, Herr Wagner. Bemused.

Rolf = Wagner

Bemused eh? Attended by the Muses. That's all right, then.

Max = Reporter

You have been working *with the orchestra of our Philharmonic Society. What is your impression, Maestro?*

Rolf = Wagner

Alas, the orchestra consists almost entirely of Englishmen. They are quite good players, mind you. But they play so mechanically. Like musical boxes. Oh, they are crude fellows.

Max = Reporter

(scribbles, murmurs) *crude fellows.*

Rolf = Wagner

And, would you believe it, they don't understand, or pretend not to understand my German. I have acquired a few useful phrases. I get by with, 'Once more, gentlemen. Once more.'

Max = Reporter

(scribbles, murmurs) *Once more. Herr Wagner, you used to live in Paris. Do the two cities strike you as similar, or are there marked differences?*

Rolf = Wagner

In Paris, the businessmen look like people taking a walk. In London, people taking a walk look like businessmen.

Max = Reporter

It seems to me, Herr Wagner, you are not as yet wholly convinced of the more pleasant aspects of life in this country?

Rolf = Wagner

Don't say that, my good man. Every day I visit your Zoo in Regent's Park. The crocodiles are simply magnificent!

Blackout.

At the end of the presentation, the audience was united in their generous applause. There was a queue outside Rolf's dressing room, mainly to thank him and wish him well. There were also a few agents, and representatives from Bamberg, Nürnberg and Bayreuth, whom Rolf was going to meet in half an hour at the pub opposite the theatre. A gentleman in a white raincoat could not wait, on account of his train to Berlin, which was leaving in forty minutes. Rolf asked him to come to his dressing room.

'Meier, Gestapo,' announced the white raincoat, showing his legitimization.

Rolf replied, 'Heil Hitler. What can I do for you?'

'That final item in your first half,' observed Meier, consulting his notebook, 'the letter by Hermann Levi to his father. Was that really necessary?'

'Not if you want to give an incomplete picture of Richard Wagner. But if you want to do him justice, you must show him and his circle of friends, as they really were. A number of devoted Jews served Wagner, and they had one thing in common - doglike devotion to their Master. Wagner was different. Composed, cool, upright and German, he tolerated the strangers, on account of their musical gifts which were useful to him, and their wealth, which they put at his disposal so that he could compose his great works.'

'Well,' announced the raincoat, 'looking at it from this angle, I suppose - there is nothing - my god, I must fly. Heil Hitler.'

Rolf met Max and Madeleine in the pub, before the arrival of the others.

'I must thank you. You were great, both of you. And Max, your compilation of answers to awkward questions proved a life-saver. I used the section, named 'Wagner and the Jews' almost verbatim. Much obliged.'

Rolf's next visitors were altogether more pleasant and pleased. They asked him, if he would consider repeating tonight's performance at Bamberg and Bayreuth. They offered him a trial period for travelling with his Wagner presentation to Nürnberg, Munich and King Ludwig's castles Neuschwanstein and Linderhof. Rolf promised to let them have a reply in a week's time.

This was to be his last week before his return home. Next morning, he sauntered up and down the main streets of Coburg, until he came to a plaque on a house:

Yossl Messing's Wire Studio, 1865.

For a moment he thought he was dreaming. Then he read the inscription several times, until he fully comprehended the importance of this discovery. 'My roots,' he considered. 'My roots. This is where it all began. O, Yossl!'

He was about to enter the house, when he drew back. No, he would first of all tell Rahel about this discovery. He would telephone Ursus Castle and tell her about this, his most important realization ever. Rolf hastened to his hotel.

'Mother! I have news, good news. Will you get me Rahel. She can tell you. You are a darling.'

The best part of five minutes elapsed. Rolf wondered - -

'Hello?'

'Listen, Rahel. I found my great-grandfather. I mean, I found Yossl. Yes. Yossl's Wire Studio. Where? There is a plaque on a house, saying that here Yossl Messing built his Wire Studio in 1865. I was so excited that I had to phone you. Incidentally, I love you. You do, too? That is good. Very good. Goodbye, Rahel.'

Rolf had one hour before his train left Coburg. He walked swiftly to the place that was for him the wellspring of his being. On arrival, he read a note, saying:

Today Closed.

Rolf shook his head. He strolled to the railway station, where he awaited the arrival of the train that took him back home. Home? He wondered.

CHAPTER 22

A frosty early November day is not the most attractive time for enticing the foreigner to the cultural allures of Paris. Herschel Grynspan crosses broad avenues and winding by-roads with equal disregard of the traffic. Now he lingers by the Place de l'Etoile and stares at the Arc de Triomphe. He wants to have a closer look. Regardless of the cars which converge upon him, he strides to the other side, guarded by his private guardian angel and an incredulous policeman, whose open mouth prevents his whistle from being blown. An hour later, he is hungry and buys a cheese sandwich with ham, and a bottle of fizzy drink. He finds himself in the Place du Palais-Royal and has his midday provender on a park bench in the Royal Gardens, attended by flocks of geese which he feeds. He is unaware of having anything himself. A lady, her faded youth hidden under congealed make-up, accosts him. He looks the other way. He has thoughts for one event alone. His parents. They were taken a few days ago from their beds in Hanover, and together with 17,000 others they were transported to the Polish border.

The clock strikes three. He takes a piece of paper from his pocket, checks the details scribbled thereon, and Herschel Grynspan sets out on his journey that will provoke cataclysmic repercussions.

He hails a taxi. 'German Embassy, please.'

Punctually, at half past three, he stands before the receptionist.

'I have an appointment with the Ambassador. Grynspan.' He shows a paper, which admits him to a room on the second floor. There, the third secretary, Ernst vom Rath, receives him.

'Have you got parents?' the visitor asks. 'Are they likely to be arrested?' he now shouts. 'And abducted?'

Herschel, convinced that it is the Ambassador himself who shook his hand, draws a pistol from its holster and shoots him. Two days later, vom Rath dies of his wound.

The god-forsaken man races down. He gains the front door. He disappears in the crowd.

In the night of 9th November 1938, few people in Germany would have enjoyed a wholesome slumber. Bands of uniformed and civilian marauders roamed the streets, smashing their way into all shops owned by Jews, and totally emptying their contents. Fire engines were heard up and down the country, looking at the Synagogues and houses of Jewish inhabitants, without turning their hoses on the flames. Only when neighbouring dwellings were in danger, did they spring into action.

Amongst the people who awakened to horror that night was the Cantor of the Synagogue in the Oranienburger Strasse. His neighbour yelled to him, 'Quickly! They are burning our temple!'

Herr Reimann swiftly dressed, ran outside, where the mob celebrated its victory. Within minutes he disappeared into the burning building. Within minutes he was outside again, the Torah in his arms, just as his wife had painted him in peaceful times. Several SA men tried to stop him. Others shouted, 'Break your neck!' - 'Perish Judah!' - 'Bleed to death!'

These exhortations came from the mouths of crazed men who under normal circumstances would not have considered it possible that such words could ever escape them. They had caring mothers. They were caring lovers, husbands, sons. They came from a nation that had produced Beethoven, Goethe, Dürer. And yet.

The Cantor now raced down the road, his eyes transformed into harbingers of joy. In his arms he cradled the Holy Writ, his baby that he had rescued from imminent death. When he reached his home, his wife stood outside to receive him. At the same time a shot was fired from the crowd. The Cantor collapsed into his wife's arms. The Torah spilled to the ground, where it lay, a monument of an irrelevance dwarfed by a monumental savagery. Rolf, how will you build your bridges here?

In German, they called this night *Kristallnacht* (Plate Glass Night).

Hanna's mother went out, next morning, to shop for their dinner. Her daughter, together with forty-two children and the whole staff of Ursus Castle, were listening to the radio, reporting the events of the Kristallnacht:

'Last night several Synagogues and living quarters of Jewish citizens in Germany were burnt by an irresponsible crowd. We understand a certain amount of damage has been done.'

In Berlin Herr Rosenbaum, the butcher, was busy clearing up his devastated shop. Frau Gutmann had no loaves to sell and a burnt out shop to bewail. She did not dare to enter a non-Jewish retailer's, and bought a newspaper instead. At home, her husband read to her:

Immediately after the death of vom Rath, due to the Jewish assassin Herschel Grynspan, the deeply outraged soul of our people gave vent to its anger against the intrigues of the Jews. After last night's demonstration of the people, all Jewish establishments are suddenly visible as such, due to the shattered windows and display cases, and to the merchandise which has been fundamentally cleared out.

On the German radio, the comfortable voice of the news reader, Joseph Messing, announced:

All synagogues have been destroyed by the spontaneous indignation of the people.

Among the goods plundered from shops were such items as priceless pictures, superb jewellery, costly artefacts and manuscripts. This made Hermann Göring exclaim:

'I had rather see you strike two hundred Jews dead, than let valuable assets disappear.'

These were terrible times. But in comparison with what followed, they were beds of roses. Twenty-six thousand Jews were transported to concentration camps in Dachau, Buchenwald and Sachsenhausen. All damage to shops and dwellings of Jews had to be made good by the former owners. The sum of One billion Marks had to be paid to the state as atonement, Jewish pupils were forced to leave their Christian schools. Jews were forbidden to visit operas, concerts, theatres, cinemas, baths, sport arenas, and whole districts of towns. There was a curfew for Jews, and it was illegal for them to own cars or motor cycles. In other words, a pogrom without parallel, sanctioned by the state, designed to expire only when no victim was left.

If we are to return to the Synagogue in the Oranienburger Strasse, it is to celebrate the chief of Police Station 16, Wilhelm Krützfeld. Shortly after the Cantor had escaped, but not survived, with his Torah, he arrived at the scene, and with his revolver in one hand and the preservation order for a historical monument in the other, he chased the mob of SA men away. He could not prevent the temple's destruction, but the rare example of a man who, when all around him lost their senses, dared to speak a thunderous *Don't You Dare*, encourages the chronicler of the Kristallnacht to continue with this story.

Rolf was the only spectator. Nobody else wished to witness the burnt out shell of the Synagogue in the Oranienburger Strasse. He stood there for a long time, a dilettante among so many truant professionals.

'Please let me in,' Rolf called at Frau Reimann's door, as he tried several times to attract her attention. At last she opened. Was it Rahel's mother, or perhaps a relative? Her face looked changed, fatigued and drained. No words were spoken. Rolf followed her into - what had been their front room. Devastation. Broken furniture. The sofa at a crazy angle.

'Herr Reimann?' he asked. Rahel's mother merely shook her head.

'Have they -?'

And here she spoke, with some difficulty, but forcing herself to be communicative seemed to restore her somewhat:

'He is with the God of his fathers.' She recounted the night of terror. How he ran into the burning building and out again. The way he dashed back, with the Torah in his arms, his face restored to its look of thirty years ago, when she had painted him. Then she paused, exhausted.

'Frau Reimann, you must leave. As soon as you can. Apply for a Visa today. I and some friends will help you. When you have it, I'll take you to England. To Rahel.'

CHAPTER 23

Once again, Rolf took the passenger boat from Hook van Holland to Harwich. From there to London. From there to Penrith. From there by car, provided by the school, to Ursus Castle. But this time he did not give warning of his arrival to Rahel. He wanted to talk to his mother first. The melancholy reunion would be faced next morning.

'Our newspapers have been cleansed for parochial consumption, designed not to give us indigestion over our breakfast reading,' said Mrs Messing. 'For an independent report I rely on you.'

'Mother. Herr Reimann - poor Rahel - they have killed him.'

She rose and held his hands in hers. 'Poor girl, indeed. Who is to tell her? You or I?'

'You, mother. Speak to her first about her father, before mentioning that I am here. Then - O God, why have the cultured Germans descended to the level of vipers?'

'Try to get some sleep, now. In the morning I shall break the bitter news to Rahel, and then tell her you are here. Goodnight, my son.'

Prepared by his mother, Rahel sat silently in her room. Rolf was next to her. Both in sombre understanding. Her joy at the unexpected meeting with Rolf was drowned in her grief. A long time passed, before Rahel spoke:

'How? Could it have been an accident?'

'That depends on how you look at it. Some fool with a gun must have seen your father running from the Synagogue. That sufficed for him. What is a single life these days in Germany? If it is a Jew, his killing becomes a blessing.'

Rahel's black eyes were veiled with moist despondence:

'O, Rolf! If life is really like this, I do not want to live.'

'No, Rahel. No. Life also contains hope, justice, uprightness. The artists, poets, philosophers, writers, musicians of the world are the living testament for their exertion in comforting us over the iniquities in our lives. The present situation in Germany

140

presents the darkest chapter in its history. But it will come to an end. And I swear to you, Rahel, there are millions of Germans, who remember their past and their obligations. Decency is not dead. It is awaiting its day.'

'It is strange, Rolf, that until last night I took my father as the stern, unbending man, who thought females were a necessary lesser creation. Now he is father.'

'Your mother had a similar experience. She once showed me a picture she had painted of him, before they married, of him flying through the air into her arms, while clasping a Torah roll.'

'Yes, yes. I know it. I have always known it. It is her best work.'

'And when he raced down the Orianienburger Strasse in that unholy night, he clasped a Torah roll, and she was waiting for him.'

Rahel surrendered herself in silent tears. Then she whispered:

'Thirty years of married life were washed away. Her last view of him must have been glorious.'

That evening in Mrs Messing's study, a serious discussion took place about the immediate future of Frau Reimann. How to get her out of Germany? How to persuade her, if she was unwilling to leave? How to dispose of her flat and her belongings? What to take on the journey? Since Rahel insisted on living with her mother, where to settle them both? And all the while, in Rolf's mind, revolved the question, Coburg or Ursus Castle?

'First things first,' announced Mrs Messing. 'To obtain a Visa for your mother, Rahel, we need a place of employment and a guarantor. That is, luckily, quite easy. Your mother can combine house duties here with supervising the art classes, and I shall write the necessary applications tomorrow.'

'Knowing my mother, I am afraid she will make difficulties. In spite of what has happened and what will happen, she will want to stay. Why? Because she believes it will all come to a sudden end. The English and the French, led by Mr Chamberlain, will march through Berlin, and the nightmare will be over.'

'Leave this to me,' said Rolf. 'I think I can win her over. And I shall conduct her across the water, as Tristan conducted Isolde from Ireland to Cornwall. To a new life.'

'How long will it take for the Visa to be issued,' asked Rahel. Mrs Messing replied, 'It has been known to reach the applicant within a month, but it may be delayed for up to half a year, depending on the backlog.'

'It is lovely of you to offer my mother an occupation and lodging at Ursus Castle. I cannot tell you, how grateful I am - we are.' She looked gravely at Rolf.

'Well, that is settled then,' said Mrs Messing. 'After the *Kindertransport* comes the *Muttertransport*.'

The three tried to keep the news of the killing away from the pupils. During the following week, Rolf held several singsongs and an evening with readings from HG Wells' *Joan and Peter*, and a memorable outing, with Rahel, to their beloved Mount Skiddaw. It was there that they discussed the future, their future.

'What will it be, Rolf? Ursus Castle or Coburg? England or Germany?'

'If I want to become a teacher, then the Training College in Berlin offers the best tuition. It would take three years. After that I would apply for a post at mother's school.'

'Is that what you truly want to do - better than anything else you could be doing?'

'I don't know.'

'What else is there?'

'Composing. Conducting. Drown myself in music. Help the Germans through music. I have sketched out a Cantata. There is the beginning of a most wonderful tune. It breaks off. A second, equally magnificent tune is similarly interrupted. A third and a fourth, all going towards a goal, but always stifled. After a pause, you hear a melody that could have been conceived by Bach, but orchestrated by Wagner. Another pause. And then you have the four discontinued tunes woven into the web of the new one, with a chorus celebrating their union.'

'What will it be called?'

'*The Blessed Bridge.*'

Nobody spoke for some time. Then Rahel asked:

'Ursus Castle? With me?'

'Yes, Rahel. A thousand times Yes! That is where my heart is. No more wishful thinking. Let us make plans for our future together, with our mothers, in the new mother country.'

'No. Your eyes were scintillating, when you told me of *The Blessed Bridge*. You must go to Coburg to your roots. You must steep yourself in all aspects of your craft. And when you have mastered it, you and I shall live, where freedom will be. In England or in Germany. I shall wait and I promise not to complain. I belong to you.'

'So do I, Rahel.'

Their lips dovetailed.

Hans-Joachim had invited Sven and a high-ranking officer of the Hitler Youth to his house for a discussion. After strong coffee and biscuits, they sat on two chairs and on his bed.

Hans-Joachim started the debate:

'We have met to discuss how religious rites, prayers and beliefs stand in the way of rational thinking, as is advocated by our leaders. National Socialism has taken on an implacable defender of the faith in the Church, but is slowly winning what seems to be its most formidable campaign so far.'

'Do you mean both Churches,' asked Egon, the Hitler Youth leader, 'the Protestant and the Catholic one?'

'Yes, of course. But the Catholic is by far the more obstinate one. Its tentacles are world-wide, and you wrestle with Rome at your peril. Even Henry VIII must have wished he had not provoked the ruthlessness of Rome.'

'Let us begin with the beginning,' said Sven. 'The Bible tells us God created the world in six days. Darwin teaches that natural selection took rather longer, that life evolved over millions of years, with man as its latest manifestation. So, is there a God or not?'

Egon frowned. 'God loves us. See how He loves us. He sends plagues, cancer, hunger and child exploitation. God listens to us. See how He listens. He makes us multiply beyond the capacity of the earth. He smiles at murder, rape, condemnation without trial. He is a God of peace. But He endorses war between nations. Each war is bloodier than the last.'

'Careful, Egon,' said Hans-Joachim. 'Some misguided person might take your examples as a condemnation not only of Rome, but much nearer home. In fact, home. You said, God smiles at murder and rape. Your misguided fellow might be tempted to add, He smiles at murder and rape in our concentration camps. You mentioned condemnation without trial -'

Sven interrupted with a laugh: 'Yes, Hans-Joachim. We have got the message. We would be well advised to leave examples of God's goodness or badness alone, and concentrate on the question, is there a God?'

'It seems to me,' said Egon, 'that the question is superfluous. 'In the face of all the known scientific data there can only be one conclusion. There can only be a God, if that idea is a synonym for natural selection, if it includes a benevolent and at the same time a merciless God, who is utterly uninterested in any morality, and therefore deaf to any personal intercession or prayer on our part.'

Here Hans-Joachim rose from his bed and paced up and down the room. As he halted, he gripped the side of his table for support and addressed the two listeners, as if he addressed a meeting of a hundred:

'I agree with Egon. If there is a God, then He or She or It must necessarily be unmerciful. As cat is unmerciful when it eats mouse, and as nature is unmerciful when it follows its pre-programmed instinct for self-preservation. That would render most prayers for intercession useless. Such phrases as *Remember, oh Lord and Help me, and I will praise Thy name for ever,* have always struck me as heathenish. Even if God were merciful, to remind Him of anything would be presumptuous. And if He is unfeeling, it is pointless. But - the vital concern for all people of an independent mind is this: why do so many brilliant men and women, with minds as sharp as a razor, succumb unquestioning to the same web of time-sanctioned mystification as their parents and their grandparents and their great-grandparents and so forth until, as they would erroneously maintain, they had reached the beginning of their line in Adam. That brings us to the second point of equal importance. What happens to the mind of such a person, doctor, teacher, writer or statesman, who allows his mind to be taken over by an unknown force he does not know, while in communion with a power that does not exist? Can we really trust such people to be in total command of their thinking, when it comes to vital decisions, such as saving a person's or a nation's survival?'

The other two listened carefully, considering every word. Then Sven took over:

'The history of our churches, and not only in our country, but world-wide, is interlaced with horrific examples of blunders, committed in the name of God. The crusades. The ruthless persecution of so-called unbelievers. The burning at the stake of those who questioned the Church's teaching that the earth is flat. The condemnation without trial, and the condemnation with a predetermined trial.'

Egon looked embarrassed. He thought of the Kristallnacht and the part he played in demolishing shops and arresting their owners. Was that not condemnation without trial? No, this cannot be. It was an order he had pledged to obey. An order that came directly from the Führer. And, by definition, that could not be wrong. Or could it? Stop! No more! That way lies mutiny. At last he spoke:

'Well, I don't know. At first it all seemed straightforward. But the more I ruminate, the more involved it becomes. I need time to ponder.' 'We all do,' replied Hans-Joachim. 'It is remarkable, is it not, that our condemnation of the Churches runs parallel with that of the state.'

'That is comforting,' said Sven. 'And vindicating.'

Egon exchanged cautious glances with Sven and Hans-Joachim. They fixed a date for their next meeting.

Joseph Messing, Hans Eifer, Dr Greifer, Peter Schleifer and Horst Kneifer, a phalanx of SS men with identical stripes, had assembled in the interview room, which had served for the interrogation of Church Councillor Kietz, but today it shed its quotation marks and functioned as an ordinary space for ordinary business, conducted by ordinary people. The bonhomie which enveloped the uniformed monotony, hid everyone's attention to the other's slightest slip or inattention, which could be used for some unspecified future purpose.

The five had settled along the desk in the centre. Hans Eifer began the proceedings:

'We have been called to examine the application of young Rolf Messing for release from National Service, in order to study music in Coburg. I must emphasize that I find such a desire, in these days, a little - shall we say out of the ordinary.'

'Out of the ordinary, perhaps,' said Dr Greifer, but let us hear his reasons for making this request. We have his father here. So, over to you, Joseph.'

Mr Messing polished his reading glasses. 'I have his application here. In it he states that - and I quote - I see my future as a composer and conductor, travelling with my fellow musicians to centres in the *Reich,* where I could bring strength through the experience of music to workers by hand and brain.' Joseph Messing was well pleased with his pleasantly modulated announcer's voice.

'He wishes to study in Coburg, I hear,' said Peter Schleifer. 'I have obtained the prospectus of the place he has in mind. It mentions a three years' duration of the course. That would be acceptable, I suppose?'

'No, gentlemen, no!' This was Horst Kneifer's sour voice, that sounded as though some unseen assailant was for ever trying to harm him. 'Music, to my mind, makes people grow soft. A young man today,' and here he elevated his short body to its full 5ft 6in. 'needs to have the experience of the normal run of things, that is from the Hitler Youth straight to the SS. Serving the war-like Adolf Hitler does not stand comparison with serving Frau Musica.' He shook his flowing fair locks vigorously as if to rid himself of an invisible grappler. Then he dwindled by sitting down.

Four alarm bells sounded in four pairs of ears. Here was a new danger. Nobody had heard of the little Kneifer before, but everyone knew whom to beware of in future.

'Time for coffee and biscuits,' proposed Hans Eifer. 'They have laid their hands on really marvellous Italian macaroons.' He rang the bell.

During the break for snacks they discussed the relative value of Frau Musica in a militaristic world. The National Anthem. The Horst Wessel song. The hundreds of tunes to which the Hitler Youth, the SA and the SS marched on their field trips and parades.

Hans Eifer appropriated the last two macaroons for later consumption, as the remains of their repast were taken away.

'I think we can ask young Messing to come in now. What do you think, Herr Kneifer?'

'Yes, yes. By all means.'

Rolf entered, a picture of the young upholder of the regime, blond, blue eyes, upright, he gave the Hitler salute, and stood to attention, until permitted to stand at ease.

'Rolf Messing,' Peter Schleifer addressed him, 'we have before us your application for exemption from conscription, to enable you to study music. Please tell us, in your own words, what made you take this somewhat unusual step.'

'Honoured gentlemen of the SS,' Rolf began, 'Any young man now alive, in these times of regeneration of our fatherland, would regard it not as his duty, but as an honour to join the ranks of his contemporaries for national service. If I opt for studying music, I do not regard this request as an alternative, but as another form of national service. Music is a necessary way of expressing the feelings of soldiers marching towards their goal. Think of those glorious tunes *Perish, Juda* or W*hen the traitors' blood from the dagger drops.* I intend to write many similar songs, when I have got the necessary qualifications. You, gentlemen, have seen the samples of my compositions, as yet untutored, enclosed in my application, and you will have arrived at an estimation of my native talent or otherwise. In the course of my studies I intend to form my own orchestra, train and inspire them, and travel with them to halls and meeting places, indoors and outdoors, where soldiers and workers can relax, and gain the strength and enthusiasm derived from the inspiration that flows from listening to fine music. Thus, our Führer's words, *Strength through Joy*, would be fulfilled.'

Rolf resumed his stance of attention, awaiting the 'Dismissed' signal. It arrived, after a short discussion between members of the commission. Rolf gave another smart Hitler salute and marched out of the room.

'What do you say now, Herr Kneifer?' asked Dr Schleifer.

'I am impressed, I must say,' answered Kneifer, with alarm in his voice.

Further discussion. Smiles all round. Application granted. Unanimous.

When Rolf arrived at home, he quickly went to the bathroom, where he took a shower, scrubbing his whole body vigorously, as if to make sure that all signs of a shameful interview had been washed away. His consolation was the conviction that he fought the system with its own means, with shabby disregard to truth, and that he probably had won. He would wait for his father's return.

'Hello Rolf. Well done. Well done. Your speech convinced them. Just my sentiments. Let us celebrate.'

'As a matter of act, father, I used just one aspect of music, their kind of music, in my argument. The other, the far more valuable side of *Frau Musica,* is not for them. But, as you say, let us celebrate.'

CHAPTER 24

22nd February 1939

Dearest Rahel
I would like to share my jubilation with you. But I cannot. The first
hurdle was taken today, when I obtained my exemption from military
service. And I do not know whether to be glad about it or not. It
means that I can study at Coburg. But it also means that I can only
see you three times a year, in between semesters. That is more than
affliction. Dearest, dearest Rahel. My term begins in early April. So
expect me at Ursus Castle in a week's time. The Blessed Bridge is
progressing. I compose without really having learnt it, and I do not
miss it. O, that tune of all tunes at the end, the one that is underlined
by the chorus, as it weaves its way into the four initial melodies¬ I
shall play it for you, when we meet. I have plans for repeating
programmes, such as my previous ones. Perhaps a mixture of
Wagner and my own composition? Think it over. I want your help. I
have been asked, although not directly, but through an agent, to
Bayreuth, Nuremberg, Bamberg, Munich, and King Ludwig's castles
at Neuschwanstein and Linderhof. And I do not know what my
director of studies will have to say. 'Premature,' I suppose. But I
need your advice, and mother's about this, as about everything.
Sleep well, my dearest, watched over by your special guardian
angel. And may you live all the days of your life.
Be embraced and be much made of by your Rolf.

It was now several months ago, that Leni Eifer gave birth to
Josefine, the utterly teutonic looking baby with no hint of an
aquiline nose. Leni had engaged a competent nurse to look after her,
while she was taking up her school position again. She had missed
contact with her pupils, and they missed her. On her last free day she
made a phone call.

'Is that you, or Rolf?' she asked.

'Joseph Messing here.'

'Jo. Leni speaking. Yes, I know. Yes. I am aware it has
been ages. I thought it is time we made up. No I - I genuinely

missed you. I hold no grudge - I wonder, can we meet? At the Café Alexander. Well, I can make it in half an hour. For old time's sake. So long, Jo.'

Leni hung up, a satisfied smile slightly expanding her lips. No, this was not a ruse, nor was it sheer boredom. It was the fact that her relations with her husband were by now worse than ever, and that she genuinely longed for Joseph.

Punctually, after half an hour, he arrived at the Café, claiming a table away from the crowd, in a corner. She sauntered in, five minutes later, without make-up, which pleased him. He wore his uniform, and his eyes and his boots were gleaming. They kissed, twice on the cheeks and then on the lips.

'O, Jo, I missed you so much, I just had to phone. Am I forgiven?'

'I suppose so,' he said, while straightening his tie. 'How is the baby.'

'Josefine is a cradle of delight. I have brought you a few pictures.' She showed them to Joseph, who pored over them, quizzical, concerned, triumphant.

'Ours,' he applauded. 'Your eyes, my nose. Yours and mine. When can I see her?'

'Today. Nurse will wheel her in, unless I phone her.'

'Do not think of it.'

They ordered cheesecake, the speciality of the house, and coffee. Leni Eifer spoke nothing for a while, wondering how to introduce the subject. Then she began:

'Hans is not unreasonable. He just shows lack of interest. In our marriage, our house, our child. Progress in the SS is all he is concerned about. The higher, the sooner, the better. That and his gorging himself with sweet stuff. In the few months since Christmas, he has put on another ten kilos. That means another uniform. His third in three years.'

'Has he settled for a mistress?' asked Joseph. 'A girlfriend?'

'I do not think that would occur to him. He dropped me three years ago. He seems quite happy pursuing the two courses that will kill his soul or his body. Intrigues and Vienna Strudel. He is rather good at both.'

'What about the baby?'

'He does not want to know.'

Joseph took a cigarette from its golden case, offered it first to Leni, and as she refused, he stubbed it very carefully and superfluously several times on the ashtray, before lighting it with the silver cigarette lighter. He blew the smoke in little circular clouds, meditating. Then he said, slowly, deliberately choosing each word:

'All this might affect both of us. But before going into this, I would like to clear up a little matter. You remember the ill-starred Wannsee episode?'

'Why ill-starred?' asked Leni. 'Look at the outcome. Look, Jo!' She pointed at the revolving door, through which a nurse in a white uniform wheeled a baby in its pram.

The father's first meeting with his baby daughter. He had jumped up from his chair, bent over the pram, and cautiously, as though he was handling a priceless vase from the Ming dynasty, he lifted her out and looked at her. Then he carried her slowly to his chair, and sat down, while the baby daughter snuggled into the harbour of his arms. His melodious voice hummed a sleeping song. She liked that. So she wetted his recently pressed trousers with a stream of contented, warm liquid. He handed her back to the nurse, and asked to be excused. When he returned, he asked for the baby again. This time he took the precaution to place the table napkin on his lap. For a long time they studied each other's faces, wordless but with growing delight.

Leni Eifer announced: 'Bedtime approaching. Say bye bye.'

Joseph kissed his daughter. Not once, but many, many times, before the nurse dispossessed him and carried her off.

Joseph said, 'Leni, I never knew what it was like - to be a baby girl's father. There is the matter I wanted to discuss with you, just as they came in. But not now. Next time.'

'When?' asked Leni.

'Tomorrow of course. Same time, same place.'

'Make it five o'clock.'

'All right. Leni, can you get a divorce, do you think?'

After their evening meal, father and son settled in their armchairs for a chat. They talked about the recent interview with the commission, and Rolf's bravura performance. Then the thunderbolt arrived.

'Rolf, what would you say to a female in the house?'

'A cook?'

'No. Yes, she could also cook. I was thinking - I want to get married.'

'Good heavens!'

'Wait, till you hear who it is. Who, would you say, is the most unlikely candidate?'

Rolf gave the matter some consideration. Then he said:

'Leni Eifer.'

'You said it.'

Consternation. Astonishment. Open mouth. Admiration. Stroke of genius.

'Hold on,' Rolf demanded. 'What made you change your mind about Leni? Will she obtain a divorce? And what about yourself?'

'All perfectly sensible questions. I saw Josefine today. I held her in my arms.'

Rolf thought. His father had dropped his bright announcer's voice. He neglected to brush the specks of cigarette ash that had assembled on his sleeve. He looked positively human.

'You have my blessing, father. You deserve it. Both of you.'

They discussed the two divorce proceedings. Their own should be straightfoward, provided Yvonne Messing would not object. Hans Eifer? They had different bedrooms. He never acknowledged Josefine as his. He had not asked. Did he know? He showed interest only in his advancement in the higher ranks of the SS. This could mean that he would either enthusiastically embrace any proposal for a divorce, or fight it tooth and nail.

That night, little Josefine dreamt of a giant teddy bear with facial features that bore a vague resemblance to Joseph Messing, her

- well what? The word was as yet unknown to her. The comfortable feeling was not.

At the same time, Leni and Hans Eifer experienced an uncanny sensation. They talked seriously and at length.

'Hans. I think you ought to know about Josefine's father.'

'I know.'

'What?'

'The little hotel at the Wannsee. Herr and Frau Krause. You did not seriously think, you could hide such details from an SS officer, whose attention to details are the envy of his comrades? And the Café Alexander, where Frau Krause used to meet her lover, Joseph Messing? Where she met him this very afternoon! No, Frau Krause. If you really want to keep a secret, you will find this impossible in Germany.'

'Since you know the circumstances, will you agree to a divorce?'

'That will depend.'

'On what?'

'On his judgement. Next month a high-ranking new post will be created in the Secret State Police. There are two candidates for this prestigious job. I and Joseph Messing. He can always withdraw. That would be wise. If he does not, let him look to his survival. Not only will he lose his position with Radio Berlin, but an article with documentary evidence will be launched in the morning paper, describing the little episode at the Wannsee, and its outcome nine months later. You see, Leni, it all depends on his judgement.'

Next day Café Alexander saw the same customers on successive days, an event that had never happened before. This time, though, it was just the two serious people who had so much to say to each other, the smart SS man, and the busy school teacher with no discernible make-up, but still young enough to get away with this voluntary restraint. There was no intrusion of a wheeled pram, and the whispered conversation could not be understood by waiter or cashier. It was an exclusive debate on the rights or otherwise of Hans Eifer, to set conditions for his amiable divorce, if indeed 'amiable' is the right word.

When Leni had come to an end, she looked expectantly at Joseph who ventured:

'Of course I shall step down. Tell him that, and also tell him that my decision is not a reply to his absurd threats, but is given straightaway and without hesitation. Because of you. And because of Josefine.'

It occurred to Joseph that he wanted to bring up that episode of the missing receipt for Herr and Frau Krause that mysteriously disappeared from Leni's handbag, almost a year ago. But then, he thought, events had overtaken the - theft, if Leni had even noticed it. Sleeping dogs.

Two radiant people were walking the air from the Café Alexander to the Potsdamer Platz, where Leni took a taxi and Joseph walked home, after a lingering farewell kiss. Let people think what they like.

CHAPTER 25

Peace at Ursus Castle was suspended by the director's announcement that she would be away for three days, to attend urgent business in Berlin. Rahel Reimann, the oldest pupil, would be in charge.

Yvonne Messing was on the phone for half an hour the previous night. Her husband, supported by Rolf, urged her to come for a personal discussion to Berlin and stay for two nights at their flat. She was persuaded.

She went by air, via Manchester, thus shortening the journey time considerably. At Templehof Airport she was received by Rolf who hugged her and drove her home. From the ensuing conference, Rolf learned a number of facts he had either not fully known or forgotten. Such as the drowning of his mother's parents, which was officially declared an accident, but was in reality the outcome of a suicide pact, to enable them to escape urgent operations for cancer, that would have prolonged their lives by a miserable, bed-ridden year or two. The considerable fortune which came to Yvonne and which made it possible to turn Ursus Castle into a privately run school. And the circumstances surrounding his mother's dual nationality, and her enjoying the mystification of the German embassy members in London, whether she was a bad German and a good Englishwoman or vice versa.

'I want to obtain our divorce quickly and with a minimum of publicity. Anything you can and will do, I would appreciate, Yvonne.'

'A good lawyer should manager with little fuss, I think. It is well over the required five years that we separated, and I shall, of course, not raise any objections.'

'What about the costs?' asked Rolf. 'They can be rather steep, I understand.'

'Share?' enquired Yvonne.

'Done!' said Joseph.

'Now to the infinitely harder part,' Rolf insisted. 'Father wants to marry Leni Eifer, who already has a baby from him, as a matter of anticipatory wedlock. But there is her husband.'

'Hans Eifer,' Joseph interrupted, 'who might stir up trouble in the SS, unless I agree to help him win promotion.'

Rolf cut in: 'And that is the point. One cannot be sure that he will stick to our agreement. A shameless creature like Hans Eifer is not to be trusted.'

Mrs Messing considered for a while. 'You need a lawyer who has a record of outwitting the most unscrupulous operator.'

'That is undoubtedly Siegfried Levin, but he is forbidden, of course, to practise,' said Joseph.

'Of course,' Rolf retorted with a bitter laugh. 'Anyway, let us have some coffee.' He retreated to the kitchen, from where the comforting noise of the percolator was followed by the aroma of the freshly brewed coffee.

Ten minutes later they had the possible answer. Rolf announced: 'There must be somebody as efficient or nearly as efficient as Levin, who is still allowed to practise. Find him. Appoint him. Make him design a declaration which Hans Eifer is to put his signature to.'

'What is it to contain?' asked Joseph.

'Words to the effect, that Hans Eifer will agree to the divorce without hindrance, that he would refrain from any attempt to make use of adverse publicity, and that you consent to bear the cost of the case and to assist him with his forthcoming promotion.'

'In legal language, of course,' said Joseph. That seems to meet the case. Except the costs. That had better be dropped from the declaration. It can always be used as a bargain counter, if Eifer makes life difficult.'

'That seems to have settled the matter to everybody's satisfaction,' concluded Mrs Messing. 'I have tomorrow for your consultation with your lawyer, if I am required.'

'You have been your usual level-headed self. I would not know how to express my gratitude.' Joseph walked over to Yvonne and kissed her hands.

Rolf served the coffee and biscuits. While he and his mother took the refreshments, Joseph made a few phone calls. When he had finished, he joined the others and declared:

'I have been told of a lawyer who specializes in divorces and who is even dearer than Levin used to be. If that means that he is at least as good, we caught the right sort of fish. What is this?' he asked, looking at the coffee and biscuits. 'Rolf, this calls for a celebration. Go and get some Heidsieck.'

The explosion that sent the cork flying towards the ceiling, was the audible signal for an hour well spent.

Two days later, in the plane from Berlin to Manchester, Rolf and his mother talked about the outcome and possible achievements of their last forty-eight hours. The new lawyer with his staggering fees was a propitious sign, as he saw the case as good as won before it had started. Their conversation changed to Rolf's apparently confirmed career at Coburg.

'O, mother! I am in the middle of composing a Cantata, called *The Blessed Bridge*. I think, apart from meeting Rahel, this is the most exciting thing that has ever happened to me. I shall play the completed sections for Rahel. If you like, you can join us.'

'I would love to. But tell me, if you can compose, why Coburg? I mean, what can they teach you there that you do not already know?'

Rolf thought for a moment, then he replied: 'I have three good reasons. Firstly, a course of studies will enable me to take up contacts, which are so important in professional life. Secondly, it is a much saner way to occupy yourself with than conscription. And thirdly, and most importantly, it means my return to my roots, to Yossl's life there, to my building a bridge that spans almost a century.'

'And Rahel?'

'She is the one agonising source of frustration in the whole picture, mother. There is no hour of my days or nights, when the thought of leaving her for so long, does not torment me.'

'She will have me.'

Rolf leant his head on his mother's shoulder.

It was on the morning of the next day they were united. Plans for tomorrow. Plans for the nearer future. Plans for the further future. A campfire was envisaged, with readings, songs, exchange of views, and the latest from Germany. One topic that Rolf had originally thought eminently suitable for such an evening, was dropped without a single thought. Was there a God? Rolf had come to the conclusion that it was kinder to leave this topic alone, to allow each person to derive as much comfort as they needed, from contact - however illusinary - with their God. He arrived at this decision, when he contemplated debating the topic with Rahel. He felt that this would create greater harm than benefit. From here it was a logical step for his determination not to broach the topic with anyone, perhaps not even with convinced Nazis, lest his sowing doubts in their minds would result in a vacuum that might be filled with things more harmful than a little inoffensive loose thinking.

In the afternoon Rolf had taught the choir, twenty-five pupils, the closing scene from his Cantata, *The Blessed Bridge*, a difficult assignment. Now, with everybody, staff and students, assembled around the campfire, they sang:

Open the box,
the box with the seeds,
the seeds for the future,
a future that joins the priest and the heathen,
the jackboot and the slipper,
the finger on the trigger and the outstretched arms
of amnesty.
Open the box.

They sang it three times in succession, every time with greater confidence, and their last run through was accompanied by the small ensemble which Ursus Castle had managed to build up over the years. It was the third trial which produced the right spirit, the right notes. The initial line, *Open the box,* and its fellow, the final line, rang out as it rose. There was a pause after *the outstretched arms of amnesty.* Then the violin took up the composer's favourite tune, the one that sounds like Wagner inspired by Bach, had filtered through the experiences of Yossl, and finally recreated by Rolf Messing. It lasted for five minutes, with its variations. Then the final line, *Open the box,* in a four-part canon. Rolf listened while on the piano he tried to substitute the missing trumpet part, and he decided that in future performances of the cantata he would always employ a young choir, with their enthusiasm, preferably to a mature ensemble. As they ended, it was agreed to repeat the performance at the close of the campfire which was held, as always, by the far perimeter of Ursus Castle, where everybody was truly in the open. The only difference from former years was the number of participants which had doubled. There now were two circles, the younger ones forming the inner, the older the outer pack.

Yvonne Messing read from where she sat, and her voice rang out in the star-enwrapped sky. She read from HG Wells' novel, *The Undying Fire*, which she had introduced to her English class a month ago, and which had become a point of much discussion both in and out of the classroom:

I have made knowledge of what man is and what man's world is and what man maybe, which is the adventure of mankind, the substance of all my teaching. If there is no mercy, no human kindliness in the great frame of space and time, if the stars away there in the void are no more than huge empty flares, signifying nothing, then all the brighter shines the flame of God in my heart. There burns an undying fire in the hearts of men. By that fire I live. By that fire I know the God of my salvation. Once it is lit in a man, then his mind is alight thenceforth. The darkness and ungraciousness, the evil and the cruelty, are no more than a challenge to you. In you lies the power to rule all these things.

A staff member and Jonathan were the appointed fire guardians. They now brought new wood to revive the low flames, until a warm glow filled every soul with tranquillity and wistfulness.

A hand rose up.

'Yes, Abby.'

'He speaks of God. Which God does he mean? The Hebrew God of the Old Testament or the Christian of the New?'

'It is the same God, since there is only one. And this one God can stand for the originator of everything, or the unknown force that started life on our planet. The important aspect of this passage, and indeed of the whole output of HG Wells is the elimination of any intermediaries between ourselves and God. Thereby he achieves - and we achieve - direct communication with this force we call God.'

Another hand.

'Rosa?'

'We are supposed to rule over all the cruelties and the evil in the world. I cannot see that. At present there is so much inhumanity and badness in people, in Germany and elsewhere, that - that -'

Tears are never a helpful device for keeping an argument afloat, so Mrs Messing replied:

'You are right, Rosa. But you must remember what he says at the end: *The darkness and ungraciousness are a challenge to you.* If we all learn to live up to that challenge, we shall eventually be victorious. We shall probably not see it. Nor will our children or their children. But step by step we shall advance. Remember, it is barely two hundred years ago that wars between nations were the accepted facts of life, that the poor lived without hope, the sick without lasting cure, and the most unspeakable cruelties were committed by religious representatives of many creeds. When the present regime in Germany comes to an end, we shall find that progress was inexorable, that in the long run right could not be prevented from defeating might.'

Rolf meditated.. He considered his mother's description of God as the *originator of everything or the force that started life on this planet* as one with which Rahel could live. HG Wells. He had only heard him mentioned, when at school, as a writer of science fiction, like *The First Men on the Moon* and *The Invisible Man.* But in Ursus Castle they knew him as the author of *Joan and Peter, Christina Alberta's Father, Men Like Gods* and *The Undying Fire.* He seemed to be a man after his own heart, and he determined to study him in the next few months, as an adjunct to his musical studies of Richard Wagner.

Rahel handed him her guitar and beckoned him to the centre of the circle, where he stood, hard by the fire. They all sang, some more beautifully than others, some in parts, some in unison, but all with dedication and love. Songs from Ireland, like *Johnny Doyle,* from Scotland, like *the Bonnie Banks of Loch Lomond,* from England, like *Greensleeves,* and from Germany, like *Es geht eine dunkle Wolk' herein (*a dark cloud is coming). They were not aware of it, but all the time they were building bridges into an invisible future.

Letters were read from friends in the former homeland, from friends in the States, Australia, Hong Kong and South America. But as a fitting end to the campfire they all wanted to give another performance of *The Blessed Bridge.* All agreed: this was our best campfire.

Three days to go to the end of term. Rolf attended many lessons. In between he talked to new pupils and old, but spent most of the after-school hours with Rahel.

It transpired that she had been far from idle these last few months. She had been preparing for her life after school. For her livelihood. For a career. She had studied the rapidly growing market for cards covering every occasion, from celebrating special days, such as Christmas, Mother's Day, Congratulations for passing your driving tests, Apologies for not having written sooner, et cetera. She then designed her own ideas for these occasions, and with a light, often humorous touch she brought a new angle to the business. On sending her first batch, on trial, to a leading firm, she was surprised to receive the following reply:

Dear Miss Reimann

We have received the set of cards you designed for us, and we are pleased to tell you that we recognise your talent for this kind of work. Please come and see us, after phoning for an appointment.

Yours sincerely

Rahel fixed the time for the meeting with the publishers for the first day after the end of term, so that Rolf could accompany her.

Mrs Messing said farewell, with a heavy heart, to the class of school leavers, when on the last day of term she gave her address.

But thankfully, she said, there were three members who would be staying on in various capacities:

'Sigi, we are all greatly looking forward to your advance as chief cook for Ursus Castle. We all wish you well in your career which is so much in our mutual interests.'

Wild applause.

'Another school leaver, who will join the teaching staff as an auxiliary, is Jonathan. He will be responsible for sports and swimming, and he is going to teach us the art of self-defence. In the school holidays he will be joining the England squad and train for his special event, the long jump, in preparation for the next Olympic Games.'

Clamorous applause.

'I am very pleased to report that all remaining members of the top class have secured posts, mostly in cities of the north. So we hope that we have not seen the last of them. You are always, always most welcome to visit us, for short or long periods. *For they are jolly good fellows . . .*'

They all rose, their arms on each others shoulders, as they sang their tribute to friends, whom identical reasons for coming to Ursus Castle had knitted together in school and long after.

End of term. Long holidays. A mere interruption, fleeting, for adults, but for the young a whole lengthy age without end in sight. By arrangement with a local Quaker group, the majority of pupils were going on a safari that would occupy their next three weeks. The others were going for their new jobs, accompanied by staff members to help them settle in their new accommodation, which had been booked by the school. Thus, it was a pretty deserted place, from which Mrs Messing motored her children, as she called them, down to Liverpool. The approaches to the town were disheartening, dingy, row upon row of identical terraced homes, lived in by identical people, or so they thought. Matters improved the nearer they came to the centre. Broad thoroughfares with impressive looking buildings showed them that big cities had several faces.

They found the publishers near the railway station. A lift took them to the third floor, which was entirely given to the production of cards for all occasions.

The interviewer, an elderly partner in the business, was astonished to see such a young lady instead of whatever he imagined to meet. He accepted her sketches in toto, with a request for further regular deliveries. That is where Rahel asked whether her advisers might be asked to attend the interview.

Mrs Reimann and Rolf were introduced, and the negotiator repeated his proposal, and added:

'We would settle for a sum of five pounds for every card submitted and approved.'

Mrs Reimann objected. 'Considering you would obtain all the rights for selling my daughter's work world-wide, I think that sum is on the paltry side.'

The elderly gentleman thought for a minute, then he scribbled some notes and said 'We can make it seven pounds.'

'Ten,' Rolf put in.

'Very well, our last word. Eight pounds per picture.'

Handshakes all round. Rahel opened her briefcase and took out a portfolio.

'I have here suggestions for future designs. May I read them to you? Yes? Thank you. Apart from the usual ones, we might think of such cards as *Forgetfulness*, where you apologise for not remembering an important event; *Better Late,* like this one which regrets the late marriage proposal, with the old veiled lady waiting at the church door, and a white-haired, bearded man, galloping up to her; *Consolation*, where you encourage someone about misfortune, including death of a loved one, like this where you have a long ladder reaching into heaven, and a welcoming crowd with trumpets at the gate; *Bury the Hatchet,* where you invite people to let bygones be bygones.'

Here she was stopped by the elderly gentleman.

'Leave me your list, please. I must say, it is extraordinary to see someone so young and so new to us, going so deeply into the card business. I can predict a growth industry arising, and quite a slice of the market for us, that means us and you, Miss Reimann.'

Handshakes. Satisfaction. Future supplies. Cheque for £176.

The pneumatic tyres of their Landrover were filled with Euphoria. They sang. They laughed. The ladies cried a little. Rolf and Rahel sat in the back. Close embrace. At last Rolf said:

'Strange to compare the negotiator with our counterparts in Germany. There the interrogator, as he is called, sets his own terms from the beginning, and reinforces them with occasional blows, whereas in England you are prepared to bargain. He pays a little more than he proposed, and you accept a little less than you expected. Long live the compromise.'

Mrs Reimann smiled. Rahel and Rolf had solved the problem of the immediate future. What the future in the distance would hold for them, they did not know. Nor did they care. Was that wise?

CHAPTER 26

July 1869. 'Stir yourself, little woman of my heart,' cried Yossl Messing, as he woke his wife two hours earlier than usual. 'We have a momentous day in front of us.'

Having left the two smaller children under Emanuel's devoted care, they set out by coach to the town of Lucerne, where they stayed the night at a large lakeside hotel. Their initial indifferent reception was soon altered. The manager begged them to exchange their small room into a much larger one, which he described as 'royally appointed.' No, there would be no increased costs. Yes, it is our pleasure and privilege.

Little did they know that the house detective identified the strangers as King Ludwig of Bavaria, who always travelled incognito and the singer Adelina Patti, who was a favourite of the King and who had come with the same object of travel as Ludwig, to bathe themselves in the aura of the composer, and to discuss future roles for her with the famous Richard Wagner.

Yossl had sent a note to Wagner's live-in partner, the estranged wife of the pianist and conductor Hans von Bülow, asking whether he might visit him. He enclosed some press notices, which must have caught the composer's curiosity, and next day he had a letter:

Dear Sir,

You and your wife are welcome to visit us tomorrow at six in the afternoon.

Cosima von Bülow

'You will have to help me,' said Yossl to Bettina. 'He is a very great man, and we have to be on our best behaviour. On the other hand, he is also a very unpredictable man. From what I hear of him, he monopolizes the conversation and brooks no contradiction. But he is Wagner, and to be near him is a gift of the gods. Let us be thankful.'

The boat that plied form one side of Lake Lucerne to the other, took them to Tribschen at five o'clock. They found themselves admiring the garden and what they could glimpse of the house that harboured Wagner. With half an hour to spare, they gazed at the shrubs and the trees, in silent reverie. They heard children's voices from inside. They noticed the swing in the garden. They heard voices, animated. French voices. From the bushes emerged a young couple, who introduced themselves as Monsieur and Madame Mendès.

'You are perhaps also waiting for six o'clock?' asked the French lady.

'Indeed we are. This is my husband, Yossl Messing. My name is Bettina.'

'Yossl Messing!' exclaimed Mr Mendès. 'I have been waiting to meet you. You have the wire studio, have you not? Most ingenious. Most intriguing.'

He took Yossl's arm and walked away with him, leaving the ladies to themselves.

'Is this your first visit to Tribschen?' asked Mrs Mendès.

'It is. And yours?'

'O, we have been a few times. And after every visit, we feel our insides turned out, if that is the right expression. He is a sheer delight. A present from heaven to us, his worshippers. Do not mind his foibles. They are the by-product of genius. For instance, at our first visit we were asked to the dining room after four and a half hours. The meal consisted of soup and bread. On the next day we came again. This time we had an ample meal beforehand. Half an hour after arrival we were regaled to the most sumptuous five dishes, accompanied by various wines, and finished with really strong coffee. That was the sign that we were accepted. After that Cosima lit a cigar and offered me one, too.'

Meanwhile the male side of the quartet had returned, and the party made ready to visit their host. Hasty adjustments to coiffure and dress, and on the stroke of six the doorbell was answered by two large dogs and a manservant, who ushered the visitors into the reception lobby.

Cosima, tally, thirtyish, greeted them with imperious ceremony, except for Mrs Mendès, whom she embraced and called her *dearest Judith*. She announced that the *Meister* was upstairs, but would join them shortly. No chairs were offered as yet, to ensure that the visitors would receive the descending Meister appropriately.

166

When this happened, after a while, a little man with mischief all over his face, plunged downstairs, two steps at a time (he was in his mid-fifties) shouting at everybody and nobody in particular.

'Welcome! Welcome!' Then inspecting the company: 'Let us see. What have we here? O, you again. That is praiseworthy, my dearest Judith, that you repeat your way to me so soon. And with your husband. You must be Mr and Mrs Messing? I have heard of your string quartets. They tell me you compose with little black balls on wires. Intriguing. And you, dear madam, have you got a dog? I have two. Newfoundlanders. Would not, could not be without them. Make you feel alive. We also have a horse, a peacock and a pheasant in the gardens, and chickens and some sheep. Sit you down.'

When the master had assembled his disciples, he took up the conversation once more, by telling Yossl:

'Frau von Bülow has kindly come, with her children, to help me with various problems.'

Since Madame Judith had earlier intimated that her marriage to Monsieur Mendès was coming to an end, both parties, the Wagners and the Mendès practised a certain amount of masquerading. Either couple was what the other was not.

At that moment the door was opened, and led by the nurse, the children were ushered in, demure and silent. Daniela, aged 9, Blandine, aged 6, Isolde, aged 4, Eva, aged 2, and in his pram, Siegfried, who was born only a short while ago. The girls performed perfect curtsies, smiled their welcoming smiles, suffered being petted and admired, smiled their farewell smiles, and were ushered out, silent and demure. The facts that Daniela and Blandine were Cosima's and Bülow's children, whereas the rest were hers and Wagner's, was not a topic of conversation. Nor was the matter that Mendès had two, Judith one pair of Jewish grandparents.

Dinner, which consisted of two helpings of pea soup, followed by biscuits and coffee, was somewhat unusual but not unexpected. Its scantiness was amply compensated by Wagner talking about the coming first performance of *Rheingold* at Munich, which was ordered, against Wagner's wishes, by the young King Ludwig.

'I shall send a telegram to the conductor,' Wagner exploded. *'Hands off my score, or may the devil take you.* Those people will have to learn that they can learn nothing. Imagine it. The carefully constructed tetralogy. *Der Ring Des Nibelungen*, is to be dismembered. *Rheingold*, the first of the four, is to be given alone, an orphan, without explanation about what follows. And that is what I have been striving to achieve in almost a quarter of a century? O, no! But my Wotan. You see, Wotan is not only the chief god, he is also Man. Man who has released social, political and physical forces which are sliding beyond his control. And he is, in the course of *Rheingold*, experiencing the dissolution of a world order based on expediency. Yes, expediency is a new word to him, which he must add to his dictionary.'

Wagner rose, paced through the large room with the pictures and statuettes, heavy curtains and costly wall hangings, and settled at the grand piano. Then he played. The scene of Wotan's awakening and finding his dream come true. Walhall, the castle of the gods, has been built for him by the giants. He gripped those introductory low brass chords and made them sing a melody full of hope. When he stopped, he remarked dryly:

'And by the end of *Rheingold,* Wotan leads his fellow gods over the rainbow bridge into Walhall. A rainbow. Symbol of hope and instability. And that is what the people of Munich want to hear and see, without the sequels, just because the King cannot wait until it is all ready and complete? O, no! O, no! But you must hear this. A letter from a French lady who has fallen on evil days.'

He stepped over to the coffee table where unanswered letters were neatly stacked in two trays, one marked *Not to be answered,* the other *Answer if time.* From the former he extracted a sheet.

'The lady writes: *I am passionately fond of music, but alas, since our misfortune, I have not touched a piano. I feel sure that you would not refuse me admission to your house, and a place at your piano. As for me, I have five children, and I have not the means for a home. I foresee your astonishment, my dear sir, when you read my letter. But if I could only see you, you would no longer be surprised.*

I know fur sure that your house will be my house, and your piano will be my piano.'

General amusement, and surprise at Wagner's facility to jump from a serious topic to an utterly trivial one, and making either appear as of equal importance to him. He mustered the assembled company and with his eyes, blue as a lake, he rested on Yossl.

'Ah,' he summoned, 'my abacus man. I want to hear about your wire studio. Come over here.' He pointed at a sofa in the corner, away from the others, where they settled.

'So in your studio you have arranged wires, like on an abacus, only far more, and black balls which you shift one way or another, until they appear right to you. Why? Because you compose in motion. You cannot sit still. Perpetuum mobile. Yes. I can see you jumping up to the Flutes and crouching down to the Double Basses. Yes, I myself must stand while composing. I will show you my studio later. There will you see my working arrangements which include a high, slanted desk top, which I had made for me according to my design. That is where I work, and from where I test on the piano what I am writing. This constant interaction from composing at desk to checking at piano keeps me forever on the move. Your way is, at first sight, more frantic than mine, but not so far apart. A super dimensional abacus. Yes.'

With that he jumped up from the sofa, followed by Yossl.

'Herr Messing has explained his method of composing in his wire studio to me,' he announced. 'Clever. Astute. Like an abacus for giants.'

The soup which had been served earlier on, turned out to be a refreshing welcome offering. The real dinner followed now. It consisted of five courses, accompanied by wine, and followed by tea, snuff for the gentlemen and cigars for the ladies. At ten o'clock Wagner rose. That was the sign that the party was over.

On the boat trip to the hotel they talked animatedly about Wagner. What he had said. To whom he was speaking. The questions he asked and answered himself. Amazing.

Today we went again to Tribschen. The Wagners asked us yesterday. It is incredibly exhausting, but at the same it is wonderful to be near him. He took me up to his study. A picture in a golden frame shows the young King Ludwig of Bavaria. A strong scent of perfume hangs in the air. All the bright light is concentrated on his piano and on the composing desk. There are further pictures of Aeschylus, Homer and Shakespeare. I told him of my Wagner Presentations, and he was very much interested. He let me have several documents, which I copied in the course of the evening and handed back to him. But, o then he played and sang the scene from the second act of Siegfried, where the youthful hero rests in the forest and muses on his mother. I was moved to tears. Never have I heard such convincing portrayal of human purity and integrity. Gone were all his superficial foibles. What remained was the pure revelation of a great man. He sang:

'*I'd love to know what my mother was like. Alas, that is hard to imagine. A roe-deer, perhaps, lucid and light, has such eyes when they sparkle, only far fairer. But why did she have to die? Must all mothers perish, that their sons may have their lives? That would be sad indeed. The son longs to gaze at his mother. My own mother. A mortal wife.*'

I thought of my own mother, now dead so long. O, what one would give to have such moments, such occasions fixed for posterity. An invention, to enable us to hear again and again precious performances, such as Wagner singing his own works. Perhaps our children will live to experience such blessings.

The doorbell admitted the Mendès couple, who had been invited two hours later than Yossl and Bettina. While Yossl was upstairs with Wagner, Cosima and Bettina chatted in the lounge. They talked about children, their problems in growing up, and how to deal with them. Cosima was a firm believer in discipline, enforced by use of the cane. Bettina shuddered, but kept her convictions to herself. Then Cosima thought she had known Bettina long enough, to entrust her with the secret which was no secret, her own marital break-up and her non-marital partnership with Wagner, including the recently born Siegfried, Richard's first son and heir.

Wagner, with Yossl following, came to join the new arrivals, and as the sun was bright, he suggested tea in the garden, where the four children were playing, watched over by the new-born Siegfried. Cosima sat on the garden swing, when Wagner came and pushed her higher and higher. When Cosima grew at last pale with dizziness, Bettina remonstrated with him. He immediately let go and created a diversion. He climbed up the wall of the house and, with a final flourish, landed on the second-floor balcony. He had obtained the desired effect, but only by substituting one mischief for another. Shaking with fear, Cosima turned to Bettina and said, under her breath, 'Pretend not to notice him. Otherwise there is no telling what he will do next.'

At their hotel they found a letter from Emanuel waiting for them. It was a cold letter, which confirmed their recent observations of their son's strange development. It read:

'To my parents.

We are getting along fine, except that we are sometimes hungry. You could have left us more household money. But I have sold a few books, so we shall be alright for several days. If you do not send us any more, I shall sell a Spitzweg picture or two. Emanuel Messing.'

CHAPTER 27

Berlin in 1939 boiled in a fever of contradictions, invalidations and exploding arguments. So did London. And Paris. And Moscow. When Hitler at last unleashed his war, the population was initially inebriated with the progress, swift and unexpected as lightning in a blue sky. But as the war dragged on, people became sober once more, ending up in bitter recrimination. *We never wanted this war. I have never been a Nazi.* In Britain the anti-war sentiments were propped up by a disbelief of German preparations for war. When it came, the country was ill-prepared to face it. After the disaster of Dunkirk, only Churchill's Athenian oratory saved the people from being crushed. After the rapid, and quite unexpected fall of Paris, in spite of the Maginot Line, the French found themselves at the lowest point in their history, only to be awakened by the intoxication of the final retrieval of liberty. Russia, brutalized by the bloody ruthlessness of Stalin, first concluded a disingenuous pact with Germany, only to be overrun up to their capital city, and finally emerging as conquering heroes in the rape of Berlin. Thus, every nation involved in the war, began it either grudgingly or jubilantly, and ended it at the other extreme.

But let us return to the spring, and allow mankind a brief respite, before the bellowing canons will turn their minds.

Joseph Messing experienced the cautious growth of doubts, concerning the moral rights of the war. Moreover, his own divorce proceedings were delayed. He spent more and more time over his nails, hair, shaving twice a day, brushing his clothes and footwear, cleaning his teeth after every meal in addition to the morning and night ritual. That was one way in which he could avoid pondering over his future, Leni's future, Rolf's future, Germany's future.

Joseph Messing, chief announcer at Radio Berlin, read the following announcements with his well modulated, manicured voice, but with growing private suspicion over their motivation:

24th January   Field Marshall Göring gives instruction to expedite the removal of Jews from Germany with all speed.

172

30th January   The Führer Adolf Hitler declared yesterday: 'If the international financial Jewry should succeed in entangling the nations of the world once more in a world-wide war, then the result would not be the victory of Jewry, but the annihilation of the Jewish race in Europe.'

6th February   The Gestapo has dissolved the Young Catholics Association, and has appropriated its assets.

21st February   All Jews are ordered to hand in their articles made of gold, silver or platinum, as well as precious stones and pearls.

15th March   Last   night   our   troops   marched   into Czechoslovakia. The Czechoslovakian soldiers were disarmed without offering resistance. When the Führer was told that England and France have not reacted, he exclaimed, 'I knew it. In a fortnight everybody will have forgotten it.'

Hans-Joachim, Sven and Egon held their second meeting, at Sven's place. Egon reported his progress with discussions among his higher-placed contemporaries. They tended to agree with his views on the disagreeable way religious matters were handled by the innumerable intermediaries between God and His believers. By and large they were in favour of the official line, concerning the marginalization of the churches, and their substitution by the Deutsche Christen.

'It is incredible' said Hans-Joachim, 'that so-called Christians accept the Bible in toto, instead of being selective, according to its moral standards, which do not change with the changing times. In Luke 14,26 we read: *If any man come to me and hate not his father and mother and wife and children and brothers and sisters, yea and his own life also, he cannot be my disciple.'*

Sven reinforced this line of argument, by including the mighty of this world in the long line of perpetrators against humanity. 'In 16, Nero, hunted Christians dressed in animal skins, while others were set alight as human torches, to illuminate the scene. *An immense number of Christians were crucified, mutilated and sacrificed to wild beasts.* And what about Papal infallibility? In the Middle Ages anyone who dared to gainsay a Papal pronouncement, was punished by having his eyes gouged out.' Hans-Joachim pursued the matter. 'The stubbornness of the Church, as it challenges scientific facts, is quite staggering. Copernicus established in the 16th century that the earth was not the fixed centre of the universe, but rotated round the sun. He was threatened with excommunication for his sinful speculations.'

'What do you make of this?' asked Sven. 'I found this in a book written in the 19th century by George Grote, MP for London and a historian: *Suppose that any tyrant could establish so complete a system of espionage, as to be informed of every word which any of his subjects might utter. It is obvious that all criticism upon him would be laudatory in the extreme, for they would be all pronounced, as it were, in the presence of the tyrant, and there no one dares to express dissent. The omniscience of the deity is equivalent to this universal espionage.'* 'Shattering, for more reasons than one,' exclaimed Egon. 'Wait a moment - one cannot - I cannot - this would be regarded - this would be regarded as treason! Concentration Camp or death warrant!'

He looked from Sven to Hans-Joachim, bewildered and evidently just at the point where he had to make a vital decision for himself, and for untold others.

'Why?' enquired Sven, all innocence. 'This chap Grote wrote in 1822. And he was an Englishman. Any similarity to conditions in our time, in our country, is simply coincidental.'

'Anyway,' Egon disagreed, 'one could not possibly - the risk is appalling - or could one? - should one? - should I?'

Silence. Meaningful glances from Hans-Joachim to Sven, and from the two to Egon. Then Egon spoke:

'It is like staking everything you hold dear, your house, your possessions, your parents, your sweetheart, yourself. Va banque. but it must be done. I have just discovered that for six years I have been a fellow traveller, a camp follower, a yes-man, a collaborator. It has been a lovely, a lazy time, leading my Hitler Youth group, with my reasoning trampled on by forty boots marching in step. Now I must catch up. Next week we have a meeting of some thirty Hitler Youth functionaries. I shall bring to their attention what an English MP wrote in 1822. Van banque.'

On the day when this momentous exchange of ideas took place in Berlin, Rolf started his three-year course at Coburg. He rose very early that morning, to give him time to visit the place, where his grandfather had installed his wire studio. He did not find it closed and, his heart beating faster, he went inside. A young boy accosted him: 'May I explain Yossl Messing's wire studio to you, sir?'

'Yes, by all means.'

'This was the famous habitat of Yossl Messing. Some folk prefer to call it infamous. On all four walls of this very long room, where you now see but eight wires, there were over a hundred, closely almost touching one another, and at the end there were hundreds of little balls, which he . . .'

Rolf interrupted him. 'Yes, very interesting. That will do. Here you are.' He gave him a silver coin, and the little guide was gone.

Rolf settled on one of the chairs that stood by a dangling wire. He was alone. 'Greetings, Yossl,' he murmured. 'I am your great-grandson, and I am with you now. In Coburg. Where it all began. Your wire studio. Your first string quartets. The Wagner Presentations. Mischa, Pierre, Silke, Ben. All dead now. But you live in me. Support my building of bridges into the future. Never, never let me become bitter. And let your eyes rest with gentle affection on the spectacle, when your flesh-and-blood claims his Rahel.'

Jaap was a young student from Antwerp. Like Rolf, he wanted to be a professional musician, before he had learnt his trade. So it was not surprising that the two found each other. Jaap composed sonatas for violin and piano, while Rolf opted for larger ensembles, like the full orchestra and chorus he employed for his *Blessed Bridge*. The two became friends. They helped each other with their artistic efforts, with finding accommodation, with

175

gradually telling each other their life's histories and, rashly perhaps, issuing mutual invitations to their homes in Antwerp and Ursus Castle.

Joseph Messing's demeanour became more and more complex, the closer calendar proceeded towards autumn. He now consumed twelve whiskey bottles a month instead of the former six. He added another half an hour to the work of the visiting manicurist, by improving on her work after she had left. Telephone callers, personal acquaintances and shopkeepers noticed his taciturnity. But as soon as he was before the microphone, his clear, melodious voice returned. The beginnings of two Joseph Messings could be discerned. He read:

24th March   Leaders of Jewish communities have been directed to undertake the clearing of the ruins of Synagogues. Rebuilding is prohibited.

9th April   In consideration of the general situation, the Führer has ordered the discontinuation of broadcasting the religious morning programmes.

12th April   The office of Rudolf Hess announces the closure of all monastery schools and convent schools.

19th May   In a mass rally in Cologne, the Minister for Propoganda Joseph Goebbels declared: 'The German nation does not want war. The Führer is a lover of peace. It is up to our neighbours to choose. As for us, we are armed to the teeth.'

Next morning Joseph Messing received a telegram from his lawyer. 'Divorce agreed. Eifer accepts all conditions. Congratulations.'

'Thank God,' he groaned. 'Leni and Josefine will bring some spirit into this house. And I shall live again.'

CHAPTER 28

First day of term at Ursus Castle. The young had returned from their safari with the Quakers, and their tales were endless. Evidently this new experience had left them seething with tales of adventure and adversity, of incidents and accidents, of quests and quarrels. The telling and embroidering occupied speakers and listeners far beyond their bedtimes, and when they woke up they lived through it again, with the difference that a lonely valley in moonlight had become ghoulish, an invigorating afternoon at sea nightmarish, and a breezy orienteering trip was now called a gruesome enterprise.

Rahel was no longer a pupil. Her time was completely filled with turning out new designs for her card firm, and writing almost daily to her mother and to Rolf. She was eighteen now, a young woman, slender and charming. But she was steadfastly determined to wait for Rolf, however long he took.

Her mother needed much moral support. The still youngish looking widow found the urgent pleas for preparing her emigration as too much to undertake all by herself. Rahel wrote in every letter, with growing urgency, what to do, in what order, and with whose help. Her latest letter was dated 14th April 1939:

Liebe Mutti,

Ursus Castle is full of life once more. Yvonne has her hands full with arranging sleeping quarters for everybody, now that we shall have 50 plus pupils. I have got a larger room this term, with a balcony overlooking the mountain. Wonderful. My designs for the next batch of cards have been sent to the publishers, and they have approved and accepted them, together with the enclosed cheque for £296. You can change it into German currency at any bank. You will need it for preparing your emigration. Lola (agreed pseudonym for Rolf) will always be ready to help either personally or with advice. Yvonne hopes to have your visa soon. The main thing for you is to go to the Jewish Emigration Office and make them expedite your application. Do it now!

With love and kisses
Your daughter Rahel

There was another, shorter sheet enclosed.

Do come as soon as you can. It will be lovely for us to have a mother again. We all need you. Love, Sigi.

Two days after Leni and Josefine moved in with Joseph Messing, a small welcoming party took place. Rolf, Hans Eifer and Dr Runge, the successful lawyer, were invited. The latter brought the decree nisi.

Rolf had motored up the previous day from his college. Now he was sharing the sitting room with his father, his baby sister and his new mother. Leni gave him a huge arrival smile. From Josefine he got a terrified howl. Joseph patted him on the shoulder and said:

'So good to see you. It turned out for the best. At least in our small circle. Having you here is - so good.'

Hans Eifer took Joseph to one side of the room. 'You have known me for a long time, Joseph, and you are aware of my obsessive love for details. Tell me, what drove you to withdraw your application for promotion? Was it really only the lever to obtain Leni?'

Joseph looked at the baby in the pram and cleared his throat. 'When a man has been without his wife for as long as I, and when he is given a new lease of life by the acquisition of a rather wonderful new wife and a delightful child, then consideration of promotion become automatically a secondary consideration.'

Hans Eifer considered this reply. Perhaps Joseph Messing is above board? Maybe he really means what he declared? An unusual, though welcome discovery for an SS man.

The party was a successful mixture of goodwill, forgiveness and animated banter. Rolf was tired, and excused himself before it was over. There were two vases with Daffodils and Tulips in his room, one on the desk, one by his bedside. Rolf felt tired, after his long drive, but first he wanted to write a letter to Rahel, telling her about the hour he had spent in Yossl's studio. He referred to the tingling of his spine, as he felt that his great-grandfather was actually with him, and they were talking to one another. Rolf was used to banishing any thoughts which lacked a believable rationale, but this time . . . He commented on his course of studies, which embraced Piano lessons, Organ lessons, Composition lessons, Conducting lessons, Accompanying lessons and Improvisation and Movement. He was particularly intrigued by this. He asked her to imagine ten young men and women walking in time to the music, played on the piano. 'When the music got faster, they ran, when it got slower, they crawled, when it stopped, they stopped, when it stopped with the final chord being played twice in quick succession, they sat down. When the music changed from major to minor, they turned and continued in the opposite direction. For our second lesson, in the following week, we had to hop intervals. There were six lines, marked with chalk on the floor. When we heard the interval of a fifth being sounded on the Piano, we had to jump to line five. When we heard the interval of a third, going down, we had to hop back to line three, like this:

```
6-----------------------X--X---------------------------------------
5------------------X--X--------X------------------------------------
4----------------------------X--X----------------------------------
3---------------------------------------X--X-----------------------
2----------------------------------------------X---X---------------
                                                X
```

Base X X

Twinkle, twinkle little star.   *How I wonder what you are.*

Next week we shall be given Tambourines, Cymbals and Triangles to play the first, second and third beats of a Waltz tune, played for us on the Piano. From there we take over. Every one of us will have to come up with an idea to test our response to a musical situation. What fun we shall have at Ursus Castle, when I come to see you and the kids. Music lessons will never be the same again!'

August 1870   The newspaper of the French Town of Gravelotte reported the defeat of General Bazaine and his troops, by the jubilant Prussian army. It also carried an advertisement two days after the event, which featured a performance to be given by Yossl Messing's string quartet, consisting of Pierre Marchalt as leader. Yossl as second violinist, Margot Chevalier on the viola, and Hanne Schwarz as cellist. They were going to play Schubert's *Death and the Maiden Quartet,* followed by a new String Quartet by Messing, and Lalo's String Quartet in E flat.

At the night of the performance the hall was packed. This had several reasons. Firstly, the population needed cultural elevation, after the horrors of war. Secondly, the Franco-German names of performers and composers were not lost on the audience. And thirdly, admission was free, with all proceeds of a voluntary collection to be donated to the Red Cross.

The Schubert received great acclaim, with many noisy *Bravo,* and *Bravi* (from those who knew Italian), and *Bis,* which the leader graciously agreed with by letting the ensemble play the last movement again. What were they to make of the next item? Yossl Messing's name was known to several people in the audience, from newspaper reports and, in the case of two or three listeners, from personal acquaintance with his music. It was modern, no doubt, but it was always tuneful, so much so, that people in the audience nodded in appreciation, and when it was over, they whistled or hummed his music.

After their performance they made for a cosy restaurant, where Margot Chevalier, the Quartet's violist, took over. She knew the place, whose proprietors had actually been to the concert and had returned shortly before the musicians. Two burly natives occupied the table next to them. They remarked how they loathed the *Boches,* and to underline the degree of their hatred, they spat in the faces of the musicians. Yossl slowly got up, took his chair and sat down at their table. His three colleagues rose likewise, to form a vague defence, although they would not stand a chance against the well-nourished, well-endowed men of Gravelotte.

'We share the same feeling,' Yossl spoke. 'None of us wanted this war. Allow me to introduce Margot Chevalier, Hanne Schwarz, Pierre Marchalt. My name is Yossl Messing.' Only now did he wipe his face. 'Our concert tonight tried to give the people something more reasonable than the roar of cannons. There are no losers in any war. The only loss is sanity on both sides. Music tries to make peace, restore harmony and bring back sanity.'

The two stared at Yossl. Then one of them blared:

'Louis, four bottles of Beaujolais for our friends, the musicians!'

Joseph Messing did not find it easy to leave his house, to quit the unaccustomed bliss of domestic happiness with the growing tension involved in reading the news which he felt to be manufactured for an audience of lambs led to the slaughter. But he did not pursue those profitless thoughts. It was not up to him. His popular, vibrant voice reported Hitler's speech in which he addressed his general staff:

'Every air-raid shelter organisation is responsible for making instruments of self-help available, such as fire extinguishers, first-aid facilities, water buckets, sand bins and axes. Furthermore, blackouts have to be prepared throughout the country, so that they can be tested at any time.'

In late spring he prepared his listeners for a sudden change in Soviet Russian relations with Germany, together with the signing of non-aggression pacts with Denmark, Estonia and Lithuania.

On August 1st Joseph Messing proclaimed that Jews were forbidden to buy lottery tickets. His private thoughts queried what priority that item would occupy in the harassed minds of those people.

In the ears of millions of listeners, his greatest hour came on August 23rd, when he read the non-aggression pact between Germany and Soviet Russia, verbatim. His voice had a becoming tremble, mixed with the iron core of conviction. When he finally got home, he did the same as his son had done, when he returned from the interview with the SS selection board. He tore his clothes off and had a lengthy bath.

It was an oddly clad assembly, who at the stroke of midnight, met in the dining room for coffee, whiskey and biscuits.

Leni, who had just fed her baby, came in her pyjamas, Joseph with a towel covering his nether regions, and Josefine in her cradle, up to the chin in fine, fresh linen.

'Have you heard the latest?' asked Joseph. 'Germany and Russia have signed an agreement of non-aggression. That means, Poland is the victim, ready to be carved up. And for the first time in five years I have doubts about the Führer's judgement.'

'I have had quite a few,' said Leni.

'Darling,' he whispered, turning his head towards the door. 'I fear that this will lead - he will lead us to war.'

'War?' she cried aloud. Then, sotto voce: 'Thank goodness, Josefine is far too young. But you?'

'My job with Radio Berlin is secure. Normally I would volunteer to join up. But now - but this - I just do not know. I really do not know, Leni.'

'I suggest, we all have a good sleep. In the morning we shall talk again.'

'Good idea,' said Joseph.

Ten minutes later, Leni and Joseph held on to what they counted as their dearest possessions, while little Josefine in her dream saw her mother's nourishing breast, receding, shrinking, empty.

Two days later, Rolf met Hans-Joachim, under the Kolonnaden. 'It is a long time, since we last saw each other,' said Rolf. 'The old columns are still standing. But the *Ringerbude* has given way to a miniature circus.'

'Rolf, do you think we shall have a war on our hands?'

'I fear, the answer is Yes.'

'I was wondering what you meant, when you said that the old columns were *still* standing.'

'For the moment they are. Let us not think of it. Let us not talk of it. We have so little time. I shall have to leave tomorrow for Coburg again.'

'We missed you, Rolf. in our discussions about the Church and related topics.'

'I must make a confession. After a good deal of thought, I have somewhat changed my mind.'

'About religion?'

'Yes and no. My thinking began, when I excluded Rahel from my discussions about religious matters, about the easy way in which people gave up their own responsibilities and left it to parson and priest to take the burden of individual reasoning from our shoulders. I thought of widows, orphans, lonely folk like Rahel, who derived their comfort, in some cases their only reason for being alive, from religion. And I came to the conclusion, that both are right, the ones who decline religion as so much mumbo-jumbo, and those who find solace in it. Then I considered those prodigious buildings, churches, cathedrals, abbeys, monasteries, mosques, pyramids - all erected to godheads with different names, but with the same emotional appeal to their worshippers. And I considered all the world's precious masterpieces, without which we would find it hard to live. Rembrandt, Dürer, Cranach, Leonardo, Michelangelo, Haydn, Mozart, Beethoven, Schubert, Brahms, and above all Johann Sebastian Bach. Can one admire their work, and remain a non-believer? I think one can. I do not know as yet, how to do it. But I will strive. Perhaps we have to learn to build bridges even within ourselves. A bridge that leads from today to tomorrow.'

'So we shall lose you in our fight with unthinking leaders?'

'No, Hans-Joachim. Whenever I can, I will be with you. Tell that to Sven and the others. All bridges have two anchorages. Both are of equal value. Both are right.'

'Careful, Rolf. Next you will forgive those unspeakable monsters who are about to drag Germany into a war, from which it will not recover, and find a reason why they are right, too.'

'They are monsters and they cannot be right. Ever. But last month I was in Bayreuth, for the performances of Wagner's works. I saw the *Ring,* on four days. From it I hoped to see the audiences go out, with their ideas about their lives fundamentally altered, to accept that greed and love of power are the enemies of life, and that universal Love must rule supreme. After all, this is the message of the *Ring.* And I am convinced that I was right. The audience, however, saw things differently. They forgot about the *Ring* and its message, and in the intervals they rushed out, to see and hail and bow to the Führer, who awarded the Cross of Honour for the German Mother of Six or more Children (called by some wit The Rabbit Cross of Honour). Forgotten was Wagner and his message. I spoke to several participants of this charade, and I received the same reply from each. 'As long as we applaud him for peaceful matters, there can be no war.' And, you must admit, they too were right.'

CHAPTER 29

In 1939 in Germany, a knock at the door between midnight and six o'clock heralded the Gestapo. Between six and seven in the morning it indicated the baker's rolls. And shortly after - wonder of wonders - the postman delivering your mail. Without any racial prejudice. Surely this was one aspect the regime had overlooked. They could so easily have excluded Jewish households from the privilege of having their post delivered, leaving it to them to walk to a collection point of the rulers' choice. In the last days before the war, the dreaded Gestapo knock had not been heard at the Oranienburger Strasse, the baker brought another day's freedom from starvation, and the postman could bring the one letter which might prolong life to an unforeseen extent, the arrival of a visa from a foreign country.

This was Frau Reimann's experience, as she opened the telegram with the stamp from Great Britain:

Visa in our hands. Come any day. The sooner the better.
Love Rahel and Yvonne.

On 1st September 1939, Hitler unleashed his war, which initially savaged only Poland, but eventually countries all over the globe. Summoning up all his stamina and survivability, Joseph Messing read out the news:

September 1st   Last night Polish soldiers launched out at the German radio station Gleiwitz. In retaliation, two German army corps, supported by massive air forces, advanced in pincer formation against the Polish forces, with the object of encircling and crushing the enemy. An emergency meeting of the German Reichstag has been ordered for today, to hear about the war situation. The Peace Convention of the National Socialist Party, which was to be held from September 2nd to 11th, has been cancelled.

With these matter-of-fact snippets of information, the listeners were thrilled, stupefied, distressed, according to their convictions.

But Joseph Messing returned to his home past midnight, a chastened man, a newsreader with the real news hiding behind the official text. Leni had been awaiting him, with a glass of whiskey and a few nibbles.

'It has started,' he sighed, as he sank into his armchair. 'He has started it. Poland first. God knows who is next. Leni, I cannot go on like this much longer. What am I to do?'

'If you want to leave the station, you will have to give them a good reason. Either an illness, confirmed by medical certificates, or a move to another official sector.'

He tasted his drink and replaced the glass, still almost full. 'I am not sick. In fact, I have never been saner. As for applying for another post at this time, this would be regarded almost as disloyalty. No. The one way out would be the army.'

'You would be too old.'

'Depends. If the war goes well, they can do without me. But if it goes badly - -'

'Perhaps we should consult Rolf. He has only been in bed for half an hour. Shall I wake him?'

'I suppose so.'

When Rolf descended in his pyjamas, he first went to the kitchen, to make a strong cup of coffee for himself. Then he joined the others who put him in the picture of Joseph's dilemma. He was taken aback by the news of the outbreak of war. Then he considered for a long time. At last he spoke:

'This is Hitler's last, desperate throw of the dice. He will lose. England and France from the West, and Russia from the East. I know he has made a pact with the Russians, but they will break it whenever it suits them. I give him one year. Two at the most. Father, if I were in your position, I would continue at the radio station. I would convince myself that I was upholding the system, come what may.'

'Sh!' Joseph interrupted, with a glance over his shoulder.

Rolf continued in undertones. 'Make use of your training at drama school, and give a plausible performance of a trusted member of the regime.'

'And when it is all over, as you say, in a year or two?'

'Then, father, you will act another part. The one of the democrat, who knew all along - who could not until now - who had helped the persecuted. And you can make a start straightaway with Rahel's mother.'

The next fortnight saw a different Joseph Messing at the microphone. Here was the drama school's prize winner, some twenty years ago, the young man with the brilliant future. Joseph had come into an unexpected inheritance. He had joined the Communist party. After two years he changed over to the Social Democrats. He joined the new broadcasting studio in Berlin, where he worked his way up and up. He left the Social Democrats for the National Socialists, when they came to power. Now, in the first month of war, he read the news with total conviction of a swift victory. Hitler was in sole command, and he was his Führer's voice.

The fact that listening to foreign broadcasts was punishable with lengthy imprisonment and, in serious cases, with death, was elevated by Joseph Messing's vocal validation from sheer lunacy, to all-wise guidance from above.

He heralded the participation in the Polish war of the SS *Totenkopf* (Death Head) Division, as warranty of immediate collapse of the enemy. He graced the negotiations for peace, undertaken by Swedish and Italian sources with forbearance, whereas the invasion of Poland by the Soviets was hailed by him as a liberation. He read about the battle of the river Vistula which ended with 170,000 Polish prisoners, including a vast number of Jews, who were separated from the bulk and treated 'differently'. He read about the concentration of Jews in Polish ghettos. About the radios which they had to hand over. About the fall of Warsaw. About the parcelling out of Poland into West (Germany) and East (Soviet Russia). And about the Führer's announcement about the forthcoming war against the West, in which France would be 'demolished' and England 'humiliated'.

When he returned to the sanity of his home, he shed the mask and became a different Joseph Messing, a dissenter, a turncoat. After all, this was not the first time. But it might be the last.

Leni, as always, was his tender body-and-soul mate. After exchanging the news of their days, Leni asked:

'Have you decided what to do about Rahel's mother?'

'I shall go tomorrow morning to see her. I know it is risky. But we all have to take risks these days.'

He left the Mercedes two blocks from her door. Then he walked, not too slowly, not too fast, until he reached his destination. His knock, not too loud, not too quiet, was answered by several neighbouring heads vaguely scanning the scene, and finally by Frau Reimann.

'I am Rolf's father. May I come in?'

She pulled him aside. Then she peered through the muslin curtains, to see whether her visitor had come alone. She beckoned him to her back room, where they could talk without being overheard. But when she offered him refreshments, he said:

'Time is of the essence. I have come to help you. We must go to the office that deals with emigration matters, and then you can leave for England.'

'O, then you have not come to tell me -'

'Tell you what?'

'That Rolf - that he must - that he cannot -'

'No, Frau Reimann,' her visitor laughed. 'Rolf is constant. But are you ready to leave in ten minutes?'

Joseph Messing told her that he would leave before her. She would follow him in ten minutes, with her shopping bag and her personal documents. He gave her precise information where his car was waiting. Before he left he kissed her, to Frau Reimann's consternation, on her cheek.

He sat in his car, waiting for Frau Reimann. Twenty minutes, thirty minutes, forty minutes. He considered various plans of action he would take. But there were so many imponderabilities. How he missed Rolf. Suddenly she appeared, from the wrong direction. He grabbed her and placed her next to him. No talking. Start the car and away.

After a while she spoke. 'I am so sorry for being late. While I was getting my documents and my shopping bag, Herr and Frau Ruben, in the flat above me, were being collected by two people in plain clothes. Their little boy was playing with a friend in another flat. The Rubens did not volunteer the fact that they had a child. I suppose they thought it better for him to have the slightest chance to survive, than to share their exit. So I went to the flat. The doors were open. Nobody was inside. Then I heard some children's voices from one of the inner yards. I got hold of the small boy and took him to a refuge, the Children's Hospital. By the time I explained the situation, it was very late. I am sorry.'

'Never mind, Frau Reimann. You are here and you are safe. That is what matters.'

'Call me Golda.'

'I will, Golda. I will.'

Joseph Messing halted a little distance away from the office they were seeking, having had a quick glance at it while they were passing. He asked his passenger to make her own way there and join the queue they had seen from the car window. Meanwhile, he got out of the car, stretched his legs and bought a newspaper and cigarettes.

Frau Reimann stood in a long queue which had spilt over onto the pavement. Who knows how many people were waiting inside? Strangers, united by the same fate, the same hope. They talked in undertones. Where did they hope to be going? England? United States? Palestine? Shanghai? South Africa? Australia? Peru? The feeling was almost unanimous - we do not care where we land, as long as it is abroad.

After an hour an announcement was made over the loudspeaker. The office would be closing in twenty minutes. Everybody would be given a ticket with a day and an hour of their next appointment. Frau Reimann was asked to come again in two days' time at midday.

She looked fatigued when she arrived at the waiting car. Joseph asked:

'Any success?'

'Not so far. I have got to try again in two days, at twelve o'clock.'

'Good. I am on night shift. So I call at eleven. How about packing? I think you might make a start. Have you any luggage? You have? You are only allowed to take what you can carry. And ten marks. But that matters little. I have your tickets to Harwich ready for you. Your daughter will collect you there.'

Frau Reimann made her way home from where Joseph had dropped her. It was getting dark. Only a few people walked in her direction. Amongst them, on the other side of the road, was a young man whom she thought she had seen before. Then she remembered him. Heinz Benjamin, the nice boy who had come to take her to Dr Fischer for her first consultation. She was just going to hail him, when two men caught her attention. They were wearing white raincoats, a sign that street-wise inhabitants of these quarters had no trouble in identifying as Gestapo. They were walking ten steps behind Heinz. Suddenly he stopped and pointed at a small middle-aged man. His two followers accelerated and arrested the man, while Heinz Benjamin quickly walked away. Frau Reimann hurried home, greatly disturbed.

Joseph discussed the situation, as he knew it, with Leni. They agreed that it would be best to summon Rolf to Berlin. It was possible that Frau Reimann would receive her emigration certificate in a couple of days, and then Rolf would take over.

Next day Rolf arrived in Berlin. He made his way from the station to Frau Reimann, which was a shorter distance than to his home. He caught her in the middle of packing, or of packing and unpacking, of choosing which of her possessions she would take and which to leave behind her. But now that Rolf was with her, she wanted to talk to him about last night.

'I cannot understand this. Heinz Benjamin is a Jew. So is the man they arrested. Yet he betrayed him to the Nazis. That is not possible. It is against nature.'

'It is. But none of this would have been possible, if it were not for the Nazis' inhumane treatment of millions of people. Who can tell, what made him do it? And what would we have done, if - if, for instance, they held the one we loved dearest of all, with the knife at her throat, and told us they would kill her, unless - What would we, what could we do? Perhaps they did something similar to Heinz Benjamin?'

Frau Reimann resumed her interrupted packing. At the bottom of the case she placed her sketch books, after she had looked long and sadly at the picture of a young man with a Torah in his arms, flying to her, flying, flying.

Next day. The day of decision. Rolf took Frau Reimann to the vicinity of the office. She walked the short distance on her own. There was no queue outside, and only a few people waiting indoors. After half an hour it was her turn.

'Golda Reimann. Widow. I have a visa for England.' She showed the telegram Rahel had sent her. 'I should like to have permission to leave as soon as possible.'

'Wait, please.' The gentleman behind the counter vanished. His voice could be heard, discussing her case with some unseen interlocutor. When he returned, he said:

'Yes, you can leave, Frau Reimann. But not yet. First we shall have to make a few enquiries, as to any debts you may be owing, and to precious jewellery you may have overlooked to declare.'

'How long will that take?'

'See us again on Monday next week, at eleven o'clock. Goodbye.'

Rolf made a serious face, as she told him what had occurred at the office. He said, they would have to consider what to do next. Meanwhile, it would be advisable to fetch her case and handbag from home, and go - he would have to ponder where. He left the car close to where his father had left it, while Frau Reimann hurried home. In the vicinity of 17b, a few steps before her, a cold shudder overcome her: the angel of death. Heinz Benjamin. She turned back. Nobody accompanied him. She quickly walked to the waiting car, launched herself on the back seat and called out to Rolf:

'Drive on!'

She told him what had happened in the last five minutes.

'Well done, Frau Reimann. It is a pity to leave most of your belongings behind, but all that is so little compared with what you still have - your life, and the certainty of seeing Rahel again.'

'Where shall we go?'

'Home.'

When Rolf unlocked his front door and entered with Frau Reimann, Joseph was alarmed. He listened at the door, darkened the windows and beckoned to the others to lower their voices. Rolf gave a summary of the events, and ended with:

'Father, I beg you not to let Rahel's mother perish. Let her stay with us till she gets her clearance.'

Leni supported the request. Joseph Messing deliberated with himself. I am so deep in potential trouble, he thought, that the discovery of Golda hiding -

'Of course, you are welcome, Golda.'

It was decided to put up Rahel's mother in the spare room upstairs, which was windowless and served as a storage place for trunks, suitcases, unwanted gifts and such like. With a folding bed and a bedside table, she should be able to manage for the few days before her visit to the emigration office. Joseph gave her strict instructions, not to leave her room without making sure that it was safe to do so.

While Leni took her to her new abode, father and son settled in their armchairs and talked.

'Actually, father, I have my doubts whether we should go to the emigration office at all?'

'You mean, because she left her home, and they might search for her?'

'I am afraid they will.' Rolf pondered and pondered, but could not come up with any sensible alternative. Joseph, too, pondered and pondered, and at last he jumped up and declared:

'Kietz!'

Rolf looked at him, puzzled.

His father told him what he had heard about the Church Councillor's triumphant interrogation by the SS, and all the small details that encouraged him to mutter:

'Kietz. Kietz. Yes.'

'He may be reliable, but what do you have in mind? How do you think he could help? And if he could, would he?'

'As keeper of the Church registers, he would know of any deaths in Lübeck. And if he plays an active part, which I believe he does, in the struggle against the system, then -'

'I see. I see now. Daring. But feasible. Shall we both? And what about your radio commitments?'

'Tomorrow is my day off. We have forty-eight hours for getting the chestnuts out of the fire. What are our chances, would you say, mathematically?'

'Twenty per cent, father.'

'Well then. Va banque!'

They had decided on a surprise visit. A phone call might have alerted possible eavesdroppers. So, very early on the next morning they set out, having loaded the Mercedes with provisions for the journey. They passed Rheinsberg, Lake Malchow, and Rolf became dewy-eyed.

'O, father! These places, the lake embedded in those gentle hills and the endless walks on the shores almost ten years ago, when all was innocence and nobody dreamt of ever voluntarily leaving it all.'

Joseph Messing did not reply. He shook his head, then cancelled his gesture by nodding several times, emphatically.

They stopped near where they had their picnic five years ago, by the side of the lake.

'Rolf, do you remember our last visit to Lübeck? I believe you then doubted my success with obtaining the necessary papers. I then said it might end with a Canossa disaster. Well, this time it is not Canossa. It will either be an unmitigated disaster for you and me, for Rahel and her mother, and for Leni -'

'And Josefine,' interrupted Rolf. 'But do not think of that. We are launching out on a journey of freedom, of right. Together. We Messings do not surrender.'

They finished their picnic in silence. On their way to Lübeck, Rolf thought of Bach, of the little lady who gave him Yossl's Diary, and of the restaurant where they had their evening meal and where Yossl had wed his Bettina, in eighteen hundred and fifty. Joseph Messing contemplated hard on how he would handle the coming events.

At midday they were in Lübeck. Nearly every house was beflagged. They celebrated the war, their war, their inferno. As they entered the church and walked up to the door with the inscription *Church Council,* their knock was not answered. They looked around and found a warden, who informed them that the office was closed for lunch. Would they come back in two hours time?

They wandered through the town, until they came to the restaurant they knew from their last visit, and where Yossl and Bettina held their wedding party, almost a hundred years ago.

'I wonder,' said Rolf, 'if Kietz is still there.'

'If he is not, we have not lost anything, but a day's travel. But we shall have to start concocting an alternative plan.'

When they had finished their light refreshments, they found they had still half an hour left. So they inspected the Kirchstrasse, where Rolf had obtained Yossl's Diary, five years ago, from the little Arab lady. Or was she Egyptian? As they passed the house, they were struck by the alterations the small villa had undergone. Extensions to the front and the back practically doubled the extent of the property. Three cars of foreign manufacture, graced the drive. As they stood on the opposite side of the road, a fourth car arrived. The driver - no, it cannot be - was a small lady dressed in an expensive looking garment, and carrying several packets of food and drink, labelled *Kempinksi* (high class restaurant, formerly Jewish). Rolf declared:

'It is the same. There is no doubt.'

'Who?'

'The little foreign lady. The one who gave me Yossl's Diary.'

Intrigued, they strolled back to the church. This time, their knock was answered by a jovial 'Come in!' uttered by Church Councillor Kietz. Father and son entered.

'Messing. Joseph Messing. And this is my son Rolf.'

They sat down.

'Messing, Messing,' Kietz pondered. 'I have it. The Ariernachweis. And your generous contribution to the spire fund. And - there was a sequel, a journey - but that does not matter. How can I help you?'

Here Rolf took over.

'Herr Kietz. My father and I come to you as supplicants. You will either have us arrested, or you will help us. I have here a bundle of letters and telegrams, supporting the case you will hear. I beg you to give them back to me, whatever you decide. They are very dear to me.'

He left his father to continue:

'Rolf is to marry Rahel, a Jewish girl who has emigrated to England. Frau Reimann, the girl's mother, must leave the country, since she is on the *Wanted* list. Her husband, a cantor, was murdered in the *Kristallnacht.* A visa is waiting for her in England. You have the relevant information with Rolf's other data. Her passport is no good to her now.'

'Why?' interrupted the Church Councillor.

'It has turned into her death warrant. We need - can you - will you -?'

Another interruption.

'Not another word.' He packed all the documents in his briefcase, shook father and son by their hands, and said:

'We eat at twenty hours. Will you join us? My address is Wilhelm Strasse 8.'

Father and son left silently, walked silently, meditated silently. They made their way to their car, where at last they broke their speechlessness.

'What chances now?' asked Joseph.

Rolf answered, 'Fifty-fifty.'

With five endless hours before them, they made for the car and escaped the town with its flags and general excitement, engendered by the course of the war. They halted by Lake Röggelin, where they left the car and began to wander along its shore path.

Here was peace. The view across the lake was profiled by a dense wood of fir trees and sycamores.

'Fifty - fifty?' reflected Joseph. 'I make it Ninety - Ten. He would not have asked us to dinner, if he was the wrong man.'

'But if he were, would he not do exactly the same? To gain time to alarm the Gestapo?'

'Listen, Rolf! To make sure that one member of the Messings survives, I shall go alone to the dinner and make some excuse for you. Then you wait for three quarters of an hour, before phoning Kietz. From the way he replies, judge for yourself whether it is wise to keep the dinner appointment.'

'If he is evasive?'

'Run for your life.'

In the course of the four hours, they considered this plan, rejected it, considered five or six others, rejected them, and in the end judged it appropriate to continue playing Va Banque.

As the bells on the neighbouring church announced the eighth hour, father and son rang the bell at number eight. An elderly lady, whose features betrayed signs that in her youth she must have been very beautiful, opened the door. She received them with a welcoming smile. Herr Kietz joined his wife, to introduce their guests. Another man, elderly, tall, clad in a long, purple robe, joined them.

'Archdeacon Bamberg,' said Kietz. 'Let us go in.'

He opened the door to a large room, with a grand piano along one side, plenty of comfortable seats and books everywhere. When they had all settled down, Herr Kietz asked with a genial smile, whether they all liked their sherry pale. They did. After a quarter of an hour of amiable chat about everything but the war, Kietz announced:

'It is all a matter of identities. You see, Herr Messing came to me five years ago, searching for the identity of his great-grandfather. That turned out to be unexceptional. But then - see for yourselves.'

He took a leather-bound portfolio from a drawer, and removed a single page which he had kept inside a cardboard folder. It was page 217, now detached from the safety of one of the numerous Church Councillor's volumes. He folded it and handed it to Rolf:

'You had better keep this. You can peruse it later. It is amazing how easily you can lose pages from those old registers.'

Then he turned to Joseph Messing:

'Now to Frau Reimann. Her old identity is no good to her at present. In fact, it is downright dangerous. So I suggest she gets used to the new one we have provided.' He looked at the Archdeacon, and they exchanged glances. 'Anna Smith is easy to remember. There is a petrol station further down the road. Number 86. The man in charge is Herr Bauer. He is small and round, and he wears horn-rimmed glasses. Mention *French Revolution* and *Mark Twain* to him, and he will give you what you desire. Now no more of this. Let us see what we shall have for dinner.'

He rose to investigate. Archdeacon Bamberg addressed Rolf:

'How do you find Coburg and your music studies? Is everything to your liking?'

Rolf, with a look of bewilderment about the Archdeacon's knowledge, answered:

'It is fine. I am composing a little and learning much.'

'Specially since you discovered your great-grandfather's wire study?'

'Yes, this helped. In fact, the work I am struggling with at the moment -'

'The Blessed Bridge?' the archdeacon interrupted.

'Yes. It is about building bridges from the horrors of the present into an unknown future.'

'Why blessed?'

'Because I believe that God spares a little smile for the daring of a young innocent, who is obsessed with so veiled an undertaking.'

'I think he might,' said the archdeacon. Having done with the son, he addressed the father:

'And how do you manage to combine your radio announcer's commitments with your duties in the SS, Herr Messing? Do they clash, occasionally? Is that arduous?'

'At first everything was fine. I believed, you see. I was unshakeable, or so I thought.' Here the voice of the master of the house proclaimed, 'Dinner is ready,' saving Joseph's further self-reproaches.

Over their fish soup, Joseph addressed the archdeacon.

'Would you allow me a question. Where and how did you obtain all the detailed information about me and my son?'

'How do you think, Herr Messing, we have been in power, officially or underground, all those centuries since Martin Luther? To answer your question, let us put it this way: there is very little we do not know. And often we are aware of someone's thoughts, doubts or decisions, before the person himself. As to how it is done - you would not want to spoil the party, by asking the magician to reveal his tricks.'

These were the final words about this or related subjects. The rest of the meal was accompanied by conversation about artistic matters. Herr Kietz revealed himself as a passionate lover of Van Gogh. 'For him,' he maintained, 'painting was as vital as religion, as necessary as breathing. Every brushstroke jubilates.'

Archdeacon Bamberg confessed his admiration for Dürer. 'His canvas that shows the old man at his writing desk, striving to pit his daily strength against the little time he has left. He is watched over by a lion and a lamb, both lying peacefully together at his feet.'

No mention of the war!

Next morning, after a restless night at Yossl's and Bettina's bridal hotel, Joseph made his way, alone, to Herr Bauer's petrol station. Rolf, meanwhile, checked the car's tyres and oil, and loaded it with all their personal belongings, ready for the journey back to Berlin. Then he read the morning paper. In addition to Great Britain and France, the following countries have now declared war against us: Canada, Australia, New Zealand, South Africa and India. The Gestapo has been ordered to supervise the execution of saboteurs, without judicial interference. Public dance entertainments are prohibited. But our victorious armies in the east have completely and for all time eliminated the insolent behaviour of their Polish neighbours.

Herr Bauer was easily spotted by Joseph Messing, who made his way to where the little, round man with horn-rimmed glasses was sitting.

'Herr Bauer?'

'Yes.'

'I am looking for something about the French Revolution. Failing that, anything by Mark Twain.'

'Wait a moment.' He disappeared behind a door. After a minute, he returned, a little packet in his hands, carefully secured with several layers of sticking tapes and string.

'That will be five thousand marks.'

Joseph Messing had calculated, a large sum in cash would be needed, and had cashed a cheque, before the journey, for three thousand marks at his Berlin bank. He paid and left. With ten marks in his wallet, he would have to rely on Rolf for further supply, since it would be inadvisable to leave traces of his journey to Lübeck, by doing any business with a local bank. As for the packet, he would only open this when he was not overlooked. For all he knew, it could contain anything from a passport for Anna Smith to a newspaper cutting of last week's weather forecast.

When Joseph Messing returned to the Mercedes, Rolf was waiting for him. As soon as he was inside, both fingered the packet. The son produced his pocket knife, and carefully guided it across the fastenings, until - they held nothing in their hands. Nothing, except a scribbled note, saying *Call where you called first yesterday.*

'40-60 I would say,' stressed Rolf.

'And I paid Bauer 5000 marks for this.'

'Revised forecast. 10-90.'

Together they drove to the church. Herr Kietz, with a jovial gesture, made them welcome and handed them, without being prompted, the wanted passport, unwrapped, in all its fake or original glory. Who can tell?

'How much did Herr Bauer charge you,' he asked.

'Five thousand marks. For the spire fund?'

The Church Councillor laughed. 'To help people like you.'

Rolf declared, 'Words cannot express my and my father's gratitude. It could easily have cost us our lives. But my father had the notion that you -'

'No more, please. I understand, what you wanted to say. But at present it is wiser not to speak. Or to write. But I wish you every happiness. Here are the data you left with me.'

He handed Rolf's packet, wrapped up with sticking tape and string. Rolf put it away in his briefcase. They rose.

Rolf shook the Church Councillor's hand with both of his. 'I hope your embargo on writing will come to an end. The sooner the better.'

'Amen!'

Their precious belongings well secluded in the recesses of their inner pockets, they made their way to the waiting transport.

'Well, Rolf, luck has been with us. Not that we have not deserved it. And the cost of 5000 marks includes the certainty that, at the present time, there are groups at work -'

'Father,' Rolf cried, 'I did not expect to hear you utter such sentiments. Ever!'

'We have been given our minds, so that we can change them. That is the way to keep them alert. Only fools would maintain theirs in idleness.

When they had motored to Lake Malchow, they halted and unpacked their provisions. This was the moment for Rolf to examine that paper, yellow at the edges, which the Church Councillor had given him. He read:

'Moses Messingsky
Changed his name to Messing and converted to Protestant faith on 3rd June 1818.

Rolf read and re-read this as he read and re-read Rahel's letters.

He did not notice his father's somewhat erratic driving, as he frequently turned his head to see what caught his son's attention. At last he could not wait any longer.

'What is it, son?'

'The missing link! My great-great-great grandfather's name was originally Messingsky. He converted from Judaism to Christianity, one hundred and twenty years ago. So I have got a drop or two of his blood in my veins. What I always wanted. The missing link!'

'I knew' said the father, 'but it is too remote to make any difference. Besides, it is not absolutely certain that Messingsky was originally Jewish. He may have been Catholic or Hindu or anything.'

Rolf suppressed a smile. 'O, to tell Rahel the news. But Kietz. How did he manage - why did he remove the page from the register?'

'To save himself. To save us. An extraordinary man!'

They motored on, without further spoken words on the subject. When they finally stopped, it was evening, and Joseph Messing prepared for his night shift. Rolf went upstairs to greet Leni, then knocked at Frau Reimann's door.

'We have got a new passport for you. You are English. Your name is Anne Smith. And I am one sixteenth Jewish.'

It was a different Joseph Messing who glided purposefully to his desk at the Radio Station. It was difficult to tell who was the cleaner, he or his suit. He read, his cultured voice betraying neither surprise nor tedium, of the curfew for Jews after 21 hours. He read Hitler's decree that, if something happened to him, his first successor would he Hermann Göring, and if something happened to him, his second successor would be Rudolf Hess. He read about the new Euthanasia decree, which provided for the death of the terminally sick. He read about the latest films, which starred the darlings of the public, Willi Fritsch and Lilian Harvey. He bestowed each item with the same amount of impartiality. No tedium. No surprise.

Autumn 1870. Yossl and his quartet had given four concerts in aid of the French and Germans who were among the innocent victims of the war. Now the time had come for going back home. But Pierre urged Yossl to allow him to show the visitor his

201

country, away from the war. His real France. So, while the others went to Strassburg, Pierre and Yossl set off due south, via Orleans and Bourges, to the village of Domremy. They took a modest evening meal at the Café de Jeanne d'Arc and booked an even more modest room for the night. Then they made their way to the old gothic chapel. Amongst the mainly modern stained-glass windows, they found one that might go back five hundred years, to the time of Jeanne d'Arc, for it showed the warrior maid in her loneliness which was her strength. By the left of the entrance to the chapel, they found a statue of the kneeling Jeanne d'Arc, her left hand on her heart, her right skywards. Was it bronze or stone? They were surprised to see a group of men coming towards them. When they had reached the chapel, Yossl asked them what material the statue was made from? They answered, 'Bronze.' But then they asked for their papers. Pierre showed his, which satisfied them. But Yossl's were in German, with places like Lübeck and Coburg, which meant little to them. Meanwhile more people from the village arrived, to be witnesses of the spectacle, and to share in the wine and the biscuits that were offered. Their leader was the burgomaster, who took Yossl's stick and fingered it for a time. At last he found what he was seeking. 'Ah! Un poignard!' he cried, as he produced the sharp end of a dagger which, attached to the walking stick, could transform this common utensil to a weapon of self-defence. Or worse. This was sufficient evidence for the crowd to demand that Yossl be taken to Neufchateau for interrogation. The Frenchman, on the other hand, would spend the night at the inn. Thus began a month of enforced incarceration at the Isle d'Oleron, near the Atlantic Ocean. Meanwhile, however, Pierre had not been idle. After his release from the café, he informed Yossl's family, who immediately got in touch with the leading Prussian cabinet minister who had attended one of Yossl's concerts and was known as an admirer of his music. The minister replied with an urgent message to the French authorities who had arrested Yossl and kept him without trial:

It has come to my ears that Yossl Messing, a well-known musician, has been arrested and put in prison on the Ile d'Oleron. Mr Messing has given four concerts in aid of French war victims, and was on a journey of leisure and recuperation, before returning to his native Germany. There can be no reasonable justification for such a treatment of an innocent man. I demand Mr Messing's immediate release. In case this is not forthcoming, we shall arrest a number of Frenchmen in French cities under our control, take them to prisons in Germany, and hold them there, until this matter is finally resolved.

And that is why Yossl was freed from incarceration in France, why Pierre welcomed him with a bottle of champagne at the prison gates, and why, two days later, he returned to the security of his harrowed family.

It was the third week in September 1939, that the Messing couple with their two children, little Josefine and Rolf, the young man, sat down with Golda Reimann to consider their next steps.

Rolf spoke first:

'Today is Friday. We leave tomorrow. I shall book two single tickets from Friedrichstrasse Station to Harwich, via Hook van Holland. First class, but not together. For security reasons, we shall travel separately, but I shall try and obtain seats in adjoining compartments. When you see me appear at your window, let a minute go by, and then come out, Golda. Here is your book I want you to read periodically, or pretend to read.'

He handed her Charles Dickens' *Great Expectations.* Josefine expressed her approval by a lusty gurgle. Rahel's mother thought of what her husband would have said to her travelling on the Sabbath. Then Joseph took over:

'Here are two hundred marks. Put them in your wallet. More is inadvisable. Less might make you suspect. Remember that you are English and understand but a little German. Phone us as soon as you can. That is when you are in Harwich, and mention *Snow-White and the Seven Dwarfs.*' Josefine gave her full-hearted support.

Rahel's mother had one wish for her last afternoon in Berlin. She wanted to see the wide, green expanse of the *Grunewald,* where she had spent many Sunday afternoons, as a child at her mother's hand, and later as a pupil on school outings, and then, when she was courted, how many sunsets over the river Havel would have contributed to her indelible impressions. She persuaded Rolf to take her to the Grunewald, then leave her and call again after two hours.

Golda's Grunewald. She walked from the park gates along the wide central avenue, to the hills, down the hills, where the road narrows into a footpath. She smelt the autumn. She felt the autumn. An old tale, told by her mother, came back to her after half a century. Father was very ill. The doctor, at his last visit said:

'When the leaves fall, your husband will no longer be here.' And she, little Golda, climbed just one tree, with scissors and string, and tried to tie the leaves to the branches.

Punctually when two hours had gone by, she was back where Rolf had parked the Mercedes. Golda's Grunewald.

Amongst the few possessions she had rescued from her home, was the family's Menorah, the seven-armed candelabra with seven white candles, waiting to be lit. Rahel's mother invited Joseph, Leni and Rolf, to spend their last Friday evening, the last Sabbath in Berlin, as her guests, with her Menorah, with her memories. She had brought from her home the special white bread and the special white wine. Now, as evening drew near, they assembled round the festively prepared table, lit by the seven candles. Golda sang, and taught them while she sang, her Sabbath songs, her *Lecha Dodi,* which welcomed the Friday evening. They intoned songs from the Psalms. From the bowls filled with water, they washed their hands. They sliced a large portion of bread which Golda broke into small segments and distributed among the company, after she had dipped them in salt. Then she intoned a blessing, and the meal began. After two hours, she said grace.

In between Leni went up several times, to look after Josefine. She was as good as ever, and slept right through the Sabbath celebrations.

What did they talk about during the meal? The present situation in Germany? Their apprehension, their hopes, their curses? None of these. Their last evening together was to be a joyful occasion, and their talk was tranquil. Reminiscences of past, happier days, and anticipation of joy.

On the next morning, a young man and a not so young woman took the tram to Bahnhof Friedrichstrasse. They did not sit together, but kept in contact by occasional glances. They dismounted at their destination, and made their way to the crowded platform, where the train to Hook van Holland was due to leave. When it came into view, they made for the first class and took their seats in adjoining compartments. Two people shared Golda's carriage, and only one other passenger was in Rolf's. The man and his wife introduced themselves to Golda as Professor Meyer and Frau Professor Meyer, even before they settled down. Rahel's mother indicated that she did not speak German, and thus secured a quiet journey for herself. Rolf was not so lucky with his fellow-traveller, a single, middle-aged lady, who insisted on Rolf's unpaid services as procurer and carrier of mineral water, newspapers and apples. He at last bought his freedom from further incursions on his affability, when the lady asked him to fetch her a salmon sandwich, and he answered 'No!' She took umbrage, and tranquillity reigned over both compartments.

He took out Rahel's last letters to him and studied them carefully. She must have cornered a good slice of the market for seekers of original postcards for all occasions, and she was very proud of her achievements, for now she was looking forward to provide for Golda and herself. She did not mention, of course, her mother's imminent arrival, as such a lapse could have serious consequences.

In the adjoining compartment sat Golda, her English book on her lap, turning one incomprehensible page after another, and indulging in a little sleep now and then, while the Herr and Frau Professor were thinking of the golden times, when they kept open house for actors, artists and writers.

They were approaching the German frontier, and with it the passport control. Rolf heard how Anne Smith was politely dealt with, and was somewhat surprised at the long delay in returning his passport, after the officer looked at it and took it away with him. He went into the corridor, which summoned Anne Smith to his side. He murmured, without looking at her:

'Make your own way to the waiting boat. At Harwich they will expect you. I shall join you, whenever I can.'

Back on his seat, he found his troublesome fellow passenger accosting him:

'Get off the train now. Run to the wood on the left. Stay there until dark. The border is lightly patrolled. On the other side is Holland. Here is the address of a boatman who will take you to England for a thousand marks. Good luck.'

Rolf did not deliberate. He gathered his belongings, went to the end of the carriage, opened the door to his right, not the left, and jumped off the stationary train. He saw himself trapped. The passport office was under his nose. He quickly jumped on board the train again, and tried the other door, the one the lady had suggested. This looked more promising. There were bushes where he could hide. So down he went. Looking out from his cover, he saw a farmyard nearby. And a bicycle. He pencilled a note, put it in an envelope, together with fifty marks. Then he ran towards the house, grabbed the bicycle, left the envelope and was gone. Rolf cycled south, always south, and always he remained in Germany. Until he came to a small town, where he found a lorry with a Dutch numberplate. He decided to play Va Banque. He accosted the driver:

'I am a Jew, on the run from the Nazis. Here are all my belongings. Take whatever you want. Will you save my life?'

'You will have to leave that bike. Hop in.'

The driver opened the back, shoved Rolf inside, covered him with a tarpaulin and sped away. Whither?

When Frau Reimann, alias Anna Smith, got this momentous message from Rolf, she was stunned. She had marked every move of the passport controller from her window seat, and she was aware that Rolf was in trouble. She had stood still outside her carriage, and observed every move that he made. She saw him jump out, climb back, jump out of the opposite door, run to a house, grab a bicycle and make away with it. She went to the toilet, washed her face, and returned to her empty compartment. The professor and his wife were gone.

At the Dutch terminal, Hook van Holland, where everybody alighted, one would have heard a prayer of delivery from a thousand throats, if it were not for the silence that spoke louder than even this testimony of release from bondage and constant fear. Rahel's mother was one of them. Clutching her hand luggage, she made her way up the gangplank of the boat that was to take her to Harwich, to freedom. A steward showed her to the cabin which Rolf had thoughtfully booked for her, and where she unpacked and took a long shower. Then she plummeted into the armchair and remained motionless for some twenty minutes. Having collected herself, she prepared for bed, where she intended to have a long sleep. One hour went by, two, three, but sleep would not come. Instead she saw the same scene, like a film that played and re-played itself: Rolf cycling away from her, but whither?

Whenever the lorry stopped for unloading, or taking on goods, Rolf heard German spoken. At last the driver dismounted and stayed out of earshot for a while. When he returned he was in company. Another male voice joined his, and Rolf could make out the conversation.

'Well, Piet. It won't be long now.'

'What do you mean?' asked the Dutchman.

'The war. I am sorry, of course, and the Nazis have made mistakes along the line, but now they are unstoppable. The commander of a tank division told me a pretty tale recently. It concerns fifty spanking new tanks which your government bought from ours. For cash. So all our forces will have to do, is motor down into Holland, seize the fifty tanks and go on from there. Speed is the watchword of our army. We overrun, and overfly, and outmanoeuvre any obstacles with our tanks. Your country won't suffer. We just annex it and rush through. The same with Belgium. Then Franc. The Maginot line is just a joke. In no time we will be in Marseilles. And then for the big one. For England! Have another beer, Piet.'

The Dutchman shook his head. 'Possibly you are right. Possibly you are wrong. I must be on my way. Thanks for the beer. So long, Gustav.'

Early next morning Golda awoke. Within two hours she would hold her child, the young woman Rahel, in her arms. But without Rolf. She lengthily washed and dressed, and had breakfast in the restaurant. On returning to her cabin, she made the important substitution she had practised in Berlin, under the supervision of Rolf's father. She packed the passport for Anna Smith at the bottom of her suitcase, and extracted the one for Golda Reimann from the secret compartment, which would have given no headache to any investigator. Anna Smith, farewell. Welcome back, Golda Reimann. But Rolf?

He was cold, hungry and tired. This was not the most comfortable ride he had ever had, but it led to - freedom? They had driven for over an hour, and now they halted. Rolf heard voices. The German one came from a border guard, who evidently was acquainted with the driver:

'Hello, Piet. Nice to see you again. Had a good trip?'

Piet answered. 'Not bad, Emil. Do you think the war -'

'I hope to God it won't. I really do. So long.'

A handshake. A nod of mutual agreement. Piet drove on. Over the border. In the next village he halted and released his - fugitive? - prisoner? Rolf staggered from his confined space and reached for his wallet. Piet requested:

'No, my friend. I believed you from the first moment. One life saved is, in the eyes of God, as priceless as saving a whole nation. What next?'

Rolf looked for the paper with the boatman's address. He handed it to Piet.

'This is the name of a reliable man who will help me over to England. What do you think?'

Piet perused it. 'It is about five miles outside Antwerp. I'll make some enquiries. Meanwhile, do come home with me and have something to eat.'

The tears that were shed at the other side of the passport control at Harwich, were tears of separation now ended, of recalling a father murdered, of the absence of Rolf. Yvonne Messing, who had come with Rahel to welcome Frau Reimann, now assumed the initiative. On hearing the request from Joseph Messing for a call, in case of an unforeseen event, she dialled the number in the nearest phone box.

'Leni? Can I speak to Jo? O, I see. Well, when he comes home, tell him that we are fine.'

'Will you be performing the pantomime tonight? With your school?'

'Yes. We are all looking forward to it. Unfortunately, one of the seven dwarfs is missing. But we hope he will be able to make it for future performances. Anna and her daughter send their love. Goodbye, dear.'

Rolf now sat in the passenger seat. In the town of Breda they halted at a trim, small house, with a substantial front garden, in which three children were playing. Piet introduced them to Rolf, and when he opened the door he said:

'Marjanke, I have brought a friend along. I am sure he is hungry, so do your best.'

The famished stranger added: 'Messing. Rolf Messing.'

While Piet went upstairs to the phone, Rolf discovered their piano. He sat down to play a Dutch tune he knew, called *Im Namen von Oranien* (In the name of Oranien). The children heard him play and came rushing in. They knew this from their school, so they sang quite creditably, especially when Marjanke made it a quintet. Rolf then taught them to sing it in parts, with the oldest child and her mother singing their line after the others. When they had mastered this, they gave a fetching performance to Piet, who had returned from his telephone. It was an old song, but its relevance was clear even to the children. A song of proud defiance to the invader, who was driven by the Dutch into the sea. A French song, *Bonne Nuit,* followed. Then the simple *Guten Abend* (Good Evening), and an English one, *When the evening shadows fall,* which nobody but Rolf knew. So everybody hummed it, first hesitating, then with confidence. Rolf's pleasant voice had won the children's hearts and the adults' approval.

'The transport is alright. He is one of our most reliable men, a staunch fighter for freedom of Belgium and Holland,' Piet informed Rolf. 'Now we eat and drink.'

With apprehension weighing on their hearts, Yvonne, Rahel and Golda undertook the lengthy car journey to the North West, to Ursus Castle. It was evening, when they arrived. The school now had eighty-four pupils on their register, a mixture of old and new *Kindertransports* of refugee children from the continent and new British boys and girls from cities like London, Manchester, Birmingham and Liverpool.

It was a noisier school, too. Now, in the evening, preparations for bedtime were going ahead. Sigi and Jonathan, who were in temporary charge, were glad to see Mrs Messing back. But when Sigi saw Rahel and her mother, he flung his arms around Frau Reimann and kissed her, on each cheek.

'I take you down to Antwerp tonight,' announced Piet after dinner. Plentiful goodbyes and thanks for the splendid meal and hospitality, and many tears from the children. But a man without a passport was in a category of his own, and neither time nor place was at his choice.

Antwerp was a town at war with itself. Brightly lit, it tried to preserve a semblance of peace, but the presence of soldiers in the streets gave the place an eerie foretaste of the bitterness to come. They bought an evening paper. On the back page were advertisements for entertainments and reviews of cultural events. Amongst them a report of an evening with Jaap van der Veldt, who yesterday played Violin Sonatas by Beethoven, Brahms and by himself. Rolf was delighted to find his new friend Jaap making his way to what the paper called 'a significant breakthrough.' If he could find the time he would try to look him up.

What a miserable night. What a miserable day and night. What were they to do without Rolf? Golda was shown around the school. She inspected the kitchen, now under the command of Sigi. She saw some of the lessons, including the ones in sport and self-defence, given by Jonathan. She inspected closely the designs for the next batch of cards Rahel was preparing. But there was little joy in these pursuits. The whole school felt uneasy without Rolf.

It was well past midnight, when two lights could be seen at Ursus Castle. One in Yvonne Messing's study, the other in Rahel's bedroom. Both working. Both waiting. The phone bell rang.

'Leni here. How did your pantomime go?'

'Thank you. Excellent. Though still without Lola.'

'Sorry to hear it. Hope she will improve over the next few days, so that she can take part in the final performance. Here all is well. Everybody sends their love. So long.'

Another hour went by, when footsteps were heard on the stairs. They belonged to two people. One who took two steps at a time, the other more modestly lagging behind. Now they had reached the landing. A knock at the door, and before Mrs Messing could respond, the quicker of the two stood in front of her. It was Rolf.

'Mother, excuse the untimely intrusion. I also apologise for being later than planned, and for bringing a friend along with me.'

The friend stretched out his hand:

'Jaap van der Veldt. Call me Jaap.'

He wiped his face. He was clearly, on account of his corpulence, more tired than Rolf.

'First things first. I think Rahel is still awake. Tell her you are here. Then you go to your room, Rolf. And you, Jaap, can share his for tonight. And if you can possibly stay awake, you can tell me, in a few words, about the cause of your delay.'

Whoops of delight from Rahel. Tears of deliverance from Rahel. Then silence. After ten minutes, Rolf emerged with Rahel. Jaap had been waiting outside and introduced himself. All three made their way to Yvonne Messing's study, neglecting their freshening up. Instead, they dabbed their faces and hands with the tissues of eau de cologne, which Rahel let them have.

'First, all went smoothly,' Rolf began. 'But at the border control they kept my passport for a long time. Golda had no trouble with hers. I decided to make a run for it and jumped off the train. I liberated a bicycle, against cash, and found this van. The driver took me on board, hid me and got over the border, he being Dutch. He actually gave me an evening meal at his home. He then drove me to Antwerp, where I looked up Jaap, a friend from Coburg, who just had given a marvellous concert in his home town. Then we found this mysterious boatman, whose address was given to me by a lady passenger. He told us - that is myself and Jaap here - to meet him at a deserted place by the coast next evening. Jaap offered me quarters at his home, and I must have slept till midday. Then we made our way west, to the sea. At the appointed time we met our boatman who took us on board his yacht, charging us one thousand marks per head for the trip, and no further questions asked. Then came a shock. Two further passengers arrived, and they had previously shared Golda's compartment on the train, a Professor Meyer and his wife. They did not open their mouth once during the crossing. Strange. Anyway, in the early morning we arrived in England, some twenty miles east of Dover, at a seemingly deserted coast. We had to wade ashore. Suddenly four people appeared. They came towards us, furtively. They exchanged glances with us, walked past us, arrived at the yacht with wet feet, and were gone. We made our way towards the nearest village, where we got a bus to take us to Dover, and from there by several rail and bus trips to Ursus Castle. Professor Meyer and his wife, by the way, we lost in the village by the sea. And here we are.'

He looked at Rahel, and he felt what Othello must have felt, when he reported a similar tale of mishaps and deliveries to Desdemona:

'She loved me for the dangers I had passed,
and I loved her that she did pity them.'

CHAPTER 30

'All Jews are instructed to hand in their radios. Refusal to comply will be severely punished.'

This was one of the announcements by the newsreader of Radio Berlin, Joseph Messing, produced with his agreeable voice. The date was late September 1939. There followed several items about the military, the inner and the social situation, all given the same amount of impartial presentation which kept the listener guessing where the reader's sympathies were lying. Or whether he had any.

'Warsaw capitulates.'

The following was not read out, but it circulated in the house with immense rapidity. 'Leading personalities of the army have protested in vain against the policy of exterminating Poles and Jews. Hitler rejected their pleas of moderation, with the warning that he was unable to conduct a war with salvation army methods.'

Equally unspoken was the fact that General von Hammerstein had intended to arrest Hitler at a visit to the western front. All these items were dated September 1939.

October 1939: 'The outcome of the victorious campaign against Poland is 694,000 prisoners taken by Germany, and 217,000 prisoners taken by Soviet Russia. The number of German dead is 10,572.'

October 1939: 'Since the contributions in atonement for the damage of the *Kristallnacht* have so far fallen short of the sum required, all Jews are instructed that their payments have been increased from 20% to 25%.'

Strictly secret, and not for broadcasting under any circumstances are the news of Josef Miller's attempt to contact the British government about the German Resistance. Or the diary entry, after Joseph Goebels' visit to a Polish ghetto: 'These are no human beings any longer. They are animals. Therefore we have no humanitarian obligations, but chirurgical ones.' Or the abortive attempt on Hitler's life by Johann Elsers, in a Munich beer cellar. Hitler left the venue shortly before the explosion. Or the attempted assassination of Hitler by General Halder. All these were within the knowledge of many employees of the radio station, including Joseph Messing, but the betrayal of this knowledge would have been instant death.

The year ended with two announcements:

'Himmler has prohibited the appearance of all foreign newspapers in Germany.'

'The sale of chocolates to Jews is prohibited.'

While his son was invigorating, comforting exhilarating young and old at Ursus Castle, Joseph Messing read out the news of 1940, in a never wavering voice.

'Jews are excluded from receiving clothing cards.'

'A ghetto is established in Lodz.'

'German armies invade Denmark and Norway.'

'Desertion from the army is punishable by death.'

'A concentration camp is opened at Auschwitz.'

'German armies invade Holland, Belgium and France.'

'Churchill becomes Prime Minister.'

'A ghetto is established in Warsaw.'

'Evacuation of British and French armies from Dunkirk.'

'Paris falls.'

'Plans for deportation of European Jews to Madagascar.'

'French government under Marshall Pétain in Vichy.'

'Jews are forbidden to possess telephones.'

'65 nights of uninterrupted bombing of London.'

'Destruction of Coventry by German bombs.'

All in all, a propitious year for the Germans whose total victory could be foretold within a year, or two at most.

The war showed its other side at Ursus Castle, as it did in Great Britain. In spite of the increasingly alarmist news from the battlefields, the country remained quietly optimistic about the outcome, especially since Winston Churchill had taken over command. Mrs Messing's school reflected this composure. On the third day of Rolf's arrival with his friend, he had walked to Mount Skiddaw with Rahel, and talked about Golda, about the Germans, about Rahel's growing importance as a designer of cards, about the future, about their future, about themselves. Now they attended a special morning session of the upper forms of Ursus Castle. Its theme was *The World in 150 years.* Present were the director, Golda, Sigi, Jonathan, Rolf, Jaap and Rahel, together with about forty of the older pupils.

'We need time,' said Klara. 'Time to liberate women from the senseless job of cleaning the house. I can imagine that every room would have a built-in suction apparatus, that takes over from the hoover, and sets women free from time-consuming labour. Thus, the cumulative intelligence of millions of females would be released for worthwhile enterprises, and the world would become an even-handed place.'

'The same goes for cooking,' said Hanna. 'It is an utter waste of effort, to spend hours in the kitchen, when you could - and should - use your time for the common good. In 150 years I can foresee families and single people phoning for their selections from an ample menu, which would be delivered piping hot to your front door.'

'But think of the expense,' interrupted an objector. 'Who could afford such a luxury?'

'This would not be a luxury. On the contrary, since most people would make use of this service, it would be a vast undertaking and less expensive than individual preparation of meals. Quite apart from the amount of time saved.'

'What about our baths?' enquired a voice. 'Have you seen the dirty rim around the tub, which you clean at the end? Part of the dirt remains unseen on your body. Ugh! In 150 years the bath will be regarded as an unhygienic anachronism, which has long been replaced by the shower.'

Jonathan enquired: 'It seems to me that the most immediate problem to be solved, is the source of a new kind of energy, in place of the old petrol, which is slowly coming to an end. Has anybody any thoughts of that?'

A lengthy pause for deliberation. Then Peter answered:

'The cheapest commodity is water. With the addition of a substance yet to be discovered, we ought to be able to produce a cheap alternative. Since this is a matter for the chemist, I would suggest special attention to be given to our chemistry classes in future.'

General amusement. Peter continued:

'And while we are on the subject, what about the overcrowding of our roads? Increase in world population brings increase of transportation. How do you solve the problem of keeping the ever increasing number of cars from strangling our road system?'

'I have thought about this,' put in Hanna. 'In 150 years no cars will clog up our streets. They will be in the air. By that time we will have the technology to have flying cars and marked out lanes in the sky. The only times cars are below, are the take-off and the return. They fly, of course, vertically up and down, into and out of their electronically guarded lanes.'

'That reminds me,' said Debra. 'I wear glasses indoors and out. How often have I wished the streets were better lit. In 150 years from now I fully expect all roads and pavements to be uniformly brightly lit, so that there is no difference between day and night. That would add to safety, and diminish the crime rate.'

'Has anybody given thought to the slow rate of building?' asked Jaap. 'I expect we shall see a revolution in building materials and building time. The long time wasted by antiquated methods of erecting a house, of creating a road, will be superseded by prefabricated units. New techniques will facilitate the shaping of living quarters in days, and roads will be laid in similarly revolutionized ways.'

Now Rahel spoke: 'I believe the most important advance will be in medicine. Cancer, the scourge of mankind for so long, will be eradicated. Heart disease will have become a rarity. New methods of detection, prevention and curing will be evolved. Body parts, artificial and real ones, will feature large. In 150 years people can look forward to reaching an average life span of a hundred healthy years.'

'And morally?' asked Rolf.

Here Yvonne Messing took over. 'Morally we have always lagged behind scientific and general progress. While artists created the most wonderful images and while we can enjoy the advances in medicine, technology and communications, morally some of us are still tree-dwellers. Hand in hand with the explosion of the world's population, goes the rising number of people with a very high and a very low intelligence level. That is perhaps the greatest problem, which must be tackled in our schools. In all schools. In Ursus Castle.'

Rolf and Rahel climbed up the familiar snaking route to Mount Skiddaw. It was an autumn day like none before. The heat was intense, and lingered under their eyes and in their cheeks the whole day. Arm in arm. Up and up. The occasional words spoken were offsprings of their great love. On the summit they rested. Rahel stretched herself out on the grass and cradled Rolf's glowing head in her bare bosom. He sank his lips into the swelling billows, and both lay thus for time without end.

At last he spoke: 'I have told you almost all my adventures on the journey to you. But the big surprise I have left for now.'

He reached for his wallet and extracted a carefully folded page. It was the one he had received from Church Councillor Kietz.

'Here, read this.'

The words, written in a calligraphic hand, contained the message that Yossl's father, Moses Messingsky, had changed his name to Messing and converted to Protestantism in June 1818.

Rahel could not speak. After a long time, she drew Rolf down to her and whispered:

'Take me. Now I am entirely yours.'

It was evening before Skiddaw released them from their bewitchment.

Ursus Castle was now in full swing. Christmas, New Year came and went. Occasional snow flurries decked the surroundings with a light mantle. The eighty odd children were content with their work. Jaap had long left. Jonathan was a favourite teacher. His art of self-defence was based on Japanese principles, and he performed minor miracles in the long jump, both as a demonstrator and in his eager pupils' results. But - the sensational news that gripped them all was the wedding, next weekend of Rahel and Rolf. Both mothers, Golda and Yvonne, had toiled tirelessly with the bride's dress, her dowry, presents of all kinds to set them up, and invitations to the festivities which were to be held at their home, at Ursus Castle.

The day began with a strange ceremony, arranged by the couple. They had long agreed that no special building, no church, no cathedral was needed for two people to confirm their willingness to serve one another. Therefore they had obtained their marriage certificate from the registry office in the nearby town. Now the great hall of Ursus Castle was filled with every member of the school and the staff, when Rahel and Rolf walked in, arm in arm, clad in their festive clothes. Rolf had assembled a small orchestra and a choir, and they performed, under his direction, the Mass in G-major by Schubert.

Next, Rolf and Rahel had prepared a reading of Shakespeare's sonnet. They declaimed:

Rolf	*Shall I compare thee to a summer's day?*
	Thou art more lovely and more temperate.
Rahel	*Rough winds do shake the darling buds of May,*
	And summer's lease hath all too short a date.
Rolf	*Sometimes too hot the eye of heaven shines.*
	And often is his gold complexion dimmed,
	And every fair from fair sometimes declines,
	By chance or nature's course untrimmed.
Rahel	*But thy eternal summer shall not fade,*
	Nor lose possession of that fair thou owest,
	Nor shall death brag thou wandrest in his shade,
	When in eternal lines to time thou growest.
Both	*So long as men breathe or eyes can see,*
	So long lives this, and this gives life to thee.

This was received, as Shakespeare always is, on several levels of perception. The younger members of the school did not understand the language, but were struck by something mysterious and beautiful. Several felt themselves spoken to by a line or a phrase. Others, a small minority, lapped it all up, elated.

A short pause ensued, for the setting up of the orchestra and chorus. Then came the short final section of *The Blessed Bridge* which they had rehearsed, played in public and enjoyed ever since. 'If this is modern music, I can live with it,' admitted one. 'Give me excess of it,' acknowledged another.

Presentations. From Sigi, a wedding cake. From the school, a typewriter. From Yvonne and Golda, a picture, under wraps in a really handsome frame. When it was unveiled, under a growing chorus of Ohs and Ahs, it showed a ship crossing from a shore in black, to the other side which was golden. The ship was named *Covenant* and above it, in the sky, flew a young man with Rolf's features, straight into the arms of another figure, bearing Rahel's countenance. This was her present for him. Rolf was sunk in contemplation for a long time. Then he kissed her and gave her a fetching volume with many handwritten pages, entitled *Collected Poems* by *Rolf Messing.* It contained all the verses he had written in the last ten years, the original German on the left, with the English translation on the right. She perused them, then chose one, entitled *Homeland,* and Rolf read:

> The forest where slim pines aspire, where birch
> and beech for lucid inspiration search,
> where stranded leaves autumnal patterns spin,
> all yellow superfluity within,
> the distant lake on whose secluded slopes
> they cling, dear creatures, to each other's hopes,
> the city haunts that sheltered our yearning,
> our gazing, grieving, wondering, searching, learning,
> the minister's silhouette, soon Satan's throne,
> the oozy river's dark, insistent moan,
> the whole of mother's fatherland are you alone.

CHAPTER 31

The year 1941 brought several startling events, which influenced life at Berlin and at Ursus Castle in unexpected ways. Joseph Messing was now safer than ever before in his position as the leading radio voice. He was more than a reader of the news. His was an impartial, pleasing delivery, with timbre, pitch and intonation just right and unmistakably his own. A masterly performance, but at what cost. Every time he came home, it took Leni longer and longer to persuade him to continue playing his charade.

He had to read Goebbels' words of wisdom about modern music. The minister prohibited atonality. He prohibited music with distorted rhythm. And in dance music, he prohibited the use of mutes in French Horns. He had to read that Concentration Camp victims who were either mentally disordered or incapable of work, would be taken to terminal institutions, called - inoffensively - 'Euthanasia'. He had to read that Rudolf Hess, Hitler's deputy, had flown to Britain on a peace mission, and was taken prisoner instead, with the German explanation that he was not in command of his senses, when he grabbed the plane that took him to the enemy. He had to read, in May, that the 500 planes bombing London would be required for 'Barbarossa', the invasion of Soviet Russia, and that this vast land would be conquered before the onset of winter. He had to read that all Jews had to wear a yellow star, which was to be displayed on the left side of their garments. He had to read that Leningrad was encircled. That Kiev had fallen. That 665,000 Russian prisoners had been taken. And he read Hitler's speech, in which he informed the world that Russia was beaten and would never rise again.

He switched off the microphone, packed his belongings, and returned home, confident that his last stint as upholder of the regime had come to an end.

Ebullient activity at Ursus Castle. Rahel and Rolf had been married a year ago, and she was expecting her first child. But he was in limbo. Without a passport, with a dubious nationality, with his studies at Coburg interrupted for an indefinite period he was, in his own eyes, a drifter, a drone. His mother tried several times, to persuade the authorities to issue him with a British passport, citing his marriage to a Jewess, and his voluntary arrival in the country, but in 1941 the authorities had more urgent things to occupy their minds. The matter was settled when, on a bright April day, two policemen rang the bell at Ursus Castle, were admitted to the director's room, where one of them announced:

'We are very sorry, Mrs Messing, but we have instructions to collect your son, Rolf Messing. Will you please tell him that we shall call in an hour's time. That will give him an opportunity to collect his belongings and prepare himself for an absence of indefinite duration from his home.'

'There must be an error somewhere,' protested Mrs Messing. 'My son has given invaluable service to the country, by guiding eighty children along democratic lines -'

'We know that,' interrupted the other policeman, and we regret the decision as much as you do, Mrs Messing. But this is war. And your son is regarded as an enemy alien. So he will have to be interned. For the duration.'

They took their leave.

September 1941. Hans-Joachim, now fighting in the *Waffen* SS, beleaguering Leningrad. Inactivity. Boredom. Relief by talking, conjecturing, imagining.

'Untermenschen,' said Paul, his equal in rank.

'Like Jews,' said Hans-Joachim.

'Worse.'

'Worse?'

'Look at it this way. Would you - I mean, with the winter setting in, would you try and hold on to a town which is surrounded and will have to capitulate - with hunger and disease - just because Stalin tells them to? I mean, they have totally surrendered to the prophet, without seeing that he demands the impossible, that he is demented.'

'Just like -'

Before Hans-Joachim could continue, an enemy mortar landed between them, knocking them sideways and backwards.

When they regained consciousness, they wiped the blood off their faces, and stared at each other.

'What did you have in mind, when you said 'Just like?'

'I don't - remind me,' probed Paul.

'We were talking about Stalin, and you said 'Just like'.'

'O, that. Just like our Führer. Of course in his case, he is right, being the Führer. Only a traitor would attribute Stalin's motives to Adolf Hitler.'

'Of course.'

'Of course.'

'I am so weary,' Leni,' complained Joseph Messing. 'I am going to retire from my job with Radio Berlin. But how? Give me a timetable.'

Leni did not let him share her frenzy. It was, in any case, a fleeting sensation. Out of work? How would they manage? Of course they could. Neither he nor she need to do any paid work for the rest of their lives. Do not ask him why. Not yet. Help him. He asked you for a timetable.

'See Dr Fischer, and get a week's leave of absence for medical reasons. That will be a start.'

He replied, 'Good idea. What next?'

'That depends entirely on your choice. Your heart was not in the radio business for several months. It is time you looked for something you really would enjoy.'

'I could retire altogether.'

'They would not like that. They would suspect. They would dig. And they would find something. Anything.'

'You are probably right. How about a transfer request. To another department. Same organisation.'

'You are not a desk man, Jo. Nine to four, and a golden watch when you retire.'

'I have it. Emigrate. To America. Take the whole house, well, its contents with us, and start again, with Josefine and us in the States.'

'They would not like this at all, Jo. They would not let you leave the country in war time. They would call you a deserter, and you know the penalty for that. You have announced it often enough.'

'I know, I know. Just testing the water. What would you advise - but no, that is ludicrous - is it - *is it?* Tell me, what would you say to my obtaining a commission in the army, and joining up?'

'I would grieve to lose you. So would Josefine. Perhaps for ever.'

'Yes, I thought this would be a reaction. But let us go into details. The Soviets should be finished some time in 1942. That would open the way for an invasion of England. A nice country. There will be little resistance. It will be a relatively easy campaign. A chance to meet the family at Ursus Castle. Yes, the more I think of it, the better I like it.'

Commotion on the landing. Josefine had woken from her midday slumber and came, clip clop, clip clop, down the stairs.

Joseph buried her face in his, and kissed her many, many times. When he looked for Leni, she was in the next room, by the phone.

'Tomorrow at ten o'clock. Thank you, Dr Fischer.'

Later that day, the two policemen appeared again at Ursus Castle, to collect Rolf. The whole school was lined up in a double row, to give him a farewell in guard-of-honour style. At the head, the last to say goodbye, were his mother, his wife and Golda. When would he return? Would he return? From a sea of tears and depression, they could not extract an answer.

The small van took them across to the East, through breathtaking mountainsides, with Skiddaw offering a dwindling valediction, as it slowly vanished amongst its fellows. After two hours, they entered a town with a cathedral.

'This is York Minster,' said one of the policemen. 'You will be housed on the racecourse.'

After half an hour, Rolf was released from his police-escorted van, to be given over to the army, in the shape of a middle-aged lieutenant. He consulted his notebook, proclaimed 'Number 17' and left Rolf to make sense of this. He looked around, and found some fifty other inmates, all male, some of them on the grass, others in their horseboxes, which were neatly numbered from '1' to '60'. He discovered his own, 'Number 17' which had in peacetime harboured a fleet stallion or mare, but was now to be Rolf's living quarters, possibly until the war was over.

Bedding. Simple furniture. A list with directions on what to do and what not to do. The first seemed unlimited, without restriction. The latter merely warned you, not to approach the perimeter of the camp, as this would inconvenience the sharpshooters.

Rolf was one of the last to arrive at the racecourse, and by evening all horseboxes were full.

A whistle demanded attention. Rolf's colleagues, who apparently knew this sign, ambled to the assembly place outside their living quarters. No lining up, no military paraphernalia at all. Just words of communication from the commandant to the people he had to guard.

'I am Lieutenant Butler. My living quarters are over there.' He pointed to some houses by the side of 'Number 1'. 'If you wish to bring anything to my attention, do so by informing your representative. May I remind you that you are enemy aliens, or potential enemy aliens, and that it is as much in your interest as it is in ours, to keep you in the safety of this former racecourse. Let us hope that the war will not be long, and you will be able to return home in the not too distant future. That is all.'

Rolf approached his neighbour, introduced himself, and asked him:

'Who is our representative?'

'Number 35. Heinz Schmulewitz.'

'Is he -?'

'Kosher? I don't know. He seems to have been either self-appointed, or appointed by the British, before they opened the camp.'

The company he was forced to keep, turned out to be extraordinary. There were artists, writers, doctors, a few spies, all united by the wish to make their enforced change of routine as pleasant as possible. They were at peace, and they were left in it. Although no newspapers were allowed, several inmates had portable radios, so they were informed about the war. But it remained curiously remote.

A week went by. A month. What kept Rolf sane was the letters he received almost every day from Rahel, from Yvonne, from Golda, and from several pupils. And then the great day arrived. The post brought him the message of his son's appearance on this briefly so distressing planet. Rahel herself was the bearer of the news and of the child's name, Florestan. Take the first four letters and reverse them.

In the evenings people gathered together in small groups, in or outside their boxes. There was one dominated by the authors, where they read to each other from their own works, or from poets and writers of the present and past. Another group, mainly painters, showed their wares, finished and started, with much discussion about the purpose of art. There was the more clandestine meeting of the spies. This was the most harmonious one of all. Since they were only four, a Russian, a German, an Englishman and a Rumanian, they had reached stalemate. They agreed never to talk business, and were free to indulge in reminiscences of the towns they had seen, the lives they would have liked, in Hamburg, Vladivostock, Bucharest and Stow-on-the-Wold.

Rolf heard Violin sounds emanating from one of the horse boxes. On coming closer, he identified the piece, Beethoven's *Spring Sonata*. The player was an elderly refugee from Germany, and his playing was superb. What a pity there was no piano in the camp. Rolf had heard the Russian spy play on his Accordion. He wondered if he could get the two together.

'Forgive the intrusion,' he said. 'I have heard you improvising to perfection on the Accordion. There is an equally talented violinist in our midst. Do you think, if I get you the music, you could practise the accompaniment to his Beethoven sonata?'

Fjodor shook his head sadly. 'Njet - I know not - da, by every means.'

So began a collaboration that was destined to survive the time in camp, with the Russian's professional change of heart, and musical transfer from Accordion to the Piano.

One day, the fatal day, came - by the evening, the camp was denuded by half their number. Which half, the ominous Australian or the buoyant British, would Rolf find himself in?

March 1942. Leningrad had survived the rigours of winter. The German army was hungry, cold, demoralised. Something would have to be done. Hans-Joachim and Paul had much opportunity for chats, and they became more and more outspoken. One day, with the frost driving its claws through their marrow, Paul began:

'Escape?'

'Are you mad?'

'I mean it. Think of it, Chance of survival. At least we would have the prospect of finding something better than the idiotic death the Führer has chosen for us.'

'It would still be desertion. You know the penalty. And we have sworn an oath.'

'Which he has broken.'

Hans-Joachim asked: 'How could it be done. Alone? Or the whole company?'

'The whole company sounds great. But, though the majority think as we do, there are the fanatics who still believe in the final victory.'

'I have it. An order. Let's get an order to report, to request reinforcements. Material. Food. To save the army. To save the campaign. An order to see Hitler himself.'

'Damn good. Damn good.'

'And once we are on home soil, we have a chance to go underground, and work for the overthrow of the regime.'

1942. Stalingrad was to be the decisive battle of the war. General Friedrich Paulus' 6th Army, had the prize in their grasp, when they surrounded five sixths of the city. Amongst the leaders of this army was Waffen SS Colonel Joseph Messing.

Everything had not gone according to plan for him. The Russians proved a little stubborn. So Joseph, instead of enjoying his war with the British, was sent to Russia, to help with the taming of the bear.

Neither did Hitler's promises of relief during the winter months come true. He had undertaken decisive support from the air. The sky over Stalingrad remained largely clear. He had pledged vast quantities of warm clothing and plenty of food and drink. The soldiers remained frozen, hungry and thirsty. Now he issued a new order: hold your position at all costs. No retreat.

The parallel with Napoleon in Russia was only too clear. The difference was less so. Napoleon led his army into and out of the inhospitable vastness, whereas the Führer issued his orders from the safety of Germany.

Joseph Messing was popular with the troops. His unselfish enrolment. His shift from the safety of the microphone in Berlin to the Russian front. Considering his age. And family. All these were given due prominence in the press, and from there it penetrated to the frostbitten soldiers in the east.

Two wide rivers held the German fate, the Don and the Volga. Cross those two, and Stalingrad is yours, with the whole of Soviet Russia open for occupation. When will that happen? Will that happen? Why has it not happened? Even Joseph's popularity with the troops could not stem the flood of disillusionment that gripped an ever growing number of soldiers.

Joseph Messing thought hard. He kept his deliberations to himself, as he did not want anyone to be involved in the outcome. He was used to issuing commands. Now he was waiting for an order from above. The right kind of order. The only one. But what? *Contact Hitler and tell him of our plight.* No good. Remember that Hans-Joachim Greifer was not even admitted to his presence. *Contact Paulus.* Yes. The man on whom the fate of a whole army depended. Yes. Now was the time for discussion with others. He held several, semi-official debates with equal ranks, who were impressed with his proposal, and contacted higher authorities, until it reached Paulus himself. And he ordered Joseph Messing to come and see him. For the first time in his life he was required to contradict the Führer. 'In my outfit' he would say, 'there are men who have not left their trenches for months. Hundreds. Thousands. They are not capable of thinking any more. Their actions are reactions, motivated by one notion alone, the Führer will not abandon us. With frostbitten hands and frostbitten feet, starving, numbed and tired to death. Send them all they need. Send them all you promised. Now. Or allow them to go home. The alternative is too monstrous to be contemplated.' Such was Joseph Messing's order.

Telephone calls between General Paulus' headquarters and those of Hitler's in the security of the *Heimat,* smoothed the plan for a personal meeting.

Accompanied by two young officers, the staff car sped westwards. After three days they arrived at their destination. Surprisingly, he had to wait but a little while. Two SS men, for personal safety reasons, ensured that he was not carrying weapons. Then he was called into the Führer's presence. Relying on the undeniable legitimacy of his case and on the magic of his elocution, he gave the finest performance of his life. But before he had finished, he noticed that Hitler had not taken in a single word. He simply heard the tone and not the substance.

'Tell Paulus, the worst is over. My astrologer and my weather forecaster both agree. The winter will be short and moderate. The victory will be ours.'

The abortive mission over, Joseph Messing joined his two waiting subordinates in the car, and they drove away. Westwards. Always westwards. They bought civilian clothes for themselves. They abandoned their uniforms and their car. They used trains, trams, buses and hire cars, to take them ever westwards. Where?

On that day so calamitous for half the complement of York racecourse, two strange events took place. In the morning, a new arrival, and in the late afternoon, the bombshell. The newcomer was Prof Meyer, who moved into the last hut. Six hours later, a whistle was blown three times, by a new face, a superior in rank to their Lieutenant Butler. The whole company was required to line up in order and to count their numbers from one to sixty-one. Then came the order. 'Even numbers five steps forward.' Rolf was the last in line, number 60. He found himself gently, but firmly pushed forward, together with number 59, Prof Meyer.

'It has been decided, for your own comfort, to halve the number of occupants in this camp. To this end one half of the compartments will be available for your quarters, and the other half for social functions and other community projects. The gentlemen who remained in their original line-up position, will be transferred to another camp. I assure you of our meticulous care in all arrangements. You have two hours for collecting your belongings. That is all.'

It took some time for everybody to realise the extent of the proposition. Then they exploded: 'Why was nobody consulted?' 'What about our representative?' 'Yes, you Schmulewitz.' 'I had no idea. Honestly.' 'Where are they taking us?' 'There was talk of the Isle of Man.' 'And of Australia!' 'Australia? Are you mad?' 'Why did you push me to the front?' 'Why not? It stands to reason that the ones nearest to their compartments would be the ones to get their luggage ready.' 'So?' 'So I thought I might as well secure our time together.' 'Amazing!' 'Yes.'

And so it proved. The transfer was effected. They left the violinist and his Russian accompanist together. Rolf had many talks with Prof Meyer in the coming weeks. About the political and military situation in Germany. About the titanic effort needed, to reconstruct Germany, the morale of its survivors, the collapse of the Nazi system, the rooting out of the criminals who would be metamorphosed overnight into resistance fighters, the help in times of catastrophe of the arts and philosophy. Rolf told him of Rahel and of Ursus Castle. The professor replied with the tale of his own progressive, forest school, which he was forced to relinquish in 1933. They both profited from their daily conversations and togetherness.

The diabetes racket began in the spring of 1943. Heinz Schmulewitz, the camp spokesman, was seen by the doctor and certified as unfit to continue living under present conditions, unless he received medication, frequent check-ups and daily insulin injections. In the course of the following weeks, two inmates approached the diabetes sufferer, with an offer of 500 marks each for two samples of his urine. They produced this, on successive days, in the doctor's office, and obtained their release into freedom in the coming week. By now the authorities guarding the racecourse and its inhabitants had either grown careless, or the war looked too auspicious for the thirty men in York to do too much damage, or they simply wanted to get rid of them, and diabetes was their sovereign solution. The price of urine was changeable, according to what the bidder could afford. Sometimes a book or two, or some food and drink would assist the donor's flow. Amongst the last to obtain their release, were Rolf and Prof Meyer. They exchanged addresses and made arrangements for future meetings.

Rolf visited York. The Minster. The *Shambles,* where he bought a shirt for himself and two vases, one for Rahel and the other for his mother. Then he hired a car, and in under an hour he was on his way home, to Ursus Castle, where nobody would expect him just yet, although they knew about the urine.

Hans-Joachim and his comrade had the same plans, the same order as Joseph Messing. But, arriving at Hitler's headquarters, they had the humiliating and much publicised experience of not being admitted to speak to him.

Plan B came into operation. After about a hundred kilometres they stepped out of their car and used the public phone box. A female voice answered. Hans-Joachim asked:

'May I speak to General Beck?'

'Your password, please.'

'I have no password. My name is -'

Here Paul's slamming hand interrupted the call, just in time.

'Cretin,' he whispered. 'What next?'

'I have in my memory bank several phone numbers. Nothing written down, you understand. Let us try the *Bamberger Dom.* He dialled, and this time he was successful. Surprised that the recipient of the call was a *Bauer* from Lübeck in the north, and not from Bamberg in the east, he managed to negotiate a visit for the coming day.

They stayed in a small hotel, had a bath, and a meal of beet soup and beet cutlets, and slept for sixteen hours. Then they made their way to Lübeck. They had decided to be open about their plans, and for that reason made no pretence about their uniforms. Herr Bauer asked how they had got his telephone number. When they gave him the name of the staff officer as the source, he seemed satisfied. He asked them to come to a meeting the same evening, at 8 Wilhelm Strasse. As they left, they noticed two burly characters following them.

The meeting was attended by middle-aged man in a cassock, by the houseowner, a mellow gentleman, his wife, and two other younger women, apart from themselves, the only ones in uniform. What they remembered most, was the summing-up, given by Monsignor Bamberg:

'We agree that at the present time it would be suicidal to attempt an overthrow of the regime. We, the members of Bamberger Dom, pledge ourselves to the energetic observation of any acts of brutality, persecution or other wilful and illegal behaviour on the part of members of the Gestapo, SA or SS, with the intention of meting out the full vigour of the law, after the collapse of the present regime. Germans, like other people, are on the whole patient, peaceful and upright. We shall not allow their name permanently to be defiled by those who have wilfully strayed from the path of serving God.'

Hans-Joachim and Paul left the meeting, in a state of greater confusion than before. They decided it was time to return to the front, and to make excuses for not being able to get through to the High Command. They stayed in the same small hotel as before, and on the next day - it was the coldest day they could remember - they began to travel to the east.

Poland. Utter misery and devastation everywhere. Hordes of robbers were on the lookout for a quick kill. Natives? Germans? Five unkempt individuals stopped their car. Five revolvers enforced their wishes. Their uniforms, their boots, their weapons, their watches, their money. Then they allowed them to continue their journey, in their underwear and without means. Their petrol soon gave out. Now they were truly stranded. They decided to abandon the car and to call for help. It was getting dark. No footpaths. The earth was lacerated by the frost and by man. In their socks they trudged, arm in arm, to hold on to the illusion of warmth. The snow, which had fallen all day in thick, lengthy flakes, now dropped from the sky, layer by layer. It is thus, enveloped by the snow, themselves two men of snow, that we lose sight of Hans-Joachim and his comrade.

CHAPTER 32

1895. For Yossl's 70th birthday, the French government awarded him with an exceptional recognition. A specially created prize for the understanding between nations, consisting of a sum greater than his total earnings of a lifetime. He accepted it calmly, invested it shrewdly and continued to exert his powers in the pursuit of the twin direction of his own composition in his Coburg wire studio, and the organising of small orchestras consisting of French and German members.

Bettina had started her writing career some thirty years ago, when she composed articles for the programmes of Yossl's concerts and presentations, giving the listener an easy introduction to the works they were going to hear. From there she advanced to writing modern fairy tales, which the younger members of the family lapped up, but which Emanuel found beneath his dignity to tolerate. Now, with the century coming to an end, she wrote the story of her life with Yossl. It was a fine book which Yossl received and opened on his birthday. A worthy companion to his own diary. The testimony of two 19th century Europeans.

The final year of the century. While Paris, Moscow, Berlin, Coburg, London, Ursus Castle were preparing their festivities, Emanuel finally overcame, at the age of forty-seven, his reluctance to surrender his single status. He married Annemarie Dorn, thirty years his junior. Such was the allure of the older man, and such was the dedication of young Annemarie. Their only child was born, somewhat naughtily, a few months later. It was a son by the name of Joseph.

Yossl and Bettina chose to see the century out at Lake Lucerne, where memories still lingered of the Wagners and Judith Gautier.

They sat, close together, on a bench by the waterside, with a view of Tribschen, which had lost its occupants some thirty years ago.

'How can I ever thank you,' said Yossl, 'For your unselfish support. For your patience. For being Bettina?'

'I could say the same. It was - it is quite natural. The days of youthful enchantment in the church in Lübeck. When your singing fascinated me. And how disappointed I was that your name was Messing and not Lessing. But then you read to me. *Was it the wind, spring's postillion, that has cradled your dreams in such rueful ease?* And I knew that we would belong to one another. And your plaintive request of *Teach me. I know nothing.*'

'And you fulfilled that request. I shall be your debtor till the end.' Two snowy-haired people on a bench, shed half a century, as they buried their faces in their embrace.

Rolf had returned to Ursus Castle, unannounced, from Yorkshire. All the inmates were unrestrainable with ecstasy. Rahel showed little Florestan to him. Rolf sat him on his lap and stared long at his oval face, his hazelnut eyes, the wisps of fair hair. Florestan stared back at him, the new person, of whom his mother had told him incessantly. The war was approaching its final phase. The landing of allied forces in Normandy. The revenge, VI, unmanned bombers. Hundreds of thousands of German prisoners taken by the Russians. The ill-fated assassination attempt on Hitler's life, with the resultant butchery of Stauffenberg and his helpers, including Ludwig Beck. Over a thousand V2 rockets against London. German conscription of all men between 16 and 60. American bombers kill more than twenty thousand Berliners. Allied air attack on Dresden kills 35,000 inhabitants. Red army units capture Berlin. Hitler shoots himself.

Now for the rebuilding of Germany, of Russia, of Great Britain, of Poland, Holland, Belgium, France, Czechoslovakia, Italy, Austria, Hungary, Bulgaria, Rumania, Yugoslavia.

Prof Meyer, who had visited Ursus Castle several times since their days at York, now disclosed a promising plan to Rolf.

'Suppose we were asked to travel to Germany, hungry and torn to shreds, and undertook to sort out who was a Nazi and who was not, and starting with a set of data which would enable us to know whom to propose as reliable workers in the rebirth of Germany.'

'Interesting. But who would ask us?'

'The British Army. The Pioneer Corps which I have joined, in spite of my age, are looking for reliable people with the right sort of background, who would call men and women to de-Nazification courts. They would give us lists of likely candidates and as much information about them as possible. Are you interested?'

'Am I? This would fit in with my plans for building bridges into the future. Give me a day, until I discuss the matter with my wife.'

And that is why Rolf Messing walked into the recruiting office of the British Army, accompanied by Prof Meyer, and was accepted for his future role as court supervisor in Germany.

On the evening of that consequential day, they were sitting on the couch in their living room. Florestan, now over two years old, was asleep.

'Rolf, before we part, there is something I must tell you.'

'I am listening, my love.'

'You remember Dolf Stechlin? You don't? He is the proprietor of the publishers that deal with my cards, the one in Liverpool. I wrote to you about him, and that I changed over to an American publishing house. Well, there was more to it. For months I have been trying to tell you. I always postponed it. Now or never.'

Rolf looked at her beautiful face, which was now distorted by fear and sheer doubt whether, when her tale was finished, she would still be the same Rahel, Rolf's Rahel.

He smoothed her hair with a caressing hand.

'Whatever you have done, is it over? It is? Then there is no need for telling me, if it distresses you.'

That was the sign for acquainting him with the story of her visit to Liverpool, with the latest batch of her cards. How Mr Stechlin liked her ideas and their presentation. How he invited her to dinner. That she accepted. That he was attractive. That she had too much to drink. How he offered her a strong coffee in his flat. And then - this was the one and only time - 'I swear it will never happen again. I told Yvonne. If I had not had her, I think I would have run away. Or worse.'

Here Rahel began to weep so long and so devastatingly, that her face was a ravaged landscape. Rolf was overcome with compassion.

'You know, my love, in my years away from you, I have often dreamed or imagined you and your embraces. Then, when you were not there, I thought of others, back in Berlin. And I truly believe, that thinking is as futile, as pointless as the deed. Perhaps more so. What we have done is due to the war. Millions are dead. We are the survivors.'

It took Rolf a long time to kiss all those tears away.

Two visitors rang the bell at Ursus Castle that evening. They were a couple, emaciated to the point where they resembled nothing seen by anyone at the school. They seemed ageless. But in their eyes flickered the fire of righteousness. In the weeks to come, the world would know their likes from pictures, in the press, of people released from concentration camps. The two asked, in a small voice, for the teacher, Jonathan.

'We are his parents.'

They were ushered into the entrance hall, offered seats and told to wait a few minutes. Jonathan came. Their non-comprehension and their recognition was baleful, was awesome.

Next morning, after emerging from their guest-room, Jonathan's parents, their son, Rolf, Rahel and Yvonne Messing reminisced, filled in the missing links in their memories of ordeals and triumphs, and talked about the future, the future of Germany and their part in it. Jonathan's mother observed:

'The world knows very little, even now, about the unspeakable cruelty of the Nazi regime. Their orders issued between 1939 and 1944, show their determination to accompany the slaughter of the Jews in Germany with all the paraphernalia of humiliating constraints. I have a list, mainly from newspapers at the time, that I smuggled in and out of concentration camps.

1939. Jews are excluded from being represented in court by lawyers or barristers belonging to the party.

1939 Jewish doctors, dentists and veterinary surgeons are forbidden to treat Germans (Aryans). In future they are allowed to treat Jews only, as auxiliaries in the Healthcare.

1939 Jews are no longer allowed to sell their wares in markets.

1939 Hitler proclaims at the opening of parliament 'If the international financial Jewry should succeed to throw the nations again into a world war, the result would be the eradication of the Jewish race in Europe.

1939 Jews will lose their driving licences.

1939 Jews are ordered to take care of the removal of the ruins of Synagogues, following the Kristallnacht.

1939 Jews will have to live in Judenhäusern (Jewish houses).

1939 Jews are prohibited from buying lottery tickets. Winnings are not payable to Jews.

1939 Jewish Ration Cards are to be marked 'J' and will entitle holders to less and partly inferior food.

1939 Curfew for Jews: Summer from 21.00 hours. Winter: from 20.00 hours.

1939 Jewish 'Atonement' payment for damages in the Kristallnacht are being increased from 20% to 25%.

1941 Himmler orders the commandant of Auschwitz concentration camp to procure large numbers of showers/gas ovens.

1941 Jews over six years must wear a yellow star.
1941 Jews are not allowed to leave their neighbourhood without written permission.

1941 Jews are forbidden to wear decorations.

1941 Jews are excluded from public transport.

1941 Jews are no longer allowed to emigrate from Germany.

1941 Former German Jews, now living abroad, lose their nationality and their assets.

1941 Jews are forbidden to use public phone boxes.

1942 At his Wannsee conference, Heydrich discloses plans for the 'Final Solution' of the Jewish problem.

1942 Jews are excluded from holding pets.

1942 Jews are prohibited from buying newspapers and periodicals.

1942 Jews are not allowed to buy any cigarettes and eggs.

1942 Jews are ordered to give up their bicycles, typewriters and electrical and optical goods.

1942 Jewish ration cards exclude meat and milk.

1943 Berlin declared 'Free of Jews'.

1944 Himmler orders the cessation of mass murders by poison gas in Auschwitz concentration camp.

Silence. Like hearing of the death of a beloved person. Then Jonathan's father demanded to be allowed to speak. Jonathan had lighted a cigarette for him. His right sleeve was empty.

'My wife has left out the horrors of the concentration camps, the slaughter of millions on their forced marches or in their houses and towns in Germany and neighbouring countries. Where was the *resistance,* you may ask. The Nazis had answered that question. Within a month of the takeover of power, they had locked up trade union houses, professors, writers, army personnel, political officials of the right and the left, in concentration camps. So, when resistance to the Nazis was required, it simply did not exist, because the majority of potential leaders were under lock and key. So powerful was the machinery of the Nazi state, that people dared not risk their lives by showing the slightest sign of dissent. You may query the attitude of professional folk, like authors, artists, actors, conductors, doctors. Why, if they were not under arrest, did they not leave Germany? Because their living depended on their language. Because they could eventually do more good by staying. Because they simply loved Germany, despite the Hitler tyranny. Like us.'

At that moment Rolf knew that he would need Jonathan's parents for his attempts at rebuilding his motherland. He asked if he might be excused, if he and Rahel discussed some private matter in a corner of the room. This was granted, of course, and while Jonathan lit another cigarette for his father, Rolf said to Rahel:

'I think we shall have to contact Prof Meyer. I need at least another fortnight to prepare for Germany. We must try to get the two victims as fit as possible, so that they can accompany us. What do you think?'

'I had a similar idea. Take me too. And Florestan.'

They returned to their former positions, where meanwhile Jonathan's father had taken up the story of German resistance to Hitler.

'Attempts on his life were always thwarted by some unexpected occurrence. He seemed to be protected by some unseen power. In the Munich beer hall, Hitler made a speech and was shot at by a Swiss Theology student, Maurice Bavaud. He missed, escaped and was apprehended. When General Halder laid a bomb near Hitler, it failed to detonate. A cognac bottle which contained a time-bomb, placed by Schlabrendorff and Treskow in Hitler's private plane, did not explode, because of a malfunction of the detonator. An attempt on Hitler's life by Axel von dem Busche, which was to have taken place during a parade of new army uniforms, had to be cancelled, as the uniforms were destroyed during an air raid. Another essay on Hitler's life in a Munich beer cellar by Johann Elser came to nothing, since the intended victim left early. Claus Graf Schenk von Stauffenberg came nearest in his attempt to kill Hitler. The briefcase he left by the Führer's side at his headquarters, exploded but only wounded Hitler. Colonel Stauffenberg and his helpers, among them General Beck, were shot. A bullet put an end at last to the master criminal, and it came from his own revolver.'

Jonathan's father looked near collapse, but he was determined to continue. His son lit another cigarette for him, and Yvonne remarked:

'It is extraordinary, how you remember names and events, without any help of written words.'

'I have had plenty of time, and I do not wish to forget. Neither the hangmen nor the hanged. The good Germans, millions of them, were either killed or taken prisoners in the war, and those who dared resist, were slaughtered. So few of them are left. But I must warn you. I have seen a growing number of leaders of the regime burning their past and declaring: 'I have never been a Nazi!' That may become a problem. But allow me to return to my recollections. Of church leaders, like Cardinal Faulhaber, Bishop Graf von Gahlen, Cardinal Bertram, Pastor Martin Niemöller, Pastor Dietrich Bonhoeffer, all of whom risked their lives by protesting, from the chancel or in discussion with the regime, against the treatment of Jews and other members of different religions. Organisations, like the *Red Chapel,* who worked against the regime from the inside, that is from the air ministry. Like the *Kreisauer Kreis,* led by Helmut Graf von Moltke and former Burgomaster Carl Goerdeler. The demand that Laws which have been *trampled underfoot shall be restored.* The Gestapo put an end to their endeavour. But the one group which is closest to my heart, is the *Weisse Rose (white rose).* They were the brother and sister Hans and Sophie Scholl, students from my home town, Munich. Helped by their friends, they distributed considerable numbers of leaflets and pamphlets. They pleaded for a *renewal of the seriously wounded German spirit, and for the annihilation of National Socialism.* They were betrayed by their caretaker and executed.'

An undying fire lit his eyes from within.

The next fortnight was given over to much rethinking of arrangements for the journey into chaos. Prof Meyer agreed to the postponement, and Jonathan's parents were offered daily increasing, choice meals, prepared and served by Sigi. Florestan, who meanwhile had celebrated his third birthday, sensed the new adventure ahead of him, while Rahel was exuberant at the thought of accompanying her husband into his new mission.

The day arrived. Accompanied by sincere good wishes from Yvonne and her school, seven people went by air to Berlin. Rolf, Rahel, Florestan, Jonathan's parents, Prof Meyer and his wife. Rolf and the professor went in their official capacity, in the British uniforms of army captains. On their arrival in Berlin they were told that, due to the destruction of the road system, their transport could not be arranged with any guarantee of security. Therefore the plane would take off again, to the relative safety of Freiburg in the Black Forest. The town was in a mess. Piles of rubble stood next to houses untouched. Roads obliterated, side by side with wide avenues, and the Minster still remaining, with its angel of peace looking down at the madness of man. The first hearing was arranged for next morning at eight o'clock.

CHAPTER 33

'Are you sure you have eliminated all articles of clothing, such as brown and black shirts, badges, stripes, medals et cetera? Safely, Lore?' 'They have all disappeared, never to return, my love. So have the paintings, pictures, snaps. Nothing is left to prevent your emerging from tomorrow's hearing as a staunch anti-Nazi, my love.'

Rolf arrived half an hour ahead, accompanied by Jonathan's parents. He asked them to take their place at the end of the long table. Rolf sat down in the middle section. Prof Meyer and wife arrived a little later, and were invited to sit next to Captain Messing.

Eight o'clock. The door opened, and a private of the British army announced: 'Herr Walter Tunichtgut.'

'Come in,' Rolf called, and pointed to the chair opposite his own. 'We have here your application for a post in the new administration of your home town, Freiburg. Will you tell us about your affiliation to any political parties, both before and during the war.'

'Well before the war, I did not belong to any political organisation, but my sympathies were strongly on the side of the lawful government, that is of democracy. Among my best friends were Jews. Then came the war, and I was appalled at what the Nazis did. I helped several Jewish friends to escape, and I certainly was never a Nazi.'

'Herr Tunichtgut,' interrupted Captain Messing, 'what about SA man Tunichtgut before the war, and SS man Tunichtgut during the war? Are the two identical? Are they some other person than yourself? Or could they be, in fact, yourself?'

'O, that? You must understand, we anti-Nazis were forced to hide our true intentions behind a safe identity, such as working against Nazis whilst appearing -'

Here Captain Messing cut in with a curt reply:

'Come with the truth, if you wish. If you refuse to face it, we refuse to entertain your application.'

'Hold it!' The skeletal figure of Jonathan's father had risen from his position in the darkened corner. He now stood face to face with the man who had maltreated him, only months ago, when he was bombed out of his native Munich and had fled to Freiburg.

'You will not remember, but I do. It was towards the end of the war, when you appeared in our room, which we shared with seven others, and you kicked my wife in the stomach, and flogged me with your horsewhip, and called us *Jewish swine*. Then you took our only remaining bed cover away. You left, but not before snatching our purse and ration card. But I forgive you. The war has turned us all into demons. Now the time for healing the wounds has come. Here -'

And Jonathan's father stretched out his left arm, to shake his tormentor by the hand.

'A moment please!' The dark, slow voice was Captain Meyer's, in civilian life known as Prof Meyer. 'I am taking a party of sightseers, all people similarly placed to yourself, on a tour of inspection tomorrow. You and your wife will be welcome to join us. You will find it illuminating. We start at seven and expect to be back shortly after dark. No, this is not an order to attend voluntarily. We can always fetch you, if you prefer. So you will come? Splendid.'

There were twelve men and women waiting for their *illuminating* outing. A large van, driven by Captain Meyer, picked them up. The fact that the twelve did not look at each other or engage in conversation, indicated that they knew one another, but did not want to admit this. Of yesterday's team, Jonathan's parents were absent. So was Captain Meyer's wife. Captain Messing took the co-driver's seat.

They drove on, most of the morning, until they reached the Munich district. Around the city and to the north, until they were welcomed by the sign *Arbeit Macht Frei,* which adorned the entrance to Dachau concentration camp, by some railroad sidings. The members of Prof Meyer's party were invited to stretch their legs.

They wandered along the central avenue which was crowded with other parties of sightseers. They shuffled along the central avenue. Silently.

They saw the gas chambers. You would not have suspected them as such, had you been a prisoner. They were disguised as mass cleansing stations, where a shower would rid you of the typhoid carrying lice. There were signs reading *Shower Room* in every chamber. Only once you were inside, and the gates behind you were locked, did you realize that you were destined to die. The parties walked slowly through the twenty feet square buildings, with eighteen nozzles across the ceiling, pretending to be showers. Each chamber had a large chimney, which released the evidence of its life-into-death metamorphosis, day and night. Printed forms had to be filled in by the overseers, stating *Time of gassing. Finish Time,* and cautions for the handlers, such as *Careful, Danger to life,* and *Do not open.* The members of the quiet parties saw cans of discarded tins, labelled Zyclon-B poison, manufactured by *AEG Farben Industrie.* Quite a few, men or women, could not bear to carry any more evidence of the organised slaughter, and shielded their eyes. They plodded on, a voiceless mass of eye witnesses, slowly being turned from fellow travellers into grieving humans. Grieving at what? At their own inadequacies? At their failure, so far, to identify someone or some groups, to blame for their own present dilemma? Such was the purpose of the sightseeing party, which Prof Meyer had called *illuminating.*

It was long after midnight, when they arrived back at Freiburg. Lore Tunichtgut was relieved to see her husband. She had been pacing their lounge for the last two hours. Now he had arrived, all should be well? His welcome greeting was strangely muted.

'Have a drink, darling.'

Sip by sip, his loquaciousness returned, and with it his attempts to find an explanation for the things he had witnessed today. He found an attentive listener in his wife, who interrupted his meditation only when he intermittently slowed down to deliberate.

'Thirty thousand prisoners. In barracks. And four or five shower rooms. Or so they thought. They? Well, the inmates. What were they, if not shower rooms? Gas - ovens. Imagine, gas ovens, in

which to kill people quickly and efficiently. Can you believe it? No?
I cannot, either. The Russians, yes. We Germans? Never. Never!
Never!'

'Never. Never.' A sleepless night for Walter Tunichtgut.
One hour later: 'Never?' Another half hour. 'Yes. I have seen them
with my own eyes. They have done it. They. They. Not I.' Six
o'clock in the morning. 'O, what's the use? Has the time arrived for
complete honesty? At least between Walter and Walter? Even Lore
need never know. There was the incident in the clearing near the
Polish town of Lodz, where two hundred Jews had to be liquidated.
An order from our commanding officer. We drew our pistols and
shot them in the back of their necks. It was an order, was it not? But
an order to murder the innocent? Men, women, children. Naked.
They were only the first. More orders. More killings. And then,
when the end was near, we let the Latvian and Rumanian volunteers
do our work. So that we could have a clear conscience. And the gas
ovens? Prolific horror. How can I, how can any man live with it?'

Jonathan's parents followed a remarkable invitation to visit
the house of the Lehmanns, outside Freiburg. Klaus and Margot
Lehmann had been harbouring Jonathan's parents for the last two
years of the war, in spite of the danger of discovery, arrest and
hanging, for no other reason than their indignation at the abominable
treatment of the one-armed man and his wife, as they crawled, in the
shelter of the night, past their villa. They had been exchanging
letters ever since the ending of hostilities. Now they just stared at
one another. The Lehmanns would not credit that people could age
that much - they guessed twenty years, but kept it to themselves -,
while Jonathan's parents found their benefactors much younger
looking, say twenty years, and they volunteered their verdict:

'Our ghastly nightmare is over,' declared Margot Lehmann,
after their coffee and cake. 'Now we will build a new Germany.'

'Yes, but there are so few of us, and so many of them,' said
Jonathan's mother. They are all pleading their innocence. *We have
never been Nazis.*'

'Leave them to us,' stressed Klaus Lehmann. 'We know
who was who. We can sort them out.'

Four, incongruous people were reposing in the walled garden, sweltering in the August sun and getting caught in ever increasing tales of their past. *Do you remember?* was the repeated slogan of their late afternoon.

Klaus Lehmann reminisced, 'Do you remember the night when they came to search the house? They could not find anything, so they asked for the key to the attic. We thought, that's it. They climbed up to where we had hidden you and found the place empty. They either did not see you in the garden, or they were too tired to look. So they left, to hunt at our neighbours' for live or material booty. Your foot,' here he poked Jonathan's mother, 'took six months to heal from the accident.'

Margot remarked in her broad Swabian dialect, 'I shall never forget the kindliness of the unknown sender of food parcels during the last years of the war. We shared our ration cards with you, of course. The gifts from England arrived here like a gift from the gods.'

Jonathan's parents smiled knowingly.

On the same evening, Rolf in mufti, went to his local hostelry, where twelve men, also in civilian clothes which were too large for them, had assembled around their regular table. Rolf sat within earshot and listened to a bizarre conversation.

'Comrades. Adolf Hitler is dead. Joseph Goebbels is dead. Many of our former brothers are in hiding or masquerading as anti-Nazis. I think this is despicable. Once a Nazi, always a Nazi. That is my slogan. What do you say?'

Eleven beer glasses were raised in agreement, emptied and descended on their mats with a slamming that sounded like gunfire.

A tall, slim man with a row of decorations on his sports jacket, spoke next.

'Most of us have met the Russian, eye to eye. Many know only too well, what a beast he is. Rape, pillage, murder. And his ignorance. He has never seen a water closet. He takes it for a washing machine.'

246

'The worst is, they have committed all the crimes we are accused of. The Russians killed hundreds of thousands of Jews. Not we. This is something we have to tell our people, so that the honour of the German sword, particularly of the Waffen SS is redeemed.'

'Selma, another round of beer, please.'

Here Rolf left. On his way home he thought of the bridges he would have to help to build. An impossible mission? Perhaps. But he would not ignore his obligations.

The second hearing took place next morning. Rolf was in sole charge this time, and among the men waiting to hear their verdict was last night's speaker, the one who held forth about the Russians. Jonathan's father was there too, a figure of dread, reminding everybody of the past they were eager to forget.

First was a small, rotund shopkeeper, who intended to get a position as purveyor of cigarettes, and sweets for the occupying French.

'I, Karl Blasewitz, tobacconist in the neighbourhood for over twenty years, declare that I was never a Nazi. I have always helped my Jewish fellow citizens to the best of my skills.'

Here Rolf interrupted him, for he had done his homework on Herr Blasewitz.

'I think it would be in your interest, if we would terminate the case now. You have evidently forgotten the fact that you were a prominent member of the Gestapo from 1942 to the collapse.'

'I was coming to that,' protested the tobacconist. 'I found that I could prevent . . .'

'Shall we say next Friday at ten o'clock? And remember, truthfulness is a better companion than dissembling.'

From the background where he was sitting, unseen, the macabre figure of Jonathan's father rose, confronted the stunned tobacconist, and held out his bony hand. 'Next Friday at ten.'

Next in line was the gentleman whom Rolf had heard on the preceding night, proclaiming about the dread of the Russians. It turned out that he was unaware of an eavesdropper last night.

Herr Gottfried Lobesam took his stand.

'I wish to state that I was a member of the Waffen SS from 1939 till 1945. I served on the Westfront and in the East. I took part in the siege of Leningrad, and fought the long retreat to Germany, defending our values against the hordes of butchers. If it were not for the devotion of the Waffen Ss, this land, our fatherland would now be controlled by the beasts.'

'A remarkably frank statement,' said Rolf Messing, the presiding interrogator. 'Do you wish to tell the court more?'

'Yes, I do. We Germans have been brainwashed with false propaganda about the cruelties against the Jews. This is not so. We have always maintained that the Jews were an alien race, and had to be kept apart from the rest of us. But we were never cruel to them. We never killed them. In fact, the ones who slaughtered them willy-nilly were the Russians.'

At this point Rolf Messing took over. 'Herr Lobesam, we welcome your frankness. You have seen what happened at the front and behind it. You cannot, in your heart of hearts, harbour any doubts about the guilt of large numbers of Germans who committed crimes against their fellow citizens. Do you wish to meet one who survived? Survived not by a miracle, but by the selfless intervention of another German.'

At the sudden emergence of the emaciated figure of Jonathan's father, Herr Lobesam stood still for a long time. He felt he was a prize boxer, who had landed blow after blow on his opponent, but the apparent victim had launched an unforeseen attack on his chin, followed by a vicious swipe at his midriff that knocked him into standing oblivion. A scene that would haunt his dreams for years to come.

In the following two months the court heard and re-heard these cases and many similar cases. Rolf Messing alternated with Prof Meyer as chief judge, while the French occupation power was represented by a solicitor, who reported regularly on the proceedings to his government.

At the final session, over which Captain Messing presided, some sixty men and women had assembled in the body of the hall. This time Jonathan's parents sat next to Rolf, under the bright lamp which made their features even more ghoulish than before. As the clock struck ten, Captain Messing rose:

'Ladies and gentlemen. During the eight preceding weeks the court has heard your statements, denials, appeals, contradictions, defiance, revocations and disclaimers. We have carefully sifted through all these, helped by a number of written pieces of evidence, supported by oaths of truthfulness, both from you and from members of the public. I wish to assure you that none of us bears any malice. We are trying to be fair and just, always remembering our purpose which is the rebuilding of Germany.

Now we will have to face a task which is almost impossible - how to cope with our past. In whatever capacity you will be working, whether as repairers of our infrastructure, or as administrators of our new society, you will find that memories of Germany's past, of your past, will haunt you. What steps, then, should be taken to forget our past? Heaven forbid! Nothing will ever eradicate our guilt in Germany's collapse. All of us are responsible. Either by assisting or by standing aside. But there is a way out of this maze. Work as nobody has ever worked before, to claw back your self-respect. Enthusiastically forward-looking. Regard your task as amends. Day by day, and night by night, you will be plagued less by the past, as the promise of a new era will gradually arise. The new Germany.'

Rolf Messing sat down. His eyes were focused beyond the rear wall. Jonathan's parents who had laboriously risen stood, macabre phantoms, their gaze slowly enveloping the whole court.

CHAPTER 34

1899. Was it his father's frequent absences from home, that had made Emanuel turn from his parents? Or was it his nature to waste time?

At the age of forty-seven, he was a spendthrift, a philanderer. The older his parents, the less their restraining influence. So it came as a shock, when Emanuel announced his wedding plans to Yossl and Bettina, because the woman of his choice was thirty years younger and pregnant. Josephine Dorn was exceedingly pretty, and Yossl knew what he was doing when he arranged only part of his considerable capital to go to the bridegroom. Josephine and her first child were the chief beneficiaries in Yossl's last will. Thus, provided for life before he was born, Joseph Messing took a glimpse at the weird proceedings of babyhood, not with a wail, but with elation. Emanuel, however being assured of Josephine's devotion, lost his good looks, allowed himself to become round and sluggish, and unsurprisingly contracted a heart disease which killed him in the coming year. Yossl, in contrast, prolonged his looks and his energies, well into his seventies, imitating the ever-youthful Bettina. He worked tirelessly with orchestral ensembles, containing French and Germans, British and Russians, Austrians and Italians, men and women. With every chord played by the representatives of nations, who in *real life* were at each other's throats, bridges were built into a future that could be a little saner than their own time.

An extraordinary incident occurred in one of Yossl's frequent lectures on Wagner's opera, *Parsifal.* Incongruously, an orthodox Jew with full regalia, including black dress, a prayer shawl, and flowing locks, had seated himself among his listeners. When Yossl played them the slow prelude on the piano, the outsider closed his eyes. Then his features changed from his original gravity to surprise, to elation. He began, slowly at first, then exactly with the music, to rock to and fro, as if he were praying. His transformation did not end when the prelude ended. It remained etched on his face, witness of the new discovery that had come over him. Very much an insider now, he had created an instant bridge from one culture to another.

Another marvel was encountered by Bettina, shortly after her son's death. Emanuel's wish was to be cremated and his ashes to be strewn outside the casino at Baden-Baden, which was his favourite place of amusement towards the end. His mother took it upon herself to fulfil his final request. She travelled to the spa and waited on a park bench until it was dark. She found that the masses of gamblers frequenting the casino, were not conducive to a decent dispersal of the ashes. So she booked herself into an hotel and waited there until two o'clock. Then she proceeded with her plan. This time the place was dark and deserted. Bettina went to the front gardens, looked round, and deliberately unwrapped the urn. When she had finished her sombre business, she suddenly realized that she had been watched by an unknown. A negro in a purple cassock approached her. Bettina stood, bolted to the ground.

'You do not know me,' he said, with his deep, mellifluous voice. 'But I have been watching you and what you have been doing. I am a Baptist minister. Would you like to say a prayer with me?'

And so it came about that two strangers met, one in the act of scattering ashes after midnight in the gardens of a casino, and the other praying and hoping to bring comfort by praying. Both being tiny specks in a vast universe, but having established a bridge into a world which might be less foolish, more enlightened.

Bettina returned to her overnight place to sleep. Next morning she wrote, on the pink notepaper provided by her hotel, her sixth article for a weekly journal, on Yossl's wire studio.

251

CHAPTER 35

It was shortly before the end of the war, in 1945, that a middle-aged man knocked at the kiosk inside Herr Bauer's petrol station in Lübeck. His enquiry after the proprietor was answered by a lean woman whose clothes were several sizes too large:

'My husband is out with the emergency team, guarding the town. What can I do for you?'

'Do you recognize my voice?' asked the man. 'I have been the news speaker at the Radio. I have also met Herr Bauer. Joseph Messing is my name. When will your husband be back?'

'I cannot tell. But come inside.'

She remembered his voice indeed. And she recalled her husband telling her about him and his son.

'I need your help,' pleaded Joseph. 'The war will be over in a few days, and I shall go to England when I have found my family. But at present I am on the *Wanted* list. Will you - can you provide me with a hiding place? At a price of your naming.'

'Agreed.'

This was the first step in the rehabilitation of Joseph Messing. Hostilities were officially ended a week later. The second step proved far more complicated than the first.

There were no telephones, no public transport, no petrol. The only way to reach Berlin was on foot. A steady stream of former soldiers used the routes out of Berlin, few wanted to see the ruined capital. Joseph Messing managed the varied vicissitudes of the road, including authentic and bogus checkpoints, and reached the outskirts of Berlin after three weeks. He got a lift from a British reporter into what had been the heart of the city. His street, his house had disappeared. In their stead, a gigantic heap of bricks and charred former household goods, had arisen, constantly added to by women workers who operated a long line of buckets which stretched from the undulating ground to the top of what they affectionately called their *Mount Klamott* (Mount Rubbish). What had happened to Leni and Josefine? He accosted woman after woman, day after day. Nobody had heard of them. Some nodded sympathetically. Others did not hear, or pretended to be deaf.

After a week's searching for his family, he discovered an illicit yet vital means of information, the private sector. Those days, months and possibly years of apparent hopelessness, had promoted an extraordinarily efficient system of black marketeering, by which the customer could obtain anything, from shoelaces to bottles of vodka against payment in cigarettes, which were the standard currency. In addition several vendors undertook personal services, such as Joseph required. There was no danger of a slackening market.

'Leni and Josefine Messing,' a female racketeer scribbled. 'Potsdamer Strasse. OK. See me in three days. OK. Thanks for the commission.' She stowed the packet of cigarettes in her capacious shopping net.

On the third day, she did not show up. Nor on the fourth. But she appeared furtively, looking right and left and behind, on the fifth day.

'Meet me at the former Lützow Strasse, corner Potsdamer Strasse, at 1.30 tomorrow,' She had vanished, before he could ask any questions.

He picked his way laboriously between heaps of rubble, next day from 1 o'clock onwards, twenty packets of cigarettes in his pockets which he had acquired, at vastly increased prices, in several shops. Punctually, his informant appeared. She was accompanied by a male companion of dubious countenance who uttered:

'Your wife - hospital - we go. Two hundred marks.'

The hospital was nearby, only seventeen heaps of rubble away. His companion had disappeared, leaving him to climb over the masses of humans in varying degrees of frailness or decay. The clinic was a tented emergency structure, with inmates lying side by side on the ground. Joseph Messing made his way through the remains of a once all-powerful human race. Then he involuntarily retreated. He had recognized Leni, in the shape of a mockery of herself. Emaciated, aged by thirty years, with one eye open, the other closed behind a bandage. He waited, unseen, considering his next step. Then he stopped a passing auxiliary and said:

'It is alright for me to take Frau Messing away with me? She is my wife.' He produced some legitimisation.

The orderly shrugged his shoulders, indicating that the removal of one patient would make room for another. So Joseph picked up his comatose, drugged wife, and carried her quickly away. At the taxi rank, now served by rickshaws, he hired one that promised to take him and his load to a boarding house on the outskirts, allowing for plenty of rests and plenty of remuneration.

After a perilous journey past various diversions and checkpoints, they arrived at the boarding house that took them in, after Joseph paid them for a week's stay. He put Leni to bed and was astonished to see her open her solitary eye. She stared at him, breathed in consternation:

'Jo?'

'Yes, dearest. Yes, yes. Alright. Now get some rest. Or do you want to take some food and drink first?'

They were interrupted by a knock on their door.

'Aren't you the gentleman who always used to read the news on the radio? You are? And that's your wife? Allow me.'

She moved close to the bed.

'O dear! I'll send for the doctor.'

She left quickly. Meanwhile Leni, in between waking and drowsing, tried to claw her way back to reality. She did not succeed.

Joseph did not leave her bedside. Frau Neumann, the proprietress, came frequently up to his room, bringing fresh water, asking what else she could do, cooling Leni's forehead. After five hours, at midnight, the doctor staggered in. He did not look much better than his patient, and was clearly in need of rest and food. But he did not spare himself. He gently coaxed Leni back to her identity, to Joseph's, to her ailments, to what needed to be done. He carefully removed the bandage, revealed the eye socket, now empty, and cleaned the wound. He cautiously removed her from her bed and, with the assistance of Frau Neumann's robust arms, carried her into the bathroom. Sounds of running water, of *Careful now,* and *Keep her head over water* gave Joseph some hope. After half an hour, they returned with their precious charge who tore herself free from her guardians, and impelled herself into her husband's arms, crying over and over just one word:

'Jo.'

From this moment on, until the end of the next eight days, Leni's recovery was extraordinary.

'I married a tigress,' smiled Joseph.

And bit by bit, event by event, he coaxed from her lips the terrible tale of Josefine's death, underneath her mother's shielding presence, when the house collapsed. Of her own attempted suicide. Of the fight against the soldiers who tried to rape her. And how she lost her sight. It was the shared realization of the death of their child, that now proved an unshatterable bond between the parents.

After a month's careful nursing and feeding, Leni began to look like her former self, only very much older. So, it was with some trepidation that Joseph Messing phoned his former wife:

'Hello, Yvonne. This is -'

'Joseph. Thank heaven, Joseph.'

'Yes. It's a lengthy tale. Can we come and stay for a few days?'

'Of course. How is Leni? And the child?'

'Leni is recovering. She has lost the sight of one eye.'

'And Josefine?' Silence. 'How is Josefine?' Silence. 'Is she?' 'Yes.'

CHAPTER 36

After the downfall of Germany, Rolf's twin concerns were the creation of orchestras, consisting of earlier enemies, and performances of his most powerful work, *The Blessed Bridge*. This necessitated lengthy absences from his home. As both enterprises flourished, the establishment of a second home, in Berlin, followed. After two years of unrelenting labour, a holiday home near Ursus Castle was purchased, and his separations from Rahel and Florestan began to be of shorter duration. He now was in Liverpool, and this time wife and child accompanied him, and Jaap was the leader of his orchestra. The first desk of the violins was shared by the Dutchman Jaap and a German. The first desk of the cellos consisted of a Japanese and an Englishman. The two flutes were a Russian and an American. The three trumpeters were a Catholic and a Protestant Irishman and an English lady. The rest of the orchestra was assembled under similar considerations. In their frequent breaks from rehearsals, their talk was about the town, its attractions, its food, its drinks, their studies back home, their hopes for the future, with hardly a mention of their different nationalities and the way the recent war might have changed their attitudes to life.

A week later the first public performance of *The Blessed Bridge* by a symphony orchestra was given at Carlisle, the town at the entrance to the Lake District. The older pupils of Ursus Castle sat on the edge of their seats, wondering how the older colleagues would cope. Golda and Yvonne were there, as were several members of staff. The first half of the concert consisted of an Overture by Henry Purcell, and a Violin Concerto by Mozart, played with youthful exuberance by Jaap. Interval. Then came the great uncertainty. Would the conductor, Rolf Messing, the one who had brought together this multi-national orchestra, succeed in capturing the audience? In spellbinding them open-mouthed and open-hearted?

The Blessed Bridge formed the second half of the programme. This new work by the conductor had a good deal of advance publicity, with tales of his great-grandfather's and his own wire studio, and his efforts on behalf of progress through global conciliation, mirrored by music that had obviously stirred the players at their rehearsals.

The words the chorus had to sing towards the end of the piece were printed in the programme:

Open the box,
the box with the seeds,
the seeds for the future,
a future that joins the jackboot and the slipper,
the finger on the trigger
and the outstretched arms of amnesty.
Open the box.

The conductor pointed at the first oboist who played an A, the sound audiences all over the world connect with tuning. And so it was here, only the supposed tuning was part of the score. But when the instrumentalists had satisfied themselves that they were in tune, an unholy out of tune cacophony of sound emerged, which was, however, halted almost immediately, to give way to a violin solo. Accompanied by orchestral chords, the violin soared to the heights, plummeted to the nether regions, granting the hearers just sufficient time to regret its sudden silence. A horn solo, with similar orchestral accompaniment, followed. Entirely devoid of rhythmical features, it explored the instrument's intimate qualities, with a tune similar to the previous one, equally unfathomed, equally teasing the listeners with its unexpected cessation, which this time was marked by a shrill dissonance on three trombones. Then came a third tune. No, it was not a tune at all. A rhythm with an ever-changing palette of timpani sonorities, ceasing at its most intense, most unforeseen. And then - the most sublime melody arose from the older sister of the oboe, the cor anglais. This time it was an unaccompanied solo, played by an absolute master of this instrument, expressing with a plangency far beyond human skill a gospel which people who had been caught in the world-wide insanities could grasp, could link, could apply. Then, O what relief! that first violin melody again, uninterrupted this time, but instead, the horn solo was heard again,

257

this time combining with the violin solo, all dissonances smoothed out. And where before the trumpets terminated the proceedings, now the unearthly melody played by the cor anglais, combined with the violin and the horn in a roundelay for three voices that continued and was allowed to continue. When the trinity came to rest, an extraordinary situation occurred. Unseen by the audience, a girl pupil of Ursus Castle had been standing by a window, watching and listening for her cue. As the conductor's baton pointed in her direction, she opened the window and, with the orchestra providing a soft cushion of sound, the song of a nightingale which habitually could be heard in the neighbourhood, flooded the listeners' senses. Now the orchestra fell silent, and only the nightingale was allowed to provide a heaven-sent melody. After a minute a cello began to improvise. It tried to imitate, to counter, to underline, to echo the bird. It appeared that the two, bird and cellist, let mutual inspiration take over and, for the next three or four minutes, the listeners were incredulous, involved, enthralled. Then Rolf's baton gave another cue towards the window which was closed very slowly, and the nightingale and the cello were allowed to die together.

Now the choir arose. Fifty voices, hand-picked by Rolf, twenty adults and thirty from local schools, including Ursus Castle. They made a joyful noise indeed, with the first and the ending lines. *Open the box,* rising and rising. But before it appeared for the last time, the violin solo again produced its bewitching melody, the one with which the work opened. This time it was allowed to play itself out, uninterrupted, so that at its termination the audience had truly absorbed it, and thought of it less as an impressive yet eccentric row of notes, touching the heights and falling to the depths, but as a memorable melodic miracle. The final *Open the box* was sung, in four parts, by choir and orchestra, sacrificing unanimity to enthusiasm. With the trumpets affirming the general conviction that here was the masterpiece for our time, a bridge did not need building. It had arisen.

The conductor's slowly descending baton secured thirty seconds of silence. Then applause in wave after wave.

Critics from newspapers world-wide had descended upon Carlisle, to report on the event. Amongst the whole-hearted acceptances of Rolf Messing as a major composer, there were the usual grumbles. 'A new concept through improvisation' *(Munich)* - 'Carlisle's song of the nightingale' *(London)* - 'Misguided concept' *(Berlin)* - 'Messing triumphs' *(Milan)* 'It will be left to the future to analyse this major work, whose real significance is extra-musical.' *(Vienna)*.

The triumphant representation of his cantata was achieved. Some listeners, like the Viennese, even discerned that there is relevance beyond the music. That the meaning is in the title.

A week later a celebration took place at Ursus Castle, which united many of Rolf's friends. It was hosted by Yvonne. For the first time it saw former divergent people together at one table. Joseph Messing had arrived, with Leni, the two representing the frames of reference for the blessed bridge. Rolf and Rahel looked fondly at them, and both thought the same thought. May there be more. Many, many more.

ENVOI

It was 1950 when Rolf and Rahel went to bed, aged thirty, with fair hair and black. They awoke half a century later, aged eighty, their hair frosted with silver. The metamorphosis to reality was achieved by a considerable effort, with much brushing away of tattered remains of their old-fashioned clothes and of bits of egg shell. When they looked at one another, they did so with new eyes, discovering each other in new clothes, seated on a bench by a mountainside, overlooking a meadow traversed by a stream with ducks on it, and willows on either side.

'Do you feel what I feel?' asked Rolf.

'That we have stepped out of - -'

'A narrative?'

'About ourselves?'

Rolf said 'Not before time.'

'Are you sad?'

'Yes and no.'

'Is that an answer?'

'Such as you have taught me, my love.'

'When you begged me to teach you, sixty years ago because you knew nothing.'

'That was Yossl, my love.'

'I know. But it is not easy to tell you apart all the time.'

'Are you tired?'

'Yes and no.'

'Why yes?'

'After climbing up Mount Skiddaw I have a right to be exhausted.'

'Why no?'

'Because we are on Mount Skiddaw, and I am eighty.'

'Do you remember how you fell, and we had to phone Yvonne for help?'

'Dear Yvonne. So long departed. Sweet, sagacious Yvonne. She is in our talks almost daily. In contrast to her parents. We never mention them.'

Rolf did not reply at first. Rahel waited. When he spoke, she listened with her mouth wide open.

'It is a painful story, which I seem to have suppressed in my memory. The writer of our novel did not get all the facts. They committed suicide, true, for they had incurable illnesses. But the real reason was, they were the leading Nazis in England, and their cover was about to be blown.'

'Heavens! Why have you never told me?'

'I - don't know. I suppose, because I suppressed it. Because it is easier to let sleeping dogs - Because I did not want to distress you.'

He never could appreciate that he, for some good reason, kept distressing news from Rahel, but that the fact of keeping her in the dark was more distressing to her than the knowledge of those facts would have been.

'Which of the people who have crossed our paths through life, or were our companions, are still alive?' he mused.

Rahel took her glasses off to wipe them. Then she spoke:

'Jaap is retired, but he still plays the violin. Madeleine, who helped you with your Wagner programmes in Coburg, is a drama teacher in Paris. Of old pupils there is Sigi, and Jonathan who never made it to the Olympics, and Hanna with whom I exchange letters once or twice a year. The rest? All gone. First my Mutti. Then Prof Meyer, the Lehmanns, Sir Brian.'

Rolf continued the epitaph:

'Of the SS bandits, now dead, Eifer obtained a post in the Ministry for Foreign Affairs. Dr Greifer, Schleifer and Kneifer were committed to prison, but their sentences were reduced from ten to two years. Claus Moritz was hanged. Kietz, Herr and Frau Bauer and Archdeacon Bamberg, who was made a Cardinal, were celebrated after the war as the Lübeck Resistance Group. Their leader was the little lady who lived in Yossl's old house and had it rebuilt. Yes, my love. All of them - gone.'

Rahel gazed at him. 'Dear, dear Yossl. That is where it all began. I would like to depart the same way as Bettina. The day after him. The day after you. That would be wonderful.'

Rolf drew her close. He kissed her. A long silence, filled with thoughts of remembrances, of achievements, of losses, before Rolf spoke:

'Do you suppose we shall see Skiddaw again?'

'It all depends. If we want to achieve anything, we shall. As this view - from the bench - with you - is the most entrancing one in the wide world, I shall come here again and again, with you.'

A tinkling of bicycle bells soaked through the stillness. Sebastian and Sarah had arrived, to collect their grandparents.

'Hello, you two,' cried the raven-haired, the faithful incarnation of Rahel at fifteen, Rolf's idol in this time and that.

'Shall we tell them?' asked Sebastian.

'Don't even consider it,' replied Sarah.

Together they cycled down and down, first Sebastian, his hand over his grandmother's shoulder, followed by Sarah and Rolf in a similar defence echelon against mishaps on the road.

After two hours they arrived in their villa. What was the secret that awaited them?

'Enter!' cried the grandchildren.

With his back towards them, smoking his pipe, sat Florestan, whom they had not seen for three years, as his job as director of operas on the international circuit simply could not spare its greatest attraction who had as many antagonists as acolytes.

Leonie, his flame-haired companion for twenty years, sprang up to embrace grandparents and children.

'Now we are complete,' declared Sebastian.

When the young had cleared the dinner remains away, they went out on to the balcony, where deckchairs and a couch were prepared, together with small tables with drinks and cheese sticks. Sebastian and Sarah, Florestan and Leonie, Rolf and Rahel. Three epochs.

'I see the *Ring* did not altogether please the New Yorkers,' said Rolf.

Florestan looked over the expanse of high lands and hilltops. Then he spoke, slowly, weighing every word:

'I try to build bridges from Wagner's intentions to our time. Reporters come and ask me, what is my concept? I answer, I have no concept, except Wagner's concept. Then they write in their newspapers, *The clueless Messing.* We live in a time where thinking for yourself has become old-fashioned. It is so much easier to short-cut the process, by accepting or rejecting the result. The main ingredient of Wagner's works, of his existence -'

'Is the myth,' continued Rolf.

'O, the myth. Let my contemporaries demythologize the *Ring.* I shall not hesitate to cherish their approbation of this mainspring of our history, when he follows *Ragna Rok,* the Norse inspiration for the ending of the *Ring:*

After the conflagration of the world, a new, more blessed earth shall arise.

That is what I showed at the end of the drama in New York. The red glow of the fire subsided. The swirling waters receded. The ravaged earth began to bear shoots. And the music underpins this with the Assurance-Motif.'

Rolf regarded his only son with a look of gentleness, that made words superfluous. Yet he spoke:

'Myths offer, I believe, genuine axioms concerning our past, present and future. They hold up a mirror. The question is, *Dare we consult it?'*

'Not if you produce a Wagner opera today. Persiflage is the answer to the demands of the myth, for that is so much easier and brings in far greater sums of money, than the retracing of Wagner's steps. But once we dare, we shall be rewarded by a new understanding. You see,' and Florestan now turned to the other listeners, 'the *Ring* is about men and women living in the territory of the myth. They feel and act not as we do, but as we in ideal circumstances should feel and act. Their devotion is prodigal, their virtues indomitable.'

Sarah and Sebastian looked at one another, but did not speak. In their thoughts was the conviction that the young generation had its own ideas, and its own solutions of old problems. In short, both are right.

It was pelting next morning. A mist was drawn over the green lushness of the Lakes, like a curtain at the end of a drama. Or before the beginning.

Leonie was a great preserver. She had assiduously collected masses of reports of her husband's and Rolf's achievements, and had added memorabilia such as programmes, decorations, publications of their own, all supplemented by voluminous photo albums. Now they had assembled in their lounge, with the large table covered by documents of Leonie's thesaurus.

The grandchildren sat between Rolf and Rahel, with their arms around their shoulders, while Leonie and Florestan rummaged through their memorabilia of half a century.

'This was taken after the war,' said Leonie. 'In some courtroom. There is Rolf.'

'Dishy, dishy!' cried Sarah, while Sebastian whistled, low and lustrous.

'Next to him is a Herr Lobesam,' Leoni read, 'then comes Prof Meyer, next to him Herr Tunichtgut and Jonathan's father.'

'Who was who?' asked Sebastian.

'I helped Prof Meyer with interrogating the Nazis Tunichtgut and Lobesam, and Jonathan's father here was personifying the jury, I believe. It is a long time ago. But I remember Lobesam as the only Nazi in the post-war era. All the others stated they never were followers of Hitler, or they were forced, or they pretended, or they joined in order to prevent injustice. But Lobesam stuck to his convictions, odious as they were. I quite liked him.'

Sebastian had risen and took the old photo in his hands: 'You have told us that in a referendum the Nazis claimed 99.5% of all votes went their way. And yet Herr Lobesam was their only representative. Who swindled?'

'No swindlers. Both were right. In the referendum you went to the polling booth and handed your marked paper to the official. If he or she was satisfied, you got a badge, marked *yes,* which you put on your dress. Outside were burly SA men. You took good care to display your badge and to get home safely. From their positions, both the 99.5% and the sole Nazi were right.'

'Who is this lion-maned superman?' asked Sarah, as she raised a photo of a young man who held his cello above his head.

'O, that is one of the first arrivals of a long, long line of chamber musicians. He came from the States and his name was Elmer. He died in Vietnam.

Leonie opened a wooden briefcase and extracted from it a parchment, bearing the dedication:

In recognition of his tireless work in pursuit of the bond between nations and races through music, we are pleased to award Rolf Messing with the Peace Prize of 50,000 dollars. The Mayor and Townspeople of Pittsburgh.

'This made it possible to hold my summer schools and train my orchestras for quite a few years.'

'And your orchestras,' continued Florestan, 'the ones you picked wherever the hatred of nations threatened to block out hope and sanity. Like the Soviet/USA ensemble during the Cuban crisis. Or the British/Irish band in the eighties and nineties. They all helped to contradict the politicians, to -'

'build bridges,' Sarah and Sebastian blurted out in gentle unison, forgiving their grandfather's unuttered yet ever present obsession.

'Look at this,' called Leonie. 'A short article in a leading British broadsheet.

'Composer Rolf Messing and his wife Rahel wish it to be known that they have renounced their Christian and Jewish religions, in order to be able to wonder at and respect the creator and creations, without the benefit of self-appointed middlemen.'

'And what is this?' cried Sebastian, holding a tattered volume. He read, with difficulty, the faded inscription, YOSSL'S DIARY.

'That is the most wonderful, the most precious testament of a great man,' said Rahel. 'Your ancestor, Yossl Messing, wrote his memoirs in the 19th century. It is time for you to read it.'

A year later, Rolf and Rahel made their way laboriously up Mount Skiddaw, without bicycles. They reached the summit. The feverish heat was broiling grass and humans alike. They lay down on what they thought was the peak. They were too exhausted to speak. Their hands rested in each other's embrace. The doctor found underneath Rolf's shirt, nearest his heart, a frayed watercolour of a ship, named *Covenant*. A rainbow connected the banks of the wide river. Or was it a bridge?

The End